# Confessions from a Coffee Shop

*A novel by*

## T. B. MARKINSON

COPYRIGHT © 2014 T. B. MARKINSON

Edited by Karin Cox
Proofread by Jeri Walker
Cover Design by Erin Dameron-Hill

This book is copyrighted and licensed for your personal enjoyment only. All rights reserved. No part of this publication may be reproduced, stored in a retrieval system, or transmitted in any forms or by any means without the prior permission of the copyright owner. The moral rights of the author have been asserted.

This book is a work of fiction. Names, characters, businesses, places, events, and incidents are the product of the author's imagination or are used fictitiously. Any resemblance to actual persons, living or dead, events, or locales is entirely coincidental.

# Chapter One

"Mother, stop! Father is not boinking some slut in his office!" I yelled into my cell phone, feeling color swarm up my neck and fury rising from the pit of my stomach. It was too early in the day for one of Mom's attention-seeking stunts. "I have to go."

I looked over my shoulder, phone crooked under my chin. A beautiful woman stood at the counter, poised to order her coffee.

"Wait, don't you dare hang—"

I pushed Mom's shrill, threatening voice out of my head and set the cell phone down. I adjusted my cherry-red apron and pretended the woman hadn't just heard me yelling at my mother about my father having an affair. "I'm sorry for the wait," I said.

Why did I have to shout the word boinking? *Just act*

*casual*, I told myself.

"Cori? Cori Tisdale?"

"Uh, I'm sorry—" As I stared into the woman's amber eyes, recognition dawned on me. "Samantha Clarke?" I replied timidly.

"Yes!" Enthusiasm brightened her features. I wanted to run screaming from the store. I hadn't seen Samantha Clarke since graduation eleven years ago. Back then we were high school girls. But now she was no longer a girl. Sam was all woman, and she was standing right in front of me smiling.

"Wow, it's been a long time." I pasted on a happy face and tried to stop my eyes from roving over her navy pinstripe power suit.

My khaki pants, white button-up Oxford shirt, and apron didn't leave any doubt as to which of us had done something with her life and which hadn't. I felt like a failure—a complete and total failure.

"So, are you manager here?" she asked without a hint of derision.

"No. This is just a part-time gig … until …" Should I admit to Samantha that my jobless girlfriend had charged up our credit cards, and I was working part-time to pay down the debt? I already felt like a loser; I didn't want her to think I was a total waste of space. Plus, I didn't want her to judge my girlfriend, Kat. Yes, she had racked up a huge bill, but that didn't stop me from loving her.

"Yeah, times are tough right now." Samantha gave me a glance that managed to look encouraging without being condescending or smug.

"I have a real job," I continued. "I teach at a university."

I neglected to tell her that I taught at Adams University, which was more like a community college in my book. The people who ran the joint felt differently, but I couldn't blame them for that. All of us wanted to feel more important than we were, which was why I was doing my best to downplay the fact that I was serving coffee to Sam at six in the morning.

"Really? I always thought you would end up teaching. But I figured you would teach PE at a high school, or coach college ball." She smiled innocently. "I loved watching you play basketball," she explained.

"Ha!" I tried to laugh sincerely and not act hurt. Apparently she still thought of me as a jock—a lesbo jock with zero brains. "No, I teach English. British lit, actually." I couldn't control the snobby tone in my voice. *Why did I have to say British lit? Why didn't I stick with just English?* Because deep down, I'm a snob, and I was feeling sorry for myself.

"Figures." She gave a curt nod of her blonde head. "You always had your nose in a book when you weren't on the court."

Samantha had been a cheerleader—the popular cheerleader who all of the boys and some of the girls, myself included, had lusted after. She hadn't been stuck on herself back then, and from our brief conversation this morning, she still seemed grounded, unlike snobby me.

"What do you do?" I fidgeted with the pen on the register. The store was in the heart of Boston's Financial District, and although it wasn't officially open this early, I didn't want to tell Sam she had to leave. Soon, customers in suits would pour in, like they did all day long. Few had time to chat; most made me feel like an idiot.

"I'm a portfolio manager," Sam said. "You know, investments for 401(k)s and such." She rolled her eyes, as if it were nothing.

"Impressive. Any good stock tips?" As soon as the words left my lips, I felt like an imbecile. Flames of embarrassment burned me from neck to hairline, until I was sure she could see the blood pulsing through my veins. I waved a hand. "Just kidding, of course," I added, feeling like a bumbling teen trying to chat up the prom queen, which she had been, back then.

My former crush was kind enough to ignore my *faux pas*. Asking for stock tips while standing in a Beantown Café apron—what was I thinking? Everyone knew that insider trading was a big no-no. Remember Martha Stewart. *Jesus, Cori.*

"What can I get you, Samantha?" I changed the subject. I had enjoyed seeing her again, but I wasn't sure my ego could take much more.

"A praline latte, please." She set her shiny, patent-leather briefcase on the floor and pulled her wallet from her purse. Inside, I spied a credit card from almost every major credit company.

*She wouldn't have to get a part-time job if her partner ran up her cards*, I thought. *Stop it, Cori.*

"Sure, what size?" I chirped, sounding like an idiotic bird hoping for a breadcrumb.

"Large, please."

"All right. One Bean Supreme Praline Latte coming up." I felt like an ass saying Bean Supreme instead of large, too, but my manager encouraged such behavior. The owners of the

Massachusetts-based chain thought they were so clever using Beantown as the name that they tried to incorporate it into everything in the store. I hated my job, but I still needed to keep it. Kat only had access to one card now, and the limit was drastically lower, but I still had a lot of work to do to get us out of our hole.

I turned my back on Samantha to make her coffee, my mind racing. A cheerleader turned portfolio manager? Even as much as I hated stereotypes, I had to admit I'd figured Sam would have ended up working as a concierge at a fancy hotel or something. I certainly didn't expect her to be so smart and so successful. Don't get me wrong, Sam was intelligent back then, but most people noticed her charm—or her body—more than her brains. Oh, the dreams I had about her back in the day.

*Focus, Cori.*

But I couldn't. Samantha was the cheerleader everyone had wanted to fuck. She had to have known that back then, but she never acted as if she did, which only made her more fuckable, at least in my mind.

Behind the machine, I took in her beauty unnoticed. Long, bouncy blond hair, amber eyes, a toned body with ample cleavage, a devilish smile, flawless skin, and an ass to die for. A person could bounce quarters off her ass. It was a cliché, but also true in this case. Samantha wasn't the wholesome girl next door. I mean she was sweet, but she gave off this "I know how to be naughty" vibe. Trust me, it was a turn on. She was the whole package.

In high school, she had volunteered her time tutoring underprivileged kids, and I don't think she did that just because it looked good on college applications. Samantha actually cared about others. She sang in the choir, and her voice made me wet on more than one occasion. The paradox of it. Her looks suggested she would sound like an angel. Nope. Her voice was gravelly, more like Janis Joplin's. Back then, I sensed she didn't like the restraining quality of our choirmaster, as if she wanted to get on stage and grind out the song.

Oddly enough, she never dated anyone in school. Occasionally, I would spy her with a random guy here or there, but from what I heard, no one captured her heart. The boys respected her enough not to label her a "Wham bam, thank you, ma'am." Not that she was loose. But in high school, boys tended to say that when the hottest girl in school wouldn't give them the time of day.

Most of the girls couldn't find a reason to hate her. I lusted after her. Nobody had any idea how much I wanted to sleep with her.

We didn't hang out much, but it wasn't hard to keep tabs on Samantha. Our private school was rife with gossip. Add rich snots to the mix, and we all knew everything about everyone else, even if we didn't want to.

The minutes it took to make Sam's latte were excruciating. I felt completely ridiculous manning the humming coffee machine in front of her. When it screamed like a banshee, frothed milk flowed out of the metal pitcher to make my distraction more obvious, I wanted to melt into the floor just like the escaped foam. Samantha busied herself on her iPhone, leaving me to my shame.

When the coffee was done, I slipped on the cardboard

sleeve so she wouldn't burn her delicate hands. From the looks of her, she didn't spend a lot of time outdoors. Either that or she wore some super-duper sunblock. I thought her ivory skin made her even more appealing. Her golden hair was slicked back into a professional-looking ponytail. I wanted to let it down, run my fingers through it.

*Stop it, Cori. You're spoken for. What's wrong with you this morning?*

"Here you go." I gave her the drink, being careful not to touch her hand, fearful I might break it—or pet her.

"Thanks, Cori. How long have you been working here? I haven't seen you before." Samantha removed the lid and blew into the steaming foam. Then she dipped her pinky in, drew it out, and licked it.

*Seriously! This was how I had to start my day: all hot and bothered?*

"A little over a month," I finally answered. "I pop in a few times a week."

I felt better saying "pop in" instead of "I work here." It made me feel like I was doing the company a favor rather than slaving away for a wage barely above the minimum and with zero health benefits. Maybe I should just put *Loser* on my nametag.

"Cool. Well, I'm in here all of the time, so I'll see you around." She raised her cup to me as she headed out the door, breezing past a gentleman on his way in who stopped and held the door for her—and then leered at Sam's perky ass until she was out of sight.

Finally, the creep approached the counter. He answered his cell phone and immediately put a finger up to keep me quiet, as though I had been dying to talk to him. What a jerk!

I rolled my eyes, tapping my fingers on the countertop.

"Morning." Harold, my coworker, ambled in to interrupt Mr. Cell Phone Jerk's peace and quiet.

He was thirty minutes late, which was pretty good for Harold; usually, it was more like an hour. As soon as Harold learned that I had worked for the coffee chain before and knew it like the back of my hand, he left me to open the store by myself three times a week. I had done my first stint at Beantown Café back in high school. I'd also worked there on and off again during college. When I got my teaching job, I actually burned my apron, thinking I'd never return. Karma was a bitch. Perhaps burning my original apron had upset the Beantown Café gods.

Dammit! It wasn't even 6:30 a.m. and I was already in a crap mood. Usually, this kind of funk didn't settle in until at least nine.

As soon as the obnoxious customer had gone, Harold strolled out from the back room, tying his apron around his waist. "How was your night, Cori?"

I opened my mouth to answer, but in typical Harold style he had already launched into his own story, stopping only when another customer entered. The first time I had met Harold, he'd proclaimed he was Mr. Cool, but with a capital K.

*Kook—with a capital K*, I remember thinking.

There was absolutely nothing cool about Harold then, and there still wasn't now. Tall, gangly, and bearing remnant acne, Harold still lived with his mother. His thick, dishwater brown hair was so soft that the bowl cut he sported made it flounce around limply with every tiny head movement. Pale brown eyes appeared completely vacant above Harold's plain face and a chin that slipped into his neck. A beard might have given him the illusion of a chin, except that Harold, at twenty-seven, was still without any sign of scruff. I doubted he had ever shaved. He looked like a ten-year-old trapped in a man's body.

On my first day, I discovered that the rest of the employees called him Harry Pooper. His real name, Harold Potts, was an unfortunate coincidence. His real claim to fame was being the longest-working employee at this branch. Yet he was constantly passed over for promotion, and the manager never let him work the register since he annoyed most of the customers. About all Harold was good for was making great drinks, and fast. When there was a rush, I wanted Harold manning Big Bertha; that's the name I gave the screaming banshee coffee machine.

To say that I wasn't impressed when I met him would be an understatement. But when Harold once called out sick for three days in a row, and our pissed-off supervisor threatened to fire him, my thoughts changed a little. Harold wandered in the next day looking healthy but clutching a medical certificate, which he set down on the counter.

I peeked at it. His doctor's name was Atticus Finch, and his office was located on 643 Mockingbird Lane.

I thought for sure Mark, the boss, would know Harold was playing him for a fool. Surely Mark would recognize the name Atticus Finch from *To Kill a Mockingbird*, right?

He didn't. Harold had turned his note in as if it were just a typical morning, and then he'd trotted out of the back office and put his apron on. I studied his eyes: vacant as could be. And that was when I'd started to like Harold.

"Oh man, Cori, last night I was at this bo—" He looked up at me sheepishly as I prepared for the next onslaught of assholes in suits. "Bar," he continued.

I was positive he had been going to say bookstore. Harold loved graphic novels, but as he couldn't afford all the ones he wanted to buy, I knew he read them for hours in the bookstore, nursing a cup of coffee. He had never confessed that to me, but I'd seen him in the same bookstore on many occasions. I had never noticed Harold until I'd started working at Beantown, but then again, he just wasn't the type of guy people noticed.

Other Beantown employees bullied him ruthlessly, and Harold took it. I felt bad for him. But on this particular morning, I wasn't in the mood to listen to his whining, so I tuned him out. Not that Harold noticed.

Given a lull in the store's business, he picked up his story right where he left off. I checked my watch every five minutes, and then the clock on the wall, hoping I would somehow magically enter a time portal and my four-hour shift would be over. I still had to fine-tune my lecture for class that evening, and my ambition to make it top-notch waned with each passing minute. Ten minutes later, I was considering just pulling out notes from two years ago and going with that.

*Pull it together, Cori.* If I didn't start putting more effort into my teaching, I wouldn't be able to find a higher-paying gig, which meant never quitting Beantown Café and always saying "one Bean Supreme coming up" until my death. I tugged on the apron strap around my neck. Gosh it had felt good when I'd burned the old one.

I knew Kat wouldn't find a job anytime soon. Steady work just wasn't her thing. She was an artist. My aunt owned an art studio, so I had been around artists all of my life. Not once had I met one with a drive for self-preservation or a grip on real life. They thought on a different plane. Sometimes I wished Kat was more logical, but then I reminded myself that the world needed artists. And I needed Kat. Life without her would be miserable.

I hated working at Beantown Café to get us out of debt, but I knew I would work at the coffee joint full-time if it was the only way we could be together. I would even tattoo their silly logo—two coffee beans holding cups—on my ass, if need be.

From the moment I met Kat, I knew she was the one for me. Three years later, I still knew it.

Kat's childhood hadn't prepared her for the working world either. Her father was so old-fashioned, I wouldn't be surprised if he was 157, instead of fifty-seven years old. I felt trapped in a time capsule whenever we had to have dinner with Kat's folks.

"You'd think a university professor would make enough to cover the bills," her father once said to me.

Kat was appalled. All the color drained from her face, but she didn't say anything at the time. She was usually outspoken, but not around her parents. It broke my heart to watch her interact with them.

The night after he said that, when I got home, Kat had prepared my favorite meal—eggplant parmesan—and had run a hot candlelit bath for me. I soaked in the tub, sipping a glass of wine she'd poured me, while she put the finishing touches on dinner. She hadn't said it, but that was her way of making it up to me. And Kat has never made me feel bad about our money problems. I think she carried a lot of guilt, for obvious reasons.

But that was not to say I was entirely blameless.

## Chapter Two

Unlike Kat's family, mine appeared normal—at least on the surface. My Aunt Barbara was the one who owned the gallery. A typical Bostonian woman, she wore sensible but expensive clothes and no makeup, unless on the town or at a gallery opening. Some may have called her dowdy, but I wouldn't suggest saying it to her face, or mine. Even if I didn't play ball anymore, I was close to six feet tall, lifted weights, ran, and was in excellent shape. Plus, my uncle taught me to box when I was a kid.

Aunt Barbara loved art of all types, and she was a decent painter. My aunt also knew she wasn't the best painter, so she was content to own a gallery and showcase those who were better. I also thought my aunt preferred being out of the limelight. Organization was her thing. Need help getting life in order? Go to her.

She was also probably one of the worst cooks I knew, which didn't mean we never went to her house for dinner. Every other week, my family congregated at Aunt Barbara's to pretend we liked her meals. It was a tradition. The other weeks, we ate at my parents' house, where my mom cooked. Mom excelled in the kitchen, but none of us ever gave her too much praise. It was an unspoken rule out of kindness to Aunt Barbara.

I wasn't sure why my aunt was such a horrible cook. Her husband, Roger, had upgraded her kitchen so many times that she had gadgets and appliances that made most chefs drool. But the upgrades did nothing to improve the final product. There was not enough salt and pepper to help her bland and boring dishes. But I loved her for trying.

Aunt Barbara sounded normal, right? Here was the hitch. My aunt and uncle were happy, and they got along great and were best friends. However, they slept in separate bedrooms. Roger *always* had another woman on the side. Somehow, my aunt either lied to herself completely, or just didn't care about her husband's affairs. None of us ever talked about it. Never.

I couldn't live that way, but who was I to judge others? If they were happy, more power to them. It took a lot of restraint for my mother not to say anything in front of Roger. The youngest child, my mother idolized her sister from the beginning, and Roger's infidelities cut her to the bone. Only Mom's respect for her sister kept her mute. The revelation that my father might be having an affair was the closest Mom had ever came to criticizing Roger. But Mom was so self-involved she probably couldn't see it that way.

My mom, Nell Tisdale, was the opposite of Barbara. Her

clothes were flashy, but not over-the-top. Some women in their fifties didn't understand they couldn't dress like teenagers. My mom got that, but she was not ready to be an old woman either. She always looked put-together with flawless makeup and a toned body that she worked hard for by running every day and working out three times a week. Some might consider my aunt frumpy, although no one would think that about my mom. When I was in high school, I had to endure listening to all my guy friends talk about how much they wanted to fuck my mother. And mom knew it. She flaunted it. If I had to choose one word to describe my mom, I would cheat and say "attention-seeking."

I didn't think Mom had low self-esteem, but maybe she did in a way. It seemed more like my mother just craved attention. After all, she had always been used to getting it. Right from the start, she was a beauty.

While Barbara was an average painter, my mother was a brilliant writer. She had awards coming out the ying-yang. Mom published her first book at the age of twenty-one and received instant success and fame. None of her novels have flopped—not one. She's never failed. And even though Mom drove me completely batty, I couldn't have asked for a better mother. Oh, we didn't always get along. We loved to bicker. But my mom would kill any son of a bitch who hurt me. Think a mother bear was protective of her cub? Just wait until meeting my mom.

So what was unusual about my mom? She was sex-crazed. My mom wasn't like Roger. She didn't have affairs. But she talked about sex. *All. The. Time.* It made me uncomfortable—really who wanted to hear about their parents fucking? Not me.

Mom knew I hated hearing it, and to be honest, I thought she talked about it just to get under my skin. It was another of her attention-seeking ways. Unfortunately, I let her get to me, which only added fuel to the fire. Those were the women who raised me. Now for the men.

My father, Warren Tisdale, went by the name "Dale." He was taciturn, but not in a hurtful way. Dad didn't have the best childhood. He never mentioned it, and I didn't think he had figured out how to talk about feelings, but that didn't mean he was off-limits for me when I needed him. I could go to my father and chat with him, and he'd listen. Not once did Dad offer me advice, but he was always willing to listen, night or day. And he gave the best hugs—ones that let me know he loved me. My father may not have said it, but he showed it. It was probably a good thing he didn't talk much because Mom never shut up. It was a relief to have one parent who would listen and not try to outdo me when it came to speaking about things that were troubling to me.

My mother thought he was the most handsome fellow ever. I didn't see that, but I'm glad she did. I couldn't handle another cheater in this family. My mom also thought he was a sex machine; I always shoved my fingers in my ears when she said this.

Dad was just shy of six feet, like me. He had salt-and-pepper hair, kind brown eyes, and his stomach was starting to jut out over his belt. He had zero fashion sense, and super-skinny legs. None of that mattered. He was my father, and I loved him. He was pretty much a typical father of his generation: quiet, a good provider, and a person who stayed out of the limelight.

My uncle was also extremely involved in raising me. This shocked the few people who knew about his infidelities. Roger was handsome for his age. He reminded me of Sean Connery but without the Scottish accent. Silver hair added to his appeal and rugged good looks. If anyone needed backup in a bar fight, he was the man. In his younger days, he boxed, and his nose hadn't been straight since.

I never defended his infidelities. I didn't get it and I never will. However, over the years I learned to love the man, despite this flaw. I would feel like a shit for not recognizing all that he has done for me. He's been there for me since I was born. Roger was the one who got me interested in basketball. Neither of my parents were sporty. Yes, my mom worked out, but she had no ability at any sport, unless poker counted. I wouldn't suggest playing cards with her—she cheated, I was sure of it, but I haven't figured out a way of proving it.

Roger was an athlete, and he saw potential in me. We started with shooting hoops in the backyard. Then he signed me up for teams and clinics. One summer, he paid for me to attend an elite basketball camp. Mom wasn't happy about that since I was away for weeks. She liked having me close to home, and I liked being close to home, but I still had a blast at the camp. When Harvard asked me to play on their team, my mother was thrilled, even though they wouldn't offer me a scholarship since Ivy League schools don't allow scholarships. I didn't play for Harvard in the hope of winning an NCAA championship. (Let's face it, Harvard was never a contender.) My family had attended Harvard for more than a hundred years—actually closer to two hundred years, but I was the first

Tisdale to play any sport at the institution. I took great pride in that.

Some people were surprised when they met me, since many associated my name with basketball. I was not Shaquille O'Neal tall, although I towered over my mother. My hair was thin, mousy brown, and never held a curl. Every stylist who ever tried curling my hair quit after the first hour. My eyes were deep blue but always looked bloodshot, probably since I was always sleep-deprived. I had pale skin: fish-belly white in winter and more of a pink shade in summer. My teeth were straight, except for one at the bottom front, which jutted out because I refused to wear my retainer once my braces were removed. Being stubborn could be a total bitch. Thankfully, my teeth were as white as can be, thanks to my dentist and my obsession with brushing them. Doesn't everyone brush their teeth five times a day or more?

A few years ago, I was riding high. I was in a master's program at Harvard and had several short stories published. It'll sound smug, but my stories were brilliant. I was the new "It" girl. The daughter of famous Nell Tisdale, I was making my own splash in the literary pond. An agent approached me. Publishers wanted me to write a book. My agent brokered a deal. I had it made, absolutely made.

My book deal was an impressive arrangement for a newbie. Not J. K. Rowling or Stephen King big, but it was pretty fucking good. I even went on some local morning talk shows with my mother.

Kat loved all the attention I was getting. People started to recognize me when I was out and about. Foolishly, I proclaimed to my spendthrift girlfriend, "All of our money worries are over. From now on, you can spend, spend, spend."

At the time, I knew Kat loved to shop. I gave her a blank check, and now I could no longer cover it. God that made me feel like a failure.

I've had my life planned out since birth. Mom and Aunt Barbara used to joke that I'd grabbed the bull by the horns as soon as I popped out. Nothing stopped me.

I skipped crawling completely and started walking well before my first birthday.

Potty training—a breeze.

Sports, dancing, and school came easily to me.

I never struggled with a thing.

That doesn't mean I didn't work hard; I did. I knew how good I had it, and I didn't want to take anything for granted. It was not in our blood—being lazy. My family, from the moment we stepped off the ship and onto American soil, excelled. Ever hear of the Puritan work ethic? That fit us to the core. Toil, toil, and more toil. And when tired, we worked some more. None of us knew how to slow down. My grandfather was ninety-three when he died. He married late in life and didn't start a family until his forties. When he died, he was sitting at his desk working on his last book. He quit teaching years earlier but never "officially" retired from academia. Grandfather cranked out article after article and then decided to write a book on the Isabella Stewart Gardner Museum.

Just like everyone in my family, I knew what I was doing and where I wanted my life to go; that is, until I sat down to actually write my novel.

At first, everything went according to plan. Within a few

months I had it half finished. But as I continued, I realized I didn't have an ending. How can someone write a novel, or two-thirds of a novel, and not have a clue where it's fucking going?

My agent would like to know the answer to that as well. So would the publisher who had already advanced a substantial amount of money based on my short stories, my mom's name, and the "It" girl label.

I was teetering on the precipice of complete and total failure, and I was scared shitless. Never before had I experienced failure. Never before had I wanted something so much. No one in my family had ever failed—that was not a tradition I wanted to start.

I had been trying to put my finger on the issue for months. Everything in my life was going well. I had a beautiful, supportive girlfriend. My family, while crazy, would do absolutely anything for me. I was highly educated, motivated, in good health, and happy. I wished I could use the excuse that I was battling depression, or I was an alcoholic, or that I was a drug addict. But I was not any of those things.

I was just failing.

Maybe if I had failed earlier in life, I would know what to do, but it was too fucking late for that now! This was not the time to learn a life lesson. My reputation, my career, and my future were on the line—not to mention my mom's reputation.

Mom went to all my interviews. She sat with me on the couch, spouting off about how proud she was of me and how I would be an even better writer than her. Not once had she thrown that in my face, not even when it became apparent that something had gone horribly wrong with my novel. Mom gave me shit about my writing, or lack thereof, but she never made me feel bad about damaging her good name. If my grandfather were alive, he wouldn't be as kind. He might have disowned me.

Let's just say, I felt like crap about everything that happened over the last sixteen months. Crap really wasn't the right word, but I couldn't think of a better one at the moment. And when I walked into Beantown Café to ask for my job back, I wanted to jump off the Tobin Bridge instead. Not that I would actually do that. Suicide was not an option. Not in our family. Putting our noses to the grindstone was all that we understood. So I was donning my Beantown Café apron once again and chipping away at my debt, one fucking penny at a time. What asshole said, "A penny saved is a penny earned"? I wish I could throw him off the Tobin Bridge. I couldn't save any pennies. Everything went to American Express. Fucking bastards.

## Chapter Three

After my shift at Beantown, I headed to my mother's house. Mom sent me a text every ten minutes after I hung up on her, informing me that if I didn't stop by I wouldn't be her daughter anymore. My mother was more dramatic than a squad of high school cheerleaders on prom night. Ignoring Mom wasn't an option, unless I wanted to suffer for the rest of my life.

As soon as I entered my childhood home, she started in.

"I don't know what to do. I don't know what to do." Mom waved her arms in the air and looked as if she were having trouble breathing.

"What's wrong?" I rushed to her, thinking she was having a heart attack or something. Her breathing was erratic, her face scarlet, and she was pacing in the front room.

"Your father and that woman!" Mom sat down heavily

on the couch. "What will everyone say?"

"Mother, for the last time. Dad is not having an affair."

"Yes he is!" Her eyes bored into mine.

"All right, what proof do you have?" I crossed my arms, disregarding her distress now that I knew it was for show.

"A wife knows, Cori. A wife knows," she cried.

I studied my mother. Her usually perfect hair was a mess, and she wasn't wearing any makeup. Was this part of her act? It was hard to know with Mom.

Her beady eyes demanded a response.

"Like the time you thought he bought a sports car without telling you?"

"I admit I was wrong then, but how was I supposed to know he rented the car to surprise me for our anniversary? I always wanted a Jag. But I'm not wrong this time." Her tone told me she wouldn't budge on this.

I tried steering the subject away from my father's imaginary affair. "Do you have anything to eat? I'm starving."

"There's some leftover pizza in the fridge. Help yourself." She waved her hand in the air like a beauty queen in a parade.

I returned with a slice of cheese pizza.

"You know, Barbara's husband has cheated on her from the beginning. It was only a matter of time before your father did." Mom exhaled sharply, clutching her throat like it was on fire.

"That's why you're stuck on this. You're always competing with Aunt Barbara, but this is really low, even for you." I ripped off another piece of pizza, mumbling between mouthfuls, "Dad is nothing like Roger. You can't compete when it comes to this, so don't even try." I waggled the half-eaten slice at her.

Mom shook my words away with a toss of her head. "I know it's true, Cori. I wish you would believe me. Kat does," she murmured.

"What?" I pulled the pizza away from my mouth. "When did you and Kat talk about this?"

"This morning. When you hung up on me!" she shrieked.

"I was at work!"

Again my mother dismissed me, this time by swiping strands of hair out of her face. "She's always there for me, unlike someone else I know."

I let out a long, slow breath. "Well, then, what does my girlfriend have to say on the subject?"

"She agrees with me completely. Do you know the last time your father and I had sex? He hasn't even asked for a BJ."

I nearly fell out of my chair. "Mother! I do not want to hear about this." I jumped up, uncomfortable. God she was sex-crazed—always talking about it.

"Why? Kat listens to me."

"You've talked to my girlfriend about that?"

"Of course, dear. Women talk about this stuff. Don't be a prude."

Her steady voice unnerved me.

"Women talk about this 'stuff' with their friends. Not with their daughter's girlfriend. I forbid you to talk to her." I planted my feet firmly on the ground.

"Forbid me? Who do you think you are?" Mom crossed her arms defensively, her foot tapping out a rhythm on the floor.

"Seriously, you need to think about the stuff you blurt out

of your mouth. You can't go around talking to Kat about sex, especially when it involves you and my father." I shook my head, trying to permanently dislodge the images from my brain.

"At least Kat talks to me. All you do is hang up on me." She pouted, running her hands up and down her arms to comfort herself.

"Look at me! I'm here right now, talking to you. I should be working on my lecture for this evening, but no, I came to see how you're doing?"

Mom's expression perked up. "That reminds me. The three of us are meeting at Pablo's Café after your class." Her face clouded over as she gazed out the front window and her voice dripped with scorn as she added, "I'm sure your father will be with his hussy this evening."

I considered responding, but opted to stay quiet.

"Don't worry, I know money is tight right now, so I'll pay for dinner," she said. "And that's another thing I want to talk to you about. You need to stop making Kat feel guilty about not being able to find a job."

"What? Make her feel guilty? I never mention it. Not one bit." I really didn't. Not once had I said or suggested that she should get a job. She should, but I knew the likelihood of that happening was pretty much nil. Kat knew how to spend money, not how to make it.

"She says she can see it in your eyes. I know Kat likes to shop, but you can't lay all the blame on her. Blame the Republicans." Mom punctuated her statement with a quick nod.

Yes, it's all George Bush's fault, even though he's been out of office for years now. I was not a Republican, but unlike Mom, I couldn't continue to blame them for everything. They didn't tell her to go shopping every day. That was, unless Kat was still following George's advice after 9/11. I still couldn't believe that idiot, after the country was attacked, and how he said everything would be all right and that Americans should go shopping. Don't worry about a thing, just go shopping.

Mom's voice snapped me back to the present. "And you love Pablo's Café. Kat reminded me it's your favorite place." She tried to placate me with a smile, but then immediately bit her lower lip in distress, as if the actress in her had briefly forgotten about the "affair" and then realized she needed to put on a sad face again.

I laughed. "Oh, please. That's Kat's favorite place. They cook their rice in pig fat. It's disgusting. I can barely eat anything there."

Okay, I loved Pablo's, but I wasn't willing to admit that right then. I couldn't believe Mom was on this rant about my father. Once an idea like this took root in her head, it was trouble—with a capital T.

She ignored me completely. "And I know how much you love their margaritas. Do you remember how sick you got last time?"

"I got food poisoning."

Again, I didn't want to admit she was right. I got plastered and puked on the way home.

Nothing registered on her face. "So don't be late. As soon as your class is done, hop on the T and meet us there. I'm picking Kat up early so we can get a table. It's Thursday, so it'll be packed."

They both wanted to go early so they could get sloshed. Why not? It was the perfect opportunity for my mother to continue her campaign of "feel sorry for me, my husband is having an affair." Unbelievable.

It was as if she'd waited decades to compete with Barbara on this one. I loved her, but sometimes even Mother Theresa would want to bonk Mom on the head.

She turned back to walk into the kitchen, our conversation over. I followed. I knew she wanted to be alone now. Maybe she planned on calling Kat to talk about my father again. But I wanted another slice of pizza from the fridge to eat on my way to the T. It was time to get to my office on campus and polish my lecture. If I were diligent, I'd have time to fiddle with my novel.

I managed to stumble through my lecture. I had never got around to fine-tuning it. Afterwards, I changed clothes for dinner and briefly considered forgetting about meeting up with my mom and Kat at the Tex-Mex restaurant. Doing a no-show would allow me one night of peace and quiet, but the repercussions weren't worth it. Mom would never let me forget it. Poor Kat would be in the middle. Bless Kat. I had no idea how she spent so much time with my mother. And she never lost her cool like I sometimes did.

Kat stole my heart three years ago. Katharine Finn was not your typical beautiful woman. Unlike many hotties, Kat—please don't ever call her Katharine because she hates that name—owns her beauty and sex appeal. You'll never hear her say, "Me? Oh, I'm not beautiful. I have fat thighs."

By the way, she didn't have any fat on her, except in the

27

right places. Her ass was as scrumptious as a peach on a hot summer day, and her breasts swelled over her bra. She intentionally bought all her bras too small, just so they popped out. She wasn't afraid to show off both—her tits and ass. Usually Kat's shirts left little to the imagination, if you know what I mean.

Another quality I found sexy was that Kat wasn't stupid nor did she ever pretend to be. I liked people who could be themselves and be confident in who they were. That was sexy. Kat was not afraid to engage in scholarly debates, and she wasn't afraid to give her opinion.

My wonderful Kat knew people were attracted to her; of course, she's been known to use it to her advantage. If I were that hot, I know I would. Yet she never made me feel insecure in our relationship. From afar, people assumed Kat was a whore just because she was beautiful. In fact, she has only slept with three people, including me. She was the most loyal person I knew. When people bought her drinks, I never felt like marking my territory. If asked to dance, she would readily accept. She acted herself, which included risqué moves if her dancing partner was up for it. But at the end of the night, Kat always went home with me. Some may think she was asking for trouble: provocative dancing and skimpy clothes. A person would just have to see it for themselves, but believe me when I said that with Kat, it didn't come across the wrong way. She didn't give men and women the impression they would be taking her home at the end of the night. From what I had witnessed, they appreciated Kat's zest for life and enjoyed her company. We've been dating for three years, and I've never witnessed mixed signals. I have never encountered someone who thought Kat had duped them, or who expected more from her. Only those who didn't bother to interact with her assumed she was slutty.

That didn't mean our relationship was perfect. No relationship was. Our biggest issue was her spending. Kat was addicted to shopping, and the past year it had grown progressively worse. My savings have been wiped out. As of yet, I haven't said much to her. I didn't know how to bring up the subject, and I didn't think she did either. I knew I would never leave her because of it. Right now, I was busting my ass to pay off the debts. I needed to think of another way to help with her addiction. My brain told me I should talk to her about it, but truth be known, I was scared. She was sensitive. I didn't want Kat to think I was blaming her. I wasn't. Everyone has their demons. Kat spent money we didn't have, and I couldn't finish a novel that should have been completed a year ago. We just needed to find a way to deal with both of our demons. We just needed to fix it. And fast. Or I needed to figure out a way to make more money—a lot more money.

Lately, I was just too exhausted from busting my ass to get us out of trouble, and I couldn't focus on having a sit-down with her about cutting back expenses. Yes, that's an excuse. I'm full of them when it comes to two subjects: my novel and Kat's spending.

I spied Kat and my mother sitting in the back of Pablo's, under the Pure Louisiana Molasses sign featuring an alligator. The alligator confused me some. I got that the company was Alligator Brand, but molasses and an alligator? It just didn't make sense to me. But not much in Pablo's Café did. It was located in Harvard Square in Cambridge. The walls were covered with kitsch, they always played country music, and it stood within spitting distance from one of the finest and oldest educational institutions in the country. Kitsch, Tex-Mex, country music, and Harvard didn't jive to me, but somehow it worked. The place was always packed with students, locals, and tourists.

One look at the two of them and I knew I was in for a long night. Their eyes were already glazed over and several empty margarita glasses waited for the server to clear the table. The place was hopping. My guess was no one could have cleared their glasses fast enough.

"Hey there." Kat stood to let me slide into the booth. "I broke my seal an hour ago, so I need quick access to the bathroom," she explained, snuggling up close to me. I think she sensed I was in for a trying night, so she was offering me support. I leaned over and gave her a peck on the cheek. Jasmine perfume filled my nostrils, and her familiar scent relaxed me.

Mom laughed. "She's been running back and forth every ten minutes to pee."

I plastered a fake smile on my face and settled in for the adventure.

"So, I was just telling Kat that I've started reading cowboy porn." Mom swayed her head in an exaggerated manner.

My mom looked a lot smarter than she had earlier that morning. Her shoulder length hair was swept up into a barrette, and a silk scarf enhanced her olive skin. Only a crimson blouse hinted at her wild side. Even in public, Mom wasn't bashful when talking about sex, but she only talked that way around those close to her. Many of Nell Tisdale's fans would be shocked. When Mom gave interviews, she always came across as a prudish, middle-aged Bostonian woman. Of course, she had to uphold that image for her career's sake. It's not like Mom could wear a skimpy blouse and talk about BJs and still expect the literary world to embrace her. Male writers might be able to get away with that, but not female authors.

"Mother! Can we not discuss porn?"

"I knew you would react that way," she sniggered.

"Seriously, Cori, loosen up." Kat rubbed my arm. Her other hand, under the table, gave my thigh a supportive squeeze.

Taking the attention off me, Kat said, with an air of intellectual curiosity, "I didn't know that there was such a thing as cowboy porn."

Not that Kat would read cowboy porn—okay, she probably would. Kat was a voracious reader. Her favorite authors hailed from the Victorian period: Dickens, Collins, Thackeray, the Bronte sisters, Eliot, and Hardy. But that didn't mean she wouldn't read anything else. Kat's no prude. Not like me. Still, to my knowledge, she'd never read any erotica or watched any porn. This last revelation might shock many, since my girlfriend was a free spirit and a vixen in the bedroom.

I pondered the conundrum that was Kat, focusing on the tight shirt that barely contained her breasts, the luscious full lips, the playful eyes. Men always turned to look at my girlfriend. Even gay men admired her beauty. Most straight women hated her instantly. She was the type of woman men imagine they were fucking when sleeping with their wives or girlfriends. Not to be rude, but she was hotter than Angelina

Jolie, Sandra Bullock, Scarlett Johansson, Amanda Seyfried, Olivia Wilde, Natalie Portman … the list went on. No one compared to Kat.

I used to think I was biased, since Kat's my girlfriend, but then we were at a New Year's Eve party a couple of years ago when a woman approached me. She said she was as straight as straight as can be. She'd never slept with a woman and hadn't even kissed a girl in college. She had three children and was happily married. And then she said she'd give her left arm to fuck Kat's brains out.

I stared at her, my mouth agape. How does one respond to that? She told me I was the luckiest son of a bitch she ever met.

I felt like I should say something, so I asked if she was left-handed. If she was willing to give her left arm, I wanted to know if it would be a huge sacrifice. She looked even more appalled at my question than at the thought that I was Kat's girlfriend. Looking me up and down, she muttered, "Unbelievable how you ended up with that goddess." Then she downed the rest of her champagne and staggered off, never to be seen again.

After the woman disappeared, Kat wandered up to me and asked who she was. I told her about it, but didn't mention I'd asked whether the woman was left-handed. Kat wasn't impressed at all. She hated how people always wanted to fuck her. Yes, she loved having sex, but she hated that it was people's first thought when they met her.

Kat asked, "Well, was she even left-handed?"

I laughed.

Much like the woman at the party, I often wondered how

I ended up with such a stunning woman. My family was rich, but I was not. I would be rich when I turned fifty, but I haven't told Kat that part. I haven't told anyone. My grandfather set up my trust that way. He was a stern man who didn't want me to become a trust fund baby. So it wasn't my money that drew Kat to me. Maybe it was my cool factor.

Please! Even my own mother was cooler than me. She read cowboy porn, for Christ's sake.

Well, here's the secret to how I captured Kat's heart. I've narrowed it down to three things. First and foremost: I fell in love with Kat's brain. On our first date we had an in-depth conversation about who was a better writer: Charles Dickens or Wilkie Collins—Kat's favorite author. She said I was the first person to put her intellect above all of her other ample qualities.

Second: on our second date, I paraphrased a line from an Ani DiFranco song that went something like, "Art is my purpose in life, yet I don't understand it completely." I can't remember for sure. Kat was an artist. She lived and breathed art. At the time, I didn't know that, since she was shy talking about it. I've spent a lot of time around artists of all types—both living and in books. One of my college ex-girlfriends was a musician, too—that's probably how I ended up knowing the Ani quote. For the life of me, I still can't remember the song title.

Third: this may seem like a small thing, and I didn't have much to do with it, but Kat loved my family. Oh, we were as dysfunctional as any family in the world, but we all loved each other and spent a lot of time together. A lot of time. Kat was never close to her parents. She lived with them until she was eighteen, but they weren't close. Family dinners were silent affairs. Every week, my family got together for dinner, but we more than likely see each other several times a week as well. And as soon as I introduced Kat, they accepted her. Kat's parents never even accepted her like mine do. I don't mean about her being gay; I mean they don't accept her as a person, an individual, let alone as a free spirit, an artist, a sexual being, and an intellectual. They never appreciated what Kat had to offer. Instead, they wanted to stifle her.

My family encouraged oddness. They thought I was odd because I was the normal one, like Marilyn from *The Munsters*. Kat got a kick out of that—that I was the oddball because I wasn't a freak.

"I didn't know about cowboy porn either, until Barbara gave me some." Mom hiccupped dramatically.

Just great, not only is my mom a porn fanatic, but so is my aunt. I wanted to scream. An Edvard Munch scream.

"Why would Barbara give you porn?" I whispered the last word across the table.

"Cowboy porn," Mom corrected. "I mentioned to her that I hadn't had sex in so long—"

I put my hands over my ears. "I don't want to hear it."

Mom chortled. "Hear what? We aren't having any. I can't even remember the last time your father—"

"I'm not listening, Mother."

Kat yanked on my arm and threw me a look that warned me not to antagonize my mother. No good would come from it.

Right then the waitress arrived with our food—and I felt ridiculous.

"We ordered before you got here," Mom explained, beaming at her ability to order for me. "I got your favorite: cheese enchiladas with extra Spanish rice."

Kat piped up, "Actually, it's not their normal rice—no pig fat," whispering the last bit in my ear.

My mother didn't quite get the whole vegetarian bit. Rice to her qualified as vegetarian, so she couldn't understand how cooking it in animal fat made it inedible. To her, it just made it tasty, and since I wasn't actually eating meat, what was the harm? The pig was already dead.

"You know, maybe I should get some lesbian porn," Kat said.

I choked on my margarita.

To be honest, I was torn about the idea. Obviously, I would benefit if Kat read lesbian erotica, but I didn't want to encourage my mother either.

"You okay, Cori. Did you swallow wrong?" asked my loving girlfriend, tugging on one of her dangling earrings. Her supportive expression informed me she was just going along with my mom and that I shouldn't worry about her actually becoming crazy like my mother. Hopefully.

My mother blinked absently and said, "Oh dear, I hope it's not for the same reason." Then she gave me an accusatory look.

"Oh no." Kat waved her other hand. "Trust me, your daughter and I have no issues in the bedroom. Nope, no lesbian bed death."

Mid-bite, I stopped to stare at Kat. Did she really just blurt all that out in front of my mother? I know Kat's more comfortable talking about sex, but seriously. The woman across the table gave *birth* to me. And I'm still traumatized by being that close to her vagina.

"Lesbian bed death, what's that?" queried mom as she carved into her beef enchilada.

"Some lesbians, after being together for a while, just stop having sex altogether," explained Kat.

"Maybe Cori's father is actually a lesbian!"

They both had a great laugh at Mom's little joke.

I glanced around, completely mortified, to see if anyone could hear their conversation.

"You know, I wouldn't mind reading that cowboy erotica book." Kat plunged her fork into her chicken enchilada.

It's true she prefers Victorian authors, but she's a reader first and foremost. She'll read anything. Once, I found her in the kitchen reading all of our cereal boxes.

"Sure thing! I'll bring it to dinner tomorrow night." Mom sipped her margarita and then added, "Maybe I'll read some lesbian porn. I'm sure I would learn a few things." She giggled.

How many cocktails had Mom had before I arrived?

Mom wasn't the giggling type, so her giggle sounded more malicious than happy, almost as though she was plotting. What she was plotting, I didn't know—and I feared finding out.

Also, it wouldn't have surprised me if my mother had already read lesbian porn. Mom never cared that I was a lesbian. We didn't see eye-to-eye on many subjects, but my lesbianism never ruffled her feathers. In fact, I think she was proud to have a dyke daughter. If any of her friends ever hinted it was too bad I was a lesbian, Mom would put them in their place and more than likely never speak to them again. No one said anything negative about her daughter, which was a job reserved for her.

"You know, Nell, we should start a book club and read erotica. Wouldn't that be a hoot?"

Kat had clearly imbibed too many margs, as well.

I shot her daggers, but she shrugged them off with an evil but loving smile.

"Oh, don't mind her, Kat. She's no fun. I know Barbara will join us." Mom rubbed her hands together. "This will be so much fun." She looked across the table at me. "Who needs your father? Let him boink that other woman all he wants."

"No, no, no," I muttered under my breath.

They ignored me completely.

"Listen!" I snapped my fingers in both of their faces. "No one is starting a book club of any type."

"What's wrong with you, Cori? You're an English teacher." Kat tsked, playfully.

"It's not that." Mom leaned toward my girlfriend conspiratorially. "Cori can't talk about sex. I think ever since she came out of the bathroom—I mean—closet."

I couldn't tell whether my mother was trying to rile me or if she really was that wasted. I suspected the latter. Out of the bathroom? She was too hip to gay culture to commit that kind of mistake.

"Out of the bathroom!" Kat spewed margarita across the table with her words. "That's a riot." She dabbed her mouth with her napkin, careful not to smudge her lipstick.

Mom flashed a cunning smile, having got the desired reaction out of Kat. She always wanted to be the hippest one in any group. She lifted her glass to catch the waitress's attention, and Kat raised her arm to order another as well

Sure. Why not? I motioned for another, too.

If you can't beat them, join them.

After eating peacefully for several minutes, Mom launched into me again. "Anyway, you can't tell me what to do, Cori. Kat and I are starting a porno group, and you can't stop us."

My fork clattered onto my plate as the waitress approached, placed the drinks down, and hurried away.

Had Mom seen the waitress coming and timed her comment perfectly for maximum embarrassment?

"Thanks, Mother. You know I went to school near here. Someone might recognize me."

"So did I, Cori," she reminded me. "And your father, your grandfather … and a few others I can't remember right now." She wrinkled her brow, confused. For once, it wasn't for show. Mom was drunk.

There was no point arguing with her. The best course of action was to ignore her. If I got huffy, Mom would just push my buttons even more.

Kat came to my rescue, steering the conversation to safer waters for the rest of the evening.

Mom was too inebriated to drive home, so after dinner we put her in a cab while Kat and I made our way to the 86 bus stop to head back to Brighton, or as Kat liked to say B-Right-On. At this time of night, a single bus rumbled by every hour. We had forty minutes to wait.

Kat's imploring gray eyes focused on Charlie's Kitchen, across the street, hinting at the idea of a nightcap. After three sorrowful gazes in that direction, I gave in, chuckling. The woman had me wrapped around her finger.

The place was packed, but I made my way to the bar and squeezed between two customers perched on red barstools straight out of a fifties diner. I ordered Kat a vodka tonic, and a water for myself.

As I handed Kat her drink, I noticed a couple leave their table, so I whisked her over so we wouldn't miss our chance. I was beat. After my shift at Beantown Café, teaching, and dealing with my mother twice in one day, I needed to take a load off.

"Why can't you try to be nicer to your mom sometimes? She tries so hard to be nice to you, you know." Kat chewed on her cocktail straw.

"When you say nice, don't you mean passive-aggressive? And what's this about my father? How did she get on this kick?" I raked my fingers through my hair, forcing it back into a ponytail.

"Okay, I don't believe your father is having an affair either, but you know you can't talk any sense into her. Sometimes you just have to go along with it until it blows over. You need to try to not let it get under your skin—that's dangerous when it comes to her." Kat eyed me carefully, knowing me well enough to know I might take her comments the wrong way.

"Under *her* skin? She was the one talking about reading porn!"

A young man glanced over his shoulder and smiled at me.

I inhaled deeply.

Exasperated, I said, "She's never been rational a day in

her life. And you don't help. Please don't feed her insecurities. I know you are trying to be nice, but please stop."

"What, you want me to stop being nice to your mom?" Kat cocked her head, one eyebrow up, ready for battle. "She's more of a mother to me than my own." Her tone told me I had overstepped my boundary.

"No, that's not what I mean. I mean just don't encourage her delusion."

"Whatever, Cori." Kat bounded out of her seat and snaked through the crowd to the bathroom at the back.

All of the mirrors in this diner depressed the hell out of me. The man who eavesdropped earlier raised his drink at me. I stared back, stony-faced. He turned back around and I swore he muttered bitch to his friends. They tittered, ogling me not so discreetly.

Kat reappeared right as the 86 pulled up. It then immediately drove away, well ahead of schedule. Public transportation in this town was maddening. We were stuck for another hour.

I glanced at my watch. Eleven. Now we wouldn't get home until after midnight, and I had to be at work at 5:30. This was my punishment for not supporting Kat, who, in fact, was supporting me by dealing with my crazy mother. I sighed and draped an arm over her shoulder. "I'm sorry. She just gets to me sometimes."

Kat smiled. "I know. I have to admire her skill—she can get you from zero to sixty in less than a second."

"Hey now, don't be picking up any tips from her." I leaned down and gave her a peck on the cheek. Sometimes it was hard for me to keep my hands off Kat. She looked hot as shit, sitting there on the red stool, sipping her drink and batting her eyelashes at me.

"Truce then. Shall we just take a cab home? I'm beat." She sucked down her vodka tonic before I came to my senses and realized I couldn't afford a cab.

In the back of the cab, I nuzzled my face into her shoulder so I wouldn't be able to watch the meter tick upward. I had twenty dollars in my pocket. I hoped it didn't come to more than that.

"I like it when you're cuddly." Kat tickled my side.

I couldn't help but laugh.

"So what do you say, should we make our own porno tonight?" Her tone was alluring, even if her question was crass.

Maybe I *was* a prude. Around my mother, I definitely was.

I shook my head, needing to get the thought of Mom out of my head so I could concentrate on the beautiful woman next to me.

"I think that can be arranged."

Kat informed the driver to put the pedal to the metal. Her eagerness turned me on.

The cabbie ogled us in the mirror, pretending to be checking traffic in the rearview mirror.

I closed my eyes and ignored him.

When my alarm trilled at 4:30 a.m., Kat groaned. I silenced it immediately and popped out of bed. I never hit the snooze button—not once in my life. It would take me twenty minutes on the T to get to work, which didn't allow me much time to shower, dress, and grab something to eat before I had to make a mad dash to the subway stop.

It was still warm outside, but when winter hit, I'd likely have to forego the shower to avoid my hair freezing on my way to work. In warmer months, I was content sporting a wet ponytail, which had plenty of time to dry by the time the store opened. The only caveat was that I then had to wear it in a ponytail the rest of the day, since it dried with a permanent dent where the hair-tie held the wet strands together. Sporting a ponytail while teaching showed my dedication to research, rather than to preening, I told myself. Either that or it proved I was lazy, or a slob, or worse, both.

It was still dark outside. While I waited for the T, I nibbled on a tasteless energy bar. Peanut butter, my ass. It tasted like cardboard. Choking down another bite, I wondered how long until my mom called to talk about my dad's supposed affair again. More than likely, she'd also want me to pick up her car.

The screech of the T's brakes alerted me that the train would arrive soon. I wasn't teaching today, so I had an eight-hour shift. Then Kat and I were to have dinner with the family at Aunt Barbara's house. I rubbed some sleep out of my eyes.

When I entered the first car of the T, I tapped my Charlie card. I missed the days when you could flash your pass and enter any door. Only one other person was insane enough to get up this early. Actually, I think she was on her way home after a night out. I chuckled as she hid her face. The T-ride of shame was always humbling at five in the morning, but humorous for the rest of us. From the looks of her disheveled clothes, she had rushed out as soon as she'd opened her eyes and realized what she'd done. Her T-shirt was even inside out.

Did the guy know she was gone yet? The thought perked me up some.

She wasn't the only one regretting her late night this morning; of course, mine had nothing to do with a one-night stand.

Harold was not in the store when I arrived. I was five minutes late, but of course I didn't expect him there for another hour. How he managed to keep his job for so long, considering his habitual tardiness, baffled me. Of course, I never told on him, and maybe others didn't either. That was hard to believe of the employees who called him Harry Pooper, but maybe Harold had some dirt on everyone in the store. He seemed like the type who would collect dirt.

The first hour flew by. Samantha didn't make an appearance. I was disappointed by that. I'm not sure why, but I really thought she would pop in to say hello, or at least to grab a drink.

Of course, I couldn't pinpoint why I wanted to see her. High school was years ago, and my crush had subsided. Having an extremely hot girlfriend put the kibosh on most crushes, but it had been good seeing her—someone who knew me when I was on my way to making a big splash in the world. Even if it turned out I did a belly flop for all to see.

Oh well, I looked like I'd been up all night, which for the most part, I had, so it was probably a good thing that Samantha didn't pop in. After my second espresso I no longer felt like super-gluing my eyes open, although my heart now thumped and I had clammy hands.

"Did you sleep at all last night?" asked Harold, who looked in even rougher shape than I was. Not for the same reason, was my guess. I'm pretty sure the guy was still a virgin.

"Some. What about you? You look like shit."

"Not much. I got the new Gaiman book yesterday." Harold's entire face smiled.

"Oh, you must like it if you stayed up all night reading."

"Like it? I love it! I finished it a couple of hours ago." His eyes glowed with happiness.

"Is he your favorite author, then?" I didn't feel like talking, but it did help pass the time. Oddly, the store was quiet. Had everyone slept like crap last night and stayed in bed? I wished I'd had that option. Must be nice to be a suit.

Snuggling up to Kat was heads above standing in an empty coffee shop, talking to Harold.

"Hands down the best author." To emphasize his point, Harold slapped the countertop with one hand. "What's your favorite book of his?" He seemed eager for my reply.

"Um, I haven't read any of his books." I looked away, feeling foolish but unsure as to why. It wasn't like I was a non-reader. However, the look on my coworker's face told me I was a huge disappointment to him. An English teacher who hadn't read Gaiman? Unheard of, in his world.

He pinned me with a look of total repugnance. "But I thought you taught English."

"I do. British authors, to be exact."

He threw his hands up in the air. "Gaiman is British! Seriously, Cori, how can you call yourself a professor of British lit and not know Gaiman? That ain't right." He crossed his arms.

I heard the bell tinkle, but I didn't bother to turn around. "Maybe I should be clear, if the author isn't dead, I don't read him or her. Did Gaiman die within the past hour?"

"You're a snob. A book snob!" He refused to break eye contact, waggling a finger in my face and hopping around as if his feet were on fire.

I heard a woman clear her throat, and I turned to see Samantha. My heart stopped. Two days in a row she had arrived during an embarrassing moment.

"Well, I'm a coffee snob, if that makes you feel better." She flashed me a supportive smile.

"What can I get you?" I shot Harold a look to shut him up.

"Hey, do you like Neil Gaiman?" Harold ignored my silent plea.

Samantha cocked her head, thinking. "Did he write *Neverwhere*?"

"Yes!" Harold clapped his hands in glee, like a girl.

"Then, yes. I liked that book. I read it when I visited London last year. Mind—"

"The gap!" Harold finished her sentence.

I looked at the two of them as if they had lost their minds. Mind the gap. What did that even mean? Was it a reference to the store, Gap? Why would a British author write about a jeans store? I hated their jeans—too tight in the crotch. I preferred having blood flow down there.

"Cori, here, who teaches British literature"—he rolled his eyes—"has never read him. Can you believe it?" His voice was filled with shock and loathing.

"No! Really?" I couldn't tell if Samantha was egging him on or agreeing with him.

"I know. Crazy! We need to educate her." Harold

swiveled his head to enforce his intention.

"Doesn't say much for Harvard if they don't read the classics?" Sam's eyes sparkled, and I knew she was teasing.

"You went to Harvard?" Harold turned to me, baffled. "I thought you went to Adams."

I could tell he was impressed, and simultaneously dismayed.

"Yep, I'm Harvard alum. I teach at Adams."

*Not that my Harvard degrees helped me all that much*, I thought to myself, bitterly. Here I was, standing in a Beantown Café apron schlepping coffee. Fucking pitiful.

"Pumpkin spice latte. Bean Supreme, please." Samantha took advantage of Harold's silence.

"Hey, you're picking up the lingo."

She looked pleased at the compliment.

While Harold made her drink, I tried to start a conversation. "Got any big plans for the weekend?"

"No. Unless you count working." Sam sighed. "You?"

"Very exciting. Dinner at my aunt's."

"Ha! I'd rather do that than stare at spreadsheets all weekend. Is she a good cook?"

"Horrible! Last year I got food poisoning. But she's my aunt. What can I do?" I shrugged.

"One pumpkin spice latte!" Harold screamed, for some inexplicable reason. It was just the three of us in the entire store. I wanted to ask him if he was on crack—Gaiman crack.

Samantha picked up her cup. Harold had scrawled "Mind the Gap" on the side. "Cute, Harold." She waved goodbye to both of us and left.

"I think she's the only suit I get along with," Harold said

as soon as the door closed.

"You know her?" I was flabbergasted.

"Of course. She's one of our regs. Duh, Cori." He reached into his bag and pulled out a Neil Gaiman book. "It's eerily quiet today." He opened it up.

"Is that the one you read last night?" I gestured to the book.

"Yeah. I can't wait to read it again." He buried his nose in the book.

"If Samantha is a regular, how come I haven't seen her before yesterday?"

"Oh, she just got back from an extended trip." He didn't look up.

"Really?" I didn't mean to phrase it as a question.

"Yeah. I think she was on her honeymoon or something. She planned it for months." Harold waved his hand, his attempt to silence me.

I was relieved he didn't look up, because I didn't want him to see the look of disappointment on my face. Sure, I had a girlfriend, and sure, Samantha was rich, successful, and beautiful—totally out of my league. But I liked the idea of her. Not in the girlfriend way, but in a friend way. Married friends weren't much fun—at least not straight ones. Before too long, she'd pop out a kid and would be too busy to live life.

My phone buzzed. A texted order from my mother: Pick up the car and drive Kat to Barbara's. I wondered if Kat called her to make that suggestion. Kat hated taking the T to the Chestnut Hill stop. Even though it was only one stop past the Reservoir stop near our home, Kat claimed it was out in the boonies and she swore we would get raped or mugged and that we should take a cab each time. I agreed that the stop was a little creepy, but there were two of us, after all.

"Let's stop at the liquor store." Kat's tone implied it was an order.

I waited in the car while she ran in to get the essentials: a bottle of wine for the hostess, and a six-pack of Sam Adams for my father and uncle.

She emerged from the store carrying a box full of booze.

"Did you spend all of the cash I gave you?" I asked before she had a chance to take her seat.

"Nope. There's some left." She didn't sound flustered at all. As soon as money came in, she spent it. Saving was a foreign concept.

I rubbed my eyes in frustration. I had three outstanding bills at home.

Kat ran her finger up my inner thigh. "Come on, we'll be late."

Not wanting to ruin the night, I pulled her hand to my lips and kissed her fingertips tenderly.

I wasn't excited about this dinner, fearful Mom would burst into tears and accuse Dad of having an affair when he asked for her to pass the salt or something.

"Don't mention the affair tonight," said Kat, as if she had read my mind.

It brought me back to reality. "What?"

"Your mom called and said don't mention the affair." She drummed her fingers on my leg playfully.

"Which one? My uncle's, or the imaginary one my father is having?"

"Good point. Both."

"Will Uncle Roger be there?"

"Yes, of course." Kat's furrowed brow implied I was an idiot. Roger had never missed a family dinner.

"How my aunt puts up with him is beyond me."

Roger was discreet enough. If someone didn't know our family all that well, they'd never suspect a thing. Not one bit. In fact, if a person didn't know about Roger's affairs, he or she may have walked away saying, "What a happy couple. How do they do it?"

I started to say something along those lines to Kat, but decided to remain quiet. I just wanted to get through the night without strangling my mother. It was a tall order.

"Oh, did I mention we're having dinner with my parents tomorrow night?" Kat slipped that one in while we sat at a red light. "My father says he wants to talk to you."

"Me? Why me?" I couldn't fathom what a dentist could possibly need from an English professor.

"I dunno. Oh, we're here!" The relief was evident in her voice. Just talking about her parents made Kat uncomfortable. Before the car came to a complete stop, she had her door open and was heading towards the front door, leaving the booze in the backseat for me to carry. Oh well, I was the jock, and I would never let her carry it in anyway.

Hoisting the box into my arms, I noticed my favorite beer in the bunch. Kat never forgot me. Each day there was some type of surprise. Smiling, I wandered into the kitchen and set the box down on the counter.

"Goodness, Cori, you leave anything on the shelves?" teased Aunt Barbara as she wrapped her arms around me. She stepped back. "Are you losing weight?"

Before I could answer, Mom jumped in with, "Oh you should have seen her last night. Shoveling cheese enchiladas in her mouth so fast I'm sure she got heartburn."

"Pishposh, Nell. I tell you, she's losing weight. You work too hard, Cori." My aunt adjusted her apron and then mussed up her gray hair, which fell just below her chin line. Mom looked like she'd just walked out of a salon, but at least her clothes, while not as sensible as my aunt's, were nothing too extravagant. Boston roots didn't allow my mom or aunt to act like spoiled rich housewives from reality TV shows. Besides, they were both successful in their own right and didn't have time to act like idiots.

Despite being polar opposites, Aunt Barbara and my mother were the best of friends and were wonderful sisters. I was lucky to have two such women in my life that I could go to. Even when I was a kid, if I needed motherly advice or a hug, I went to Aunt Barbara. Mom wasn't the most nurturing person in the world, which didn't mean she was a bad mom. She just had different strengths.

"Hi, Cori. You look well," said Uncle Roger as he entered the kitchen.

"Roger, open your eyes. I swear Cori has lost ten pounds since we saw her last." My aunt looked concerned. "When did you have your last physical?"

I shrugged and munched on a carrot stick I'd taken from the appetizer platter. "School, maybe."

Seeing a doctor was a luxury I couldn't afford.

"I want you to make an appointment first thing on Monday, you hear me?" My aunt held my chin with her right hand. "First thing."

Roger peeked into the liquor box and pulled out the Harpoon Island Creek Oyster Stout that Kat had bought for me. "Oyster stout, that sounds good."

"Cori loves it," said Kat.

I cringed a little, since I was a vegetarian, but whenever the opportunity arose, I drank oyster stout. I became a veggie in high school, but there was one thing I could never give up: oysters. I was from Boston—it was in our blood. Even though I did feel guilty, momentarily at least.

Roger popped the cap off with the bottle opener on his Harpoon keychain and poured my stout into a tall mug he had pulled from the freezer. I watched the dark brown liquid gurgle into his glass. Catching a whiff of it, I wanted to grab the glass and guzzle it down; I didn't, though.

Kat looked mortified, but she remained speechless. When she looked over at me, I shook my head, letting her know it was okay. Both of us had been trained to respect our elders.

"Roger, share with Cori. It's her beer, after all." Aunt Barbara came to my rescue.

Without missing a beat, Roger pulled another glass out and poured the rest in for me.

We clinked our glasses.

"Damn, that's good." Roger wiped his mouth with the back of his hand, and then took another sip.

"Right on time, as usual, Dale," Mom piped up sarcastically as my father walked into the kitchen.

My father had never liked his first name: Warren. In high school, his football buddies started calling him "Tisdale" and then shortened it to Dale. My mother preferred the nickname.

She once told me that calling out Warren during sex was a mood killer.

I didn't want to know that.

She continued by telling me that Dale was much sexier because it reminded her of the exotic dancers, the Chippendales. I, on the other hand, thought of the Disney chipmunks Chip and Dale whenever I heard the nickname. So when Mom said she preferred having sex with a Dale, I envisioned her frolicking with a chipmunk. I was surprised I didn't need massive amounts of therapy. Maybe both Kat and I should look into getting a shrink. I wondered if we'd get a group discount if I dragged in my entire family.

My father took a seat on a barstool, settling in and crossing his ankles on the bar beneath. He wore white socks and brown loafers. As far as I could remember, Dad had always worn white socks with brown or black loafers. Mom begged and pleaded with him to buy colored socks, but he always refused. He gave in on most things when it came to her, but he would not lose the sock battle. For an entire year, Mom tied all of his white socks into knots to discourage him. She then proceeded to fill his sock drawer with beautiful, colorful socks that weren't tied together. Each morning, my father patiently untied his white socks while he waited for his bread to toast. Finally, my mother caved, and the sock war ended, although she still made fun of him. To make it worse, they were white tube socks. Secretly, I loved the man for his conviction. He crossed his arms over his chest, and I noticed that his navy polo was more wrinkled than normal. Would Mom assume he'd just had a roll in the hay with his mistress and hadn't bothered taking his shirt and tube socks off?

The snarl on her face indicated she was thinking something along those lines.

"Dad, when can we go to a game?" I wanted to play interference. My father had season tickets to the Red Sox and usually went with a buddy or with Roger. Occasionally, he'd take me.

Dad perked up and showed some life. "How 'bout tomorrow. The Yanks are in town."

I couldn't believe my luck. He had never taken me to see the New York Yankees play. I usually got the games no one wanted to watch, like the Houston Astros.

"That's great!"

My glee obviously angered my mother, but before she could say anything, Aunt Barbara said, "I love seeing you two spending time together." The tears in her eyes made her look joyful and sad simultaneously. She and Roger never had children. Aunt Barbara couldn't have any, and Roger got snipped years ago to prevent any further marital complication.

"Who's pitching tomorrow?" I asked, unable to contain my excitement, even as Mom huffed and strode out of the room with Kat on her arm.

Growing up in Boston made me a proud member of the Red Sox Nation. There was nothing like going to Fenway, indulging in a Fenway Frank, drinking a beer, and eating Cracker Jacks. My father had been taking me to the park since I was five. My mother never went. Sports weren't her thing. However, she never missed one of my basketball games, even the away games. She even learned the rules and the lingo.

"I don't rightly know." Dad pulled out his cell and started searching. "Ah, Lester."

Jon Lester was the best pitcher on the team. "And for the Yanks?"

Even Roger was curious to know. I had to keep an eye on him. I mean, the man already stole my beer; I wasn't going to let him get his grubby hands on my ticket.

"Sabathia," my father managed, struggling with his phone. His sausage fingers made operating a cell phone difficult.

I squealed. "Oh, this is going to be a great game. Both are leading in strikeouts this year. I love a good pitcher's duel." I rubbed my hands together in glee.

Dad stood and placed his arm around my shoulder as we joined Mom and Kat on the back deck. We rarely had father/daughter bonding moments, but when we did, I cherished them. And the best part was that it rattled my mother. Mom was not only competitive with her sister, but with her husband as well. If I didn't act as if she were the best parent of the two, it pissed her off. But rather than trying to woo me to her side when she felt this way, she did her best to make one or both of us suffer.

It was early in September, but humidity still clung to the air. Cicadas buzzed and the power lines marking the back of the yard hummed. I loved that I couldn't hear the T from here. I lived near the B-line, and day and night I heard the screeching of tires—a horrendous metal-on-metal sound. Out here, even beside the power lines, I felt closer to nature. I could even see Chestnut Hill Reservoir off in the distance. Someday, I hoped to have a place in the "country." If I could ever get out of debt.

"Ah, Warren, seeing you two together reminds me where

Cori got her fashion sense," hissed my mother, swirling the wine in her glass and raising her eyebrows to emphasize her point. Her eyes gleamed with the satisfaction of knocking him down a peg or two, and her tone implied he was a nitwit—a sexless, fashionless nitwit.

I looked at my father's khaki shorts and blue polo, and then stared down at my plaid Bermuda shorts, Harvard tee, and plain brown sandals.

"Hey, at least I'm not wearing white socks." I guess I could be competitive as well.

"That's because you take after your mother. White socks are the new black," said my father, victoriously.

Aunt Barbara clapped her hands. "Point to Dale."

Mom bristled. "Oh, please. The man tries to make love with his socks on."

Kat and I sensed trouble.

"Where did you get this blouse, Nell?" Kat entered the fray, reaching out for the shirt and rubbing the fabric between finger and thumb. "It's softer than a baby's butt."

The compliment worked. Mom started to tell Kat about this new boutique she had discovered on Newbury Street, and I heaved a sigh of relief. We had distracted her twice so far, but how many more bullets did we have to dodge? Dad and Roger broke off to the side and started a conversation about the Pats this season, and Barbara wandered back into the kitchen to check on dinner.

"Any more oyster beer?" Roger shouted after her.

"I only picked up one, but Cori and I can go get more if you like. Let me check with Barbara and see how soon we'll be eating."

I wanted to kiss Kat for thinking of that. I needed a break from my parents' troubled marriage.

Kat nudged my hip gently on her way back inside. "You okay?" Stopping, she waited for an answer.

"Yeah. Thanks for the help, tonight." I wove my arm around her waist.

"Anytime. I'm not ready for this blowout either, and I'm hoping it doesn't happen tonight." She sighed deeply.

Unfortunately, the liquor store was fewer than five minutes away; we were back well before I was ready for round three with my mother.

I sat heavily on one of the barstools and watched my aunt pull a vegetarian lasagna from the oven. Kat wandered back outside to keep an eye on the angry woman. Turning, I watched her go. She looked radiant in her halter-neck top and jeans. Of course, she could wear a gunnysack and still look sexy, innocent, and mischievous all at once.

"How's work going, Cori?" My head whipped back around to Aunt Barb, who was setting the steaming dish on two trivets, so she wouldn't scorch her new granite countertop.

"All right. Just wish I …"

"Have you asked your mother for help?" She pinned me with a concerned look.

"You know Mom. Loves to take me shopping, to get my nails done—but handouts—no way."

"How much?" Barbara didn't look up from cutting the lasagna into massive portions and slopping them on the plates.

"Oh, I haven't asked her for money for years."

"I mean, how much do you need now?" She was kind

enough to keep her eyes averted.

"A few hundred," I mumbled, totally ashamed.

She nodded, and I knew that before the end of the night she would slip the money into my hand. Barbara didn't dwell on shame.

Instead, she started into a story about my mother. "Once, after a school friend of your mother's lost sight in one eye following a freak Fourth of July mishap, Nell had the gall to tell him he should feel lucky. She said she always saw streaks of light in her left eye and it drove her mad, so Nell claimed he was much better off than her."

"She didn't!" I couldn't believe it, although Barbara was not the lying type. She wouldn't even think to stretch the truth for dramatic effect.

"Oh, yes she did. I was so embarrassed. When the boy transferred to a different school, I was so relieved to not have to listen to your mother go on and on about how the blinding light was killing her. She once even flopped to the ground during recess, screaming that someone should just shoot her to end her misery. After the boy left the school, oddly enough so did her mysterious eye condition. Many of us were relieved, including her teacher. Your grandfather was beside himself, poor man."

My aunt cleaned up the gooey lasagna spills on each plate so they looked more presentable, and then casually asked, "Has Kat had any luck finding a job?" She glanced at me quickly, and then turned to the fridge to take out a prepared salad.

"Nope."

Standing with the fridge door wide-open, salad bowl in

hand, Aunt Barb replied. "I'm sure she's working on some way to help you two."

I shrugged. "I wish she'd start painting again; that's what makes her happy." I took a slug of oyster stout.

Barbara set the bowl down heavily on the counter. "Well, it's not my place to say anything." She adjusted her apron and tilted her head to make eye contact, as if waiting to see if I would say anything.

Luckily, I didn't, because Mom and Kat walked in.

"Oh, Barbara, it smells wonderful in here." Kat put her arm around my aunt's shoulders. "I love these family dinners."

"And we love having you here, dear. For years, I didn't think Cori would actually settle down with anyone. She was headstrong from the moment she popped out."

Mom's laugh was genuine.

"One of her first sentences was, 'Mommy, I want to sleep in my own bed,'" Mom elaborated. "She said that when I was sitting in a rocking chair, trying to get her to fall asleep." She patted my back, somewhat tenderly. "Barbara and I never thought she would actually want to share her bed. Every time she went to a sleepover, she'd call me to pick her up early."

I sucked in air slowly, waiting for Mom to make some sexual joke.

Kat came to stand behind me and wrapped her arms around my chest. Her hard nipples prodded my back, distracting me. Until I met Kat, I hadn't understood why some men became blathering fools around beautiful women. I thought that, being a woman, I'd never be sucked in by a woman's wiles.

Dead wrong.

Kat had me wrapped around her little finger the moment she spoke to me. I'd been standing in line at the grocery store when she tapped me on the shoulder.

"Excuse me, would you mind if I cut in front of you. I only have two items, and I'm in a huge rush."

When I saw her, I couldn't utter a single word. I tried to mumble, "Sure, go ahead" but found I could only motion for her to step in front of me. All of the men in the line gawked along with me.

When Kat didn't have enough money, of course I paid for her stuff. What else could I do? In fact, I blocked the way of the man standing behind me, who was also going to offer to pay.

"I got it," I asserted.

"Are you sure? I feel like an idiot." Kat had blushed, and the reddish tint to her cheeks excited me even more. "I don't know how I can thank you."

"No worries. It happens to all of us." I waved my hand, dismissing her humiliation.

Kat had thanked me and left. Her absence immediately sucked the air out of my lungs. I felt as though I would never be able to live my life to the fullest, knowing I missed my chance of being with the most stunning woman I had ever encountered. The mysterious beauty had opened a door for me, but I hadn't entered it.

Two days later, we ran into each other near Harvard's campus. I couldn't believe my luck. Not wanting to blow my second chance, I offered to buy her a cup of coffee and clinched our first date.

Smiling at the memory, I patted Kat's arms where they

wrapped around me, and melted into her embrace.

## Chapter Four

Before heading out to Fenway for the game, I sat at my desk and eyed a stack of mail. Correction—bills. Just once I would have liked to receive a letter that didn't send shivers down my spine. I flipped through the envelopes: Gas bill, electric bill, cable bill, chiropractor—that one went to my mother—and then ... AmEx bill. Slowly, I separated it from the rest and placed it on my desk. Each month, I sat down and went over the purchases. I picked up the envelope, weighing it with my hand. It wasn't massive. Last month's bill had nearly given me a coronary. Moving my hand up and down along the envelope, feeling the pressure, the weight of it, I tried to guess the amount. Outside, I heard Kat fire up the espresso machine. She knew I was in my office, taking care of the monthly expenses. I think she dreaded this day each month more than I did.

We never discussed her spending habits openly. It was always the eight-hundred-pound gorilla in the room.

I never knew how to broach the subject. Should I say, "Hey, what in the hell did you buy at Urban Outfitters that cost five hundred bucks?" Or would a more gentle approach work, such as, "Eight hundred bucks at Bed Bath & Beyond?—I hope we have some new satin sheets to break-in tonight. Oh, and I see you went to Victoria's Secret as well," and follow it up with a suggestive wink.

A year ago, sitting in our hot tub during a dreadful snowstorm, we had talked about our childhoods. Kat had mentioned that we could both benefit from therapy. She was joking, because we had both been mad enough to get nude and hop into a hot tub during a blizzard. I had seen the comment as a small window of opportunity. Maybe if she started therapy, she'd recognize her shopping addiction. The words to tell her that formed in my head, but when I tried to speak, I choked on them. How could I tell the woman I was madly in love with that she was making my life hell by spending every dime I made? And even spending dimes I hadn't even made!

I grabbed my letter opener and tore open the AmEx bill.

Five pages.

Whew! Last month it was ten. Thank God. I scanned the charges.

Let me be clear, not all of the charges had been made by Kat. We both had cards for the joint account. I had always tried to convince myself that it paid off, since that way we accrued a lot of AmEx points. Someday we'd be able to go on an awesome trip.

Pen in hand, I read each charge, noting where and how

much. It was pretty typical. Kat loved to buy certain things: clothing, lingerie, shoes, items for the house, and groceries. She was an amazing cook.

One charge at the art shop by Fenway caught my attention. When Kat moved in, we had converted one of the small guest rooms into an art studio for her. At first, she spent the majority of her time in there, painting. But for the past year, she hadn't stepped foot in there—at least not that I could tell. I know it's awful, but I go in there to see if she's been painting again. It's her passion, and she's damn good in my opinion. But when I tell her that, she laughs. She knows I'm the only one in my family who doesn't "get" art. I can appreciate it, but I can't analyze it like my aunt. Even Mr. Tube Socks has a better eye than me. When I tell Kat she's good, she smiles and says, "Yes, but you also like paintings of dogs playing poker."

I'm not *that* bad, but I'm close. I was only in Kat's art studio yesterday, and I hadn't noticed any new supplies. The dust hadn't been disturbed on any of her paints or easels. So what in the heck did she buy at the art store?

Squinting—I refuse to admit I need reading glasses—I noticed it was dated one week ago. Damn, trash day was two days ago. More than likely the receipt had gone into the recycle bin. Kat was fastidious when it came to cleaning, and she insisted on recycling every scrap of paper, including receipts.

Sighing, I set the bill aside on my desk. Sounds coming from the kitchen suggested breakfast was almost ready. Smearing a smile on my face, I went to say good morning to my drop-dead gorgeous spendthrift.

*Make more money, Cori, and it won't matter. Or finish your fucking novel. You promised her a lavish lifestyle, and you aren't upholding your end of the bargain.*

Before I could say good morning, Kat handed me my espresso and planted a wet kiss on my lips. "Morning, darling. How do the bills look?"

I almost pissed my pants. She had never asked me that before.

"Not too bad, actually." Questions about the art supplies were forming, all I needed to do was spit them out.

I opened my mouth.

Kat looked at me, grinning like a fool in love, which forced the words back into the pit of my stomach. Instead, I licked my lips. "It smells good. What's for breakfast?"

*I'm pathetic.*

She had opened the door to that conversation, and I'd slammed it shut like a terrified child who'd just heard a noise in the attic.

"French toast."

I wanted to laugh. Kat knew it was bill day, and that French toast was my favorite breakfast food. Did she realize how obvious she was being?

"Sounds wonderful." I walked to the fridge and peeked out the glass door leading to the back deck. The recycle bin was completely empty. I gulped down half of a tiny bottle of orange juice from the fridge.

Maybe Kat had signed up for a painting class and was keeping the supplies there. I could hope, at least. When she painted, she was content. And when she was content, she didn't shop as much.

"You excited about the game today?" Kat set our plates

on the kitchen table and took her seat.

I sat opposite and poured organic maple syrup on my French toast. "Yep. I know this sounds silly, but I couldn't sleep a wink last night. I can't believe my father is taking me to a Yankees game. I usually get the tickets no one wants." I took a bite. After swallowing I asked, "What's your plan today?"

"I'm going to your aunt's today. She needs help setting up a new exhibit." Kat placed the daintiest mouthful of food in her mouth. Not once have I seen her take an enormous bite of food. She eats like a surgeon operating on a brain: slow, delicate, and calculated. I could eat three meals in the time it takes her to eat half of one. Looking up from her plate, she added, "Don't forget dinner with Phineas and my mother tonight. Six sharp." She punctuated the word sharp by stabbing the air with her knife.

Leaving Fenway, I was on cloud nine. The game hadn't started well for the Sox. In the second inning, Alex Rodriguez, nicknamed A-Rod, hit a homerun. In the third, the Sox were down six runs. Boston's manager yanked the starting pitcher, Lester, off the mound. It was clear he was having a bad day at the "office." The Yankees' pitcher already had four strikeouts and no runs.

Dad and I contemplated leaving the game and having a late lunch. Losing was bad. But getting a beat-down by New York was hideous for die-hard Sox fans.

Then the Yankees' manager pulled Sabathia, their starting pitcher, off the mound in the sixth since he thought the game was locked up. The score was eight to one. I could see why he felt safe. That's when the game turned around completely. The Red Sox lit up one reliever after another. By the eighth inning, they led by two runs. In the ninth, the Yanks tied the game.

Ortiz hit a homer in the eleventh and won the game. By the time I arrived at the restaurant to meet Kat and her parents, I was in the best mood. Nothing was going to get me down, not even Phineas Finn.

I strolled in wearing my green Sox baseball hat and a large red foam finger that proclaimed the Sox were number one. Did I look silly? Absolutely! But I didn't care. The Sox won—that was all that mattered.

Kat looked amused as I slid into the booth next to her. A child at the nearest table was eyeing my foam finger, so I happily handed it to him. His astonished parents thanked me profusely, and I was sure Kat's parents were glad I had managed to rid myself of the silly thing. Phineas Finn, Kat's father, was not a fan of frivolity.

A dentist, he seemed the type of guy who loved the music he played in his office—tunes that would make a coma patient hurtle out of bed and run screaming rather than listen to another Michael Bolton, Kenny G, or Celine Dion song. In fact, the only thing cool about Phineas Finn was his name. When I first heard the name, I loved it. I was a Trollope fan, so I asked if he were named after Trollope's famous character. Dr. Finn stared at me as if I had lobsters hanging from my eyelids.

The name had been in the family for five generations, he told me. He was Phineas Finn the Fifth. I'm not making that up.

Furthermore, he had never heard of Trollope, and the fact that I compared him to a literary figure was a downright insult to their family, which was, according to Kat's father, directly responsible for why Boston was such a thriving city today. Without the Finns, Boston would still be a backwoods town in the middle of a swamp.

According to Phineas, his family was the only one of any importance in Beantown. Forget the Adams—even if two men from that family became presidents of the United States. And don't even mention John Hancock—he was of no importance. That massive John Hancock building on Clarendon Street? Didn't mean a thing. Paul Revere was a "reckless man."

The list goes on.

One of my first dinners with Kat's parents was especially illuminating. After that night, Kat was terrified I would never want to see her again. For three hours, she squirmed in her seat while Phineas bad-mouthed all of the great names associated with the American Revolution and the founding of our nation.

All from a dentist! From the little research I've done on the Finns, no one in the family was a statesman of any type. They got their money from shipping, and, truth be known, piracy. The Finns of yesteryear were brave men who ran through blockades during the Revolutionary War and the War of 1812 and made a killing because their competitors couldn't get a ship out. If they saw a ship in distress, they would kindly relieve them of their burden. Most of Kat's ancestors would no doubt laugh in Phineas's face now—a dentist exclaiming how great their family was. They were merciless thieves and rogues. Yes, they were successful, but they certainly weren't honorable. And from the diaries I've read, they were damn proud about their lack of honor. There was no money in that.

It wasn't until the fifth Finn was born that this "legacy"

surfaced. Phineas had spent all his life being full of himself, and his attitude had isolated him, his wife, and his daughter. During her childhood, Kat was kept hidden away, attending private schools and living at home under lock and key after school hours. Luckily for Kat, she was an avid reader. I sometimes think she would have gone mad if she hadn't been a reader.

The Finns owned a TV, but only watched the news and shows on PBS. They never went on family vacations unless they involved Cape Cod. They didn't even go on picnics. Not once. I took Kat on a picnic after I found that out; she'd never been so excited. She acted like a child going to Disney World for the first time.

Kat was even denied friends unless they were relations. But all of her aunts, uncles, and cousins knew Phineas was a whack job, so they ostracized Kat anyway, thinking she was brainwashed as well. When she left home to attend Wellesley, Kat finally felt free. But her childhood still haunted. How could it not?

I couldn't imagine growing up like that. My family wasn't perfect, but compared to Kat's, we were like the Cleaver family from the 1950s television show *Leave It to Beaver*.

Kat's mother, Margaret, was the perfect mate for Phineas. She was just as boring, conceited, and unintelligent. For their honeymoon, Kat's mom suggested they go to Mount Rushmore. At first I thought she must have been a huge *North by Northwest* fan, which might have made it somewhat cooler. But she has never seen the Cary Grant classic. Never. Movies with any type of suspense are too much for her. Margaret couldn't even watch *Bedknobs and Broomsticks* with her daughter when Kat was a kid.

No, Margaret picked Mount Rushmore because she really wanted to see the presidents carved in stone—on her honeymoon. How was that for lighting the fire in the bedroom? Not to be disrespectful, but I was pretty sure most people didn't get turned on by George Washington, Thomas Jefferson, Abraham Lincoln, and Teddy Roosevelt. They might have been great presidents, but their faces were pretty much the last thing on my mind when I want to get naked.

The honeymoon was their first and last trip outside of Massachusetts. Ever since then, they go to Cape Cod every summer. They stay in their family home, go to the same restaurants, and visit the same museums when it rains. For more than twenty years, they haven't varied this routine a bit. Margaret almost cried when one of their favorite restaurants on the Cape closed. But she was a tough woman, so not one actual tear fell from her dead eyes. Her predecessors came over on the *Mayflower*. She would not disappoint them by showing any emotion, let alone happiness or sadness. Or maybe she couldn't even recognize other emotions. Everything was black and white with that woman. No shades of gray.

"I take it the Sox won." Kat squeezed my thigh, quickly so her parents wouldn't see. I could tell she was relieved when I finally arrived. She never missed the monthly dinner with her folks, but I knew she preferred for me to be there, for moral support. I was her buffer, and it was my job to keep the conversation going. Even Kat, the most bewitching of creatures, couldn't charm her parents. Not that I could either, but I was new enough to their lives that they were forced to pretend to care about what I had to say.

"Oh, Kat, too bad you missed it." I turned to face her. "Today's game will go down in history!" I slapped the tabletop, which caused Phineas's puckered face to sink further into his skull. He constantly looked like he was sucking a lime. I didn't mean to lay it on so thick, but her parents gave me the willies so I always felt uncomfortable and acted like a buffoon.

"So what did I miss?" I looked across the table at them as I placed my napkin in my lap, remembering my manners.

"We were just getting ready to order, Cori," explained her father.

I was ten minutes late. By the looks on their faces, they were not happy about it. Plus, I had been at a sporting event, mixing with the lower classes. Could they smell the beer and hotdogs on my breath?

The waiter approached and asked if I needed more time to look at the menu. I almost laughed in his face. We went to dinner once a month with Kat's parents and every time, we came here. He was our usual waiter. I hated the place, which didn't have any decent vegetarian meals, but heaven forbid we eat someplace else and break Finn family tradition. In its heyday, this joint had been popular. But now it was run-down and usually half-empty. Only tourists, who didn't know better, and the Finns patronized it. The Oriental rug on the floor was dingy and so threadbare I feared walking on it in case it disintegrated, and the grime of the place killed my appetite every time. The owners kept the lights dim—beyond dim—but I knew the truth. Anyone could smell the dust and mold.

"Not to worry. I'm ready." I motioned for him to take Margaret's order first. I knew my place.

After everyone ordered the exact same meal they always ordered, I tried to kindle a conversation. "Dr. Finn, how's business?" Pathetic, I know, but what do you ask a dentist who only watches PBS?

He sat up straighter in his chair, which impressed me since he was straight as a board already. "I'm glad you asked. I have a proposition for you, Cori."

A proposition? From a dentist?

This should be good.

I stifled a laugh. "Really?" I took a sip of my iced water; I never drank alcohol in front of the Finns.

"Yes. Our billing person quit, Cori."

"Oh, I'm so sorry to hear that." I had no idea why that was so important that we had to bump up our usual dinner plans by a week.

"Tragic, Cori. It's so hard to find people I can trust." His lips puckered again and disappeared into his sloping chin.

*Tragic*—that seemed a bit too much. The person quit. It's not like he or she died, which would be tragic.

I did my best to keep my face judgment-free. Every day, I saw ads on TV about people signing up for an online school to learn dental and medical billing. It didn't sound hard at all. How difficult could it be to find competent workers in Boston, especially now that the economy was in the shitter? He could probably find a Harvard grad who was desperate for the job. Then it hit me. I was being set up! I was a Harvard alum who was struggling financially.

*Oh no, oh no, oh no …*

Kat seemed to stop breathing. I wanted to give her a hug, to let her know it would be okay. No matter what, we'd get through this.

Instead, I grabbed a piece of bread and angrily buttered a small portion as I waited for the ball to drop. Kat and I were not allowed to show affection at her family dinners. The Finns were the coldest people I'd ever met. Rattlesnakes had more charm. Truthfully, I'd rather hug a snake than either of her parents; not that they'd ever tried to hug me. Kat couldn't even remember either of them hugging her. Not hugging your own child seemed unimaginable to me

"I know you've been working at Beantown Café part-time, Cori." He paused for me to respond.

I didn't. I wished he'd stop saying my name. I already had a part-time job. I hated Beantown with a passion, but I'd rather work there eighty hours a week than do dental billing. And working for Kat's father—shit, that sounded awful. Fucking dreadful. Why couldn't I have been hit by a bus on the way to this dinner?

"And this job would fit with your schedule because you could file the claims at any time, even at three in the morning," explained Phineas. There was an odd look in his eye. I wouldn't call it a glint—just a different shade of dull. I wondered if it was Phineas Finn's personal brand of happiness.

Neither Kat nor I spoke, but I'm pretty sure Phineas didn't expect us to. He was the type of man who thought he commanded respect.

He continued, "I'll have the software installed on your home computer, and I'll set up a fax machine for you. Each night, my secretary will fax the claims that need processing and then all you have to do is enter them in the system. Our biller has agreed to train you for a few days. If I remember correctly, you don't teach on Thursday during the day. She's expecting you at ten. And she'll be in the office this Saturday and Sunday to finish the training." He started to sip his wine—the one glass he allowed himself during these dinners—and then added, "I'm glad that's settled. What a relief." His voice and face displayed no emotion.

"Oh, of course." Either my tone wasn't sarcastic enough, or he didn't do sarcasm. There wasn't a flicker of comprehension from Phineas.

Kat picked up on it and ran her hand up my thigh, stopping at my crotch briefly. Her demonstration informed me that she was sorry but had no idea how to say no. She never said no to her parents; ergo, I couldn't say no either.

Our salads arrived. I stabbed a crouton viciously and the damn thing shot off my plate and hit the waiter in the ass.

Although I apologized profusely to the waiter, Kat couldn't hold in her laughter and some iced tea dribbled out her nose. The parents of the kid I had given the foam finger to, smiled, sensing my mortification.

Phineas, engrossed in cleaning his salad fork with his linen napkin, never even noticed the hubbub. Margaret just stared at me with empty eyes before daintily forking up some of her salad.

And that was it. I had three jobs. Four if we counted writing a novel.

Later that night, Kat ran me an extra-hot bath and actually climbed in with me. She wasn't a huge fan of baths—the idea of soaking in her own filth disgusted her—but she catered to me every once in a while. My doctor had ordered me to have one each night to help my back following a car accident I'd had ten years ago. Lately, my back had been acting up, right about the time I started working at Beantown Café. Normally, I preferred soaking in the hot tub, but it needed repairing so Mom's handyman was coming by next week.

"I can't believe that crouton!" Kat nudged me, trying to get me to smile.

I wasn't falling for it. I was in the mood to pout, and nothing was going to snap me out of it.

"I mean, the way it shot off your plate and hit William right in the ass!" Even her grin couldn't coax me.

Kat took my left foot in her hands and massaged it. Oh man, it felt good. I leaned against the back of the tub and felt the tension leave my body. She started to work on my right foot. Her plan was working. My anger was dissipating. Surely Kat could sense it.

"Why don't you lie on the bed and I'll give you a backrub as well."

She didn't have to ask me twice. I sloshed bubbles and water on the bathroom floor in my haste to get to the bedroom, Kat following me, completely naked. When she straddled me, I felt her wetness on my ass.

It wasn't just bath water.

Trying to stay strong, I didn't react at first as she dug into my tense shoulders. Kat had taken several massage classes in college as a backup plan, and she was good—too good.

I moaned, and she moved to the side to knead my lower back and buttocks, proceeding to massage every part of my body, including my pinky fingers. When she was done, I would have signed up to be her mom's kitchen maid if the Finns had asked. Actually, I don't think he even *asked* me to handle his billing. The dinner was an informal meeting. And I was told. From now on, I was expected to do it.

After the massage, I was in a much better place, but Kat wasn't done with me. As I lay on my stomach, I felt Kat's fingers run up and down my body, her light touch tickling me sensuously. Slowly, she began to kiss my back—soft kisses, up and down, never lingering in one spot for long. Then she began to lick me. Her tongue smoothed over my butt cheek, and I shivered, waiting to see what her next move would be. Wet and warm, her tongue teased at my anus—not the sexiest term, I know, but I'm not a romance novelist—and I moaned in ecstasy. It was a weakness of mine, one only Kat knew. When she had first done it, I'd jumped out of bed, shocked and disgusted.

"Shit comes out of there," I had shouted.

Kat had just laughed and said piss and mucus and menstrual blood came out of the other spot. She had a point, but I wasn't entirely convinced. The next time, I let her stay a bit longer. Soon, I always wanted it, but I never asked. It was her ace in the hole, and she knew I referred to it that way. Kat didn't do it all the time. I couldn't blame her. I never could bring myself to reciprocate. She rolled me over on my side and licked my nipple—biting it, tasting it before moving on to the other.

Moments later, she spread my legs and took my swollen pussy lips in her mouth, ignoring my juices spilling out onto the sheet.

"Oh, fuck, Kat," I moaned.

She ran her finger over my throbbing clit, and I grabbed the back of her head, guiding her mouth to the spot. "Please..."

Her tongue darted inside me, exploring my folds and hidden places with zeal. I whimpered in ecstasy, knowing I couldn't handle much more as her tongue focused on my clit in a circular motion.

My body tensed, I grunted like a cavewoman. Kat knew I couldn't climax without her inside me. For what seemed an eternity, she kept me hovering on the precipice of bliss. I wanted to beg for more, but I was so caught up in the anticipation that I couldn't formulate the words. When my hips started to gyrate madly, Kat took pity and thrust her fingers deep inside me. My muscles contracted, and I let out a yelp as her fingers explored inside while she continued licking my clit. I dug my fingers into the sheet, arched my back.

Kat thrust deeper, oblivious to my moans. When I climaxed, she held her tongue in place but forced her fingers in as far as she could.

"Fucking hell," I shouted, feeling my wetness spilling slippery over her hand. My body trembled with pleasure as Kat removed her fingers and moved up to nestle her face on my chest.

"Come here." I gently pulled her lips to my mouth. "God, I love you, Kat," I whispered. I tucked a loose curl behind her ear. "I love everything about you."

"Even Phineas," she teased.

"At the moment, yes."

## Chapter Five

Several days later, I was back in Beantown Café hell. After the morning rush, Harold said, "Can I ask you something?"

I've always hated it when people start a conversation this way, because in effect, they had already asked me something. However, I decided not to be an ass. I was too tired. "Sure, Harold. What's up?" I flashed my fake, cheerful smile.

"Do you know any good dyke bars?"

I have to admit, I was stunned. "Um, I know of some. Not sure how good they are. Why?"

"I want to go to one." He brushed some powder—or was it dandruff?—off his shoulder.

"You do know what the word means, right?" I tried not to sound too condescending.

"Dyke? Yeah, why?" He squinted.

"It's not the best place to pick up chicks, Harold. Some might get mad. And a few of them scare me, and I'm gay, nearly six feet tall, and a former jock."

"*Au contraire.*" He raised his right hand, like a magician pulling a rabbit out of a hat.

*Is that why the others call him Harry Pooper?* I wondered. *Because he pretends he's a wizard.*

"I read in this book that some dykes like to have a guy join them."

As much as I wanted to send Harold off like a lamb to the slaughter, I just couldn't do it. Harold had no idea what he was in for.

"I wouldn't believe everything you read. And I don't think you should throw the term around so loosely. Some find it offensive."

"Really?" He scrunched his face up in confusion.

"Yeah, it's like using the N-word." I lackadaisically wiped the countertop with a filthy rag. I was just trying to stay busy to keep myself awake, not to actually clean anything.

He furrowed his brow, deep in thought.

I was proud of myself for getting through to him. All Harold needed was for someone to take the time to educate him about social skills. I didn't have the time for a complete makeover, but a few helpful nudges here and there would make a vast improvement.

"Oh you mean nigger." He waved his hand. "I use that word all the time with my homeboys."

He pronounced it "hum-bas." I don't think anyone else in the world pronounces it that way—especially homeboys.

The man was an idiot. A total nincompoop. For a

moment, I considered not investing any more time in improving Harold's people skills. What difference would it make? It was like talking to a brick wall.

"Hi, sweetheart." Kat strolled into the store. "I missed you." Her broad smile was directed at Harold, and she winked at him suggestively.

Harold turned cherry-red, matching his apron. "Aw-shucks, I missed you too, Kat." He looked innocent … and desperate for a woman.

Once again, I had an urge to take him under my wing. He desperately needed guidance, and deep down he was a good guy. Just clueless. Very clueless.

But then Harold became all business. "Kat, do you know any good dyke bars?"

She glanced at me, eyebrow quirked.

I shrugged. "He doesn't get it. I tried." I poured Kat a cup of house-blend coffee and handed her the mug. She grasped the mug with both hands like she normally did.

"Tried what, Cori?" he asked.

"Telling you not to use that word."

"You said not to say nigger," he whined.

"No, I didn't. I said saying dyke is offensive and it was like using the N-word."

Harold's facial expression told me I wasn't getting through to him. He tilted his head in bewilderment and scratched his nose, lost in thought.

Kat seemed amused by this back and forth. If I were in her shoes I would find it funny watching the blind lead the blind.

"What's up, Harold? Do you have a gay sister or someone

who's coming to visit?" Kat tried to bury the dyke controversy.

"Go ahead, Harold. Tell her your plan." I leaned against the back counter and crossed my arms.

Harold took the bait. "I read in this book that dy ... lesbians like to do it in front of a dude and sometimes they invite him to, you know, join in."

To her credit, Kat stifled her laughter. Biting her lower lip, she nodded sagely, absorbing the information. "Where did you read that?" She set her mug down on the counter.

"Uh, well, I saw it, actually."

"Seriously, Harold!" I roared. "You're getting tips on how to meet women from porn!"

Kat motioned for me to be quiet.

"Tell you what, we'll go to a gay bar with you—one that has gay men and lesbians, so you won't stick out—and you can try your luck. How does that sound?" She nodded slowly, as if rationalizing with a five-year-old.

The arrangement sounded awful to me; dreadful, in fact. I supposed it might be damn entertaining, and I could use a good laugh. At least Kat would be there, in case any trouble arose; she's good at smoothing things over without any blows. Seriously, some dykes scare me.

We agreed to take Harold to his first gay club later that night. He didn't even know what Kat meant when she said it was time to pop his gay cherry! I'm pretty sure he'll be expecting a cherry as soon as he walks through the door— maybe in a Shirley Temple. Actually, I hoped he wouldn't drink any alcohol. He was a character sober; I couldn't imagine him drunk. I groaned just thinking about it, which amused the hell out of Kat.

Harold couldn't contain his glee when we walked into the gay bar. There were a few lesbians, but mostly the place was full of gay men who swarmed around the place like squirrels begging for nuts on Boston Common.

"Where are all the dykes?" asked Harold.

A couple of lesbians turned their heads. Even the clueless Harold didn't miss their meaning: shut up, asshole.

Harold moved closer to me and whispered, "Where are they?"

Kat linked her arm with his, showing everyone he was with us and that they should back off. "Harold, there's a few facts of life we want to teach you tonight. First: don't say the word 'dyke' unless you know everyone in the room. Second: lesbians love to hook-up with a woman and then move in on the second date. There's a term for this: U-Haul Lesbians. Don't worry, though, since they rush in, they'll be back on the market sooner rather than later. Third: relax and have fun." After giving this lecture, Kat turned to me and said, "Can I buy you two a drink?"

I was wowed. Usually, I was the drink fetcher. "Sure! Whatever beer is on tap."

Harold stroked his chin. "Um, a whiskey." Neither his tone nor his face proclaimed his confidence in this choice. I wondered whether he had ever had a drink before.

Kat patted his shoulder tenderly and strolled to the bar. One of the chicks in the room took notice, I saw, and sidled up next to my girlfriend at the bar. I'm pretty sure she didn't think Kat was with me—no one really does. Some might think Kat and I have an open relationship.

I whisked Harold over to a table off to the side of the dance floor, not in the least concerned about my competition. Kat loathed cheating. Her first girlfriend had cheated on her, and it had broken Kat's heart.

I wanted to meet the idiot who cheated on Kat. Seriously, the woman must have had the worst case of low self-esteem. Why anyone would cheat on such a goddess was beyond me.

The table Harold and I claimed was chest high but lacked chairs. At least we could set our drinks down. I hated leaning against the walls in these types of joints, cradling my drink. A Lady Gaga song filled the room and the dance floor shook with bumping and grinding. Harold couldn't stop staring. I noticed that he didn't look at any of the women. I had thought the plan was for him to find two women for an erotic escapade? Not that I ever thought he would actually succeed in that endeavor, but I had thought he would attempt to implement his plan.

Kat returned with the drinks. A cute little umbrella topped her over-priced, water-downed drink. Taking the umbrella, I twirled it and then placed it behind Kat's ear. She patted my hand lovingly and smiled as I took a swig of skunky Coors Light. I figured this place never cleaned the taps. It was owned by two gay dudes. Let's be honest, only lesbians ordered Coors Light in a nightclub, so I'm sure the owners didn't care much about the quality of the beer. Of course, Kat would never order a beer. In places like this, she always had to try the craziest, most expensive drink.

"What are you drinking?" I gestured to her martini glass.

"Sake martini." She looked to the dance floor. "Care to take a spin, Cori?"

I set my beer down on the tabletop. "Harold, watch our

drinks." I smiled at the look of confusion on his face.

Many think of me as a jock—and I was a jock. I played college ball and, when healthy, I hardly ever rode the pine—which meant I didn't sit on the bench much. No one thought of me as the dancing type. True, I felt more comfortable in sweats and a T-shirt, so I understand why people couldn't get the jock image out of their heads. However, ever since my mom put tap shoes on my feet at the age of four, I couldn't get enough of dancing. By the time I graduated from high school, I had taken ten years of tap lessons and occasionally dabbled in hip-hop, ballet, square dancing, line dancing, and any other type of class Mom could track down in a twenty-mile radius. Perhaps someone might think Mom hoped to waltz the lesbo right out of me. They'd be wrong. Mom preferred it that I wasn't a stereotype. True, I hated My Little Pony when I was a kid, but I had a vast Barbie Doll collection. Mom laughed her head off when she discovered I had cut the heads off all the Ken dolls. One day, I came home from school to discover she had rigged up my shower curtain using the chopped-off heads instead of shower rings. It was ingenious—and hilarious. We left it like that until I went to college.

I never had to act out during my coming-out phase to convince my family I was gay rather than just going through a phase. Yes, I usually wore (and still do) my hair in a ponytail. But when I went out on dates or attended family functions, I did my hair and even wore makeup, including lipstick. I guess that made me a lipstick lesbian—part of the time.

Mom told me once that it would be okay if I wanted to skip dance classes to take up more sports. I refused, and my mom started signing me up for more and more classes.

Coming from a successful old Bostonian family that actually had arrived on the *Mayflower* on both sides—unlike Kat's, who only did on her mother's side—I was expected to achieve from an early age. In addition to dance lessons, I had French tutors, participated in the Model UN, played sports, became class president, belonged on the debate team, joined the chess club, and held a part-time job. The job was to show our neighbors and classmates that I wasn't a complete snob. My father thought it best to show the world I wasn't afraid of hard work or of earning my own place in the world.

There wasn't a time in my life that I could remember not being busy. My schedule was packed from morning to night. And now, I was still that way. Of course, most of my time lately involved working and trying to complete my first novel. I missed all the extra activities. Recently, I'd considered taking guitar lessons. Maybe it would help me relax, and while relaxing, an ending for my novel might flood my mind, all while I was strumming away.

While I was super busy during my childhood, Kat had spent countless hours not joining groups. In fact, I was surprised Kat's parents didn't homeschool her. In high school, she didn't belong to a single group. Not one. When she found out about all of the groups I had been part of, her jaw hit the floor.

My mind returned to my stunning dance partner, and I flashed her a smile. We danced well together. Kat was a little more sexual in her dancing than I was used to, but I adjusted to it. Mrs. Chandler, my former tap instructor, would have been mortified. When we went dancing with my folks, Kat reined it in some. Actually, I think it was because of Uncle

Roger. Mom would probably cheer us on, but Roger would like it too much, and neither of us could do that to my aunt. Not to mention that the thought of my uncle lusting after Kat made me ill. We respected their relationship—even if we didn't understand it at all.

After a couple of songs, Kat motioned that it was time to quit. The crowd seemed to appreciate our efforts. Even some of the guys applauded us when we walked off the dance floor to rejoin Harold. He leaned on the table, resembling a cat dangling over a pool, about to tumble in.

On our way back to him, I whispered, "What is Harold wearing?"

He had on black pants, a brown mock turtleneck, black shoes, and white socks. And his hair looked extra soft, which would be great if he were a five-year-old boy on school picture day. This wasn't a look designed to lure in women.

"I think Harold's trying to show his true side," replied Kat.

I glanced at her out of the corner of my eye, and retorted, "If his true self is a fashion-challenged dyke, he nailed it."

Kat giggled and covered her mouth.

"Wow, Cori! I didn't know you could dance," Harold gushed when we approached. "And Kat …" He leaned in and whispered in her ear.

Kat swatted his hand away and broke into a guffaw. "Harold! No way."

I didn't hear the question, but I had a good idea what he wanted. Everyone wanted to sleep with my girlfriend. It irked me that some people considered her a tramp. People should stop judging a book by its cover. I studied Kat and chuckled to myself. I had to admit that her shirt wasn't covering much this evening.

"Why, Cori Tisdale, who knew you could dance!"

I knew, even before turning around, who it was. Blood rushed to my face and nether regions.

Harold spoke first. "Samantha! I didn't know you were a dyke!"

Kat placed her hand on Harold's shoulder to calm him down, as if he were a Jack Russell terrier jumping up and down for a piece of bacon.

Samantha burst into laughter.

I shrugged.

Kat apologized. "Sorry, he's new and hasn't learned the appropriate language." Kat put her hand out. "I'm Kat, Cori's girlfriend."

Had Kat noticed me blushing?

It was clear Kat was marking her territory. I couldn't decide if I should be flattered or annoyed. I wasn't the cheating type either.

"I'm Samantha. Cori and I went to the same high school." Sam didn't seem bothered by Harold's outburst or Kat's pissing contest. She turned to me, "How come you never went to any of the dances in school?"

"We usually had a basketball game."

"Liar! I was a cheerleader, and I never missed one of your games." She looked to Kat. "Have you ever seen her play basketball? The fans went wild watching Cori play." Again, she turned to me. "When I read that you blew your knee in your sophomore year in college and had to miss a year, I felt like crying. Hancock Prep never had a player as good as you,

Cori—before or since."

I was speechless. I never knew Samantha noticed me at all in high school. We would say hi when we ran into each other, but that was the extent of it. Sam had her own group of friends, and I had a small group I hung out with. Mostly, I was too busy running from one activity to another to have time for friendships.

Kat came to my rescue. "I've seen some footage from her games, and occasionally I can talk her into a wicked game of horse." Kat put her arm around my waist and kissed my cheek.

Her actions made me want to giggle, but I didn't dare.

"So spill it, Cori. How come you never went to any of our dances?" Samantha crossed her arms.

"No one asked me."

Harold nodded knowingly. I'm pretty sure none of the girls he asked ever accepted, if he had dared to ask.

"Can you teach me to dance, Cori?" he begged.

The thought terrified me. Harold couldn't even walk normally, how was I going to teach him to dance?

"We can!" Kat piped up.

Well, if anyone could teach him, Kat could, and clearly I was signed up to be her assistant.

"Shit, I may sign up for a lesson myself," Samantha teased.

At least I thought she was teasing.

"Come on, you don't need lessons," I said. "You were a cheerleader."

Kat's grip on my waist grew tighter. Was she scared I might chase after a former high school cheerleader?

"But I've never been able to dance like *that*." Samantha

looked completely awed.

"Can I buy you a drink?" I asked her, and then, when I saw Kat's face, added, "Harold, Kat, you need another? My turn to buy a round." It appeased Kat some, but I could tell she still felt insecure. That was new. I had never known Kat to act jealous or unsure. Something was up, and I intended to find out what.

"I'll have a beer," said Samantha.

Harold motioned to his whiskey, which he hadn't touched since taking his first sip. "I'm good, thanks."

I turned to Kat. "What exotic drink can I bring you, sweetie?" Okay, I was laying it on thick, but I didn't want to have a fight later, and I didn't want her to worry over nothing. My crush was a long time ago.

"Oh, I'll just have a beer, too," said Kat, as if that was all she ever drank. I noticed that she had moved her martini glass to the adjacent table.

*Is she actually worried about losing me?* I pondered as I left to fetch the drinks.

The bar gave the illusion of being super fancy. Mirrors behind the bottles of liquor gave the impression the supply was endless. Lights above the bar changed color every few seconds. While I waited to be served, I watched the lights. It didn't take long to figure out that they changed according to the colors of the rainbow—how gay is that? It was a perfect example of why I despise gay bars—pure cheese. I wasn't the type to proclaim I was gay. I never wore rainbow necklaces or earrings. Gay pride parade? Never been to one. Once, I got stuck in traffic in Boston. When I realized the gay pride parade was the cause, I muttered, "Damn gays."

Kat had swatted my arm, although I think she felt the same way. Why did so many have to shout from the rooftops, "I'm here and I'm queer!" Not once have I felt that need. Having said that, I usually don't mind gays who do. I may roll my eyes at flashing rainbow lights, and I may get upset sitting in a rental car that is charging by the hour because of a gay parade, but overall, I just don't care what others do. I've never felt the need to care. Kat thinks it's because I grew up in an accepting family, so not once have I been made to feel different. She might be right. Or it could be that I just don't give a crap about my gayness.

"What'll ya have?" the bartender asked me in a silky voice. She was butch with short, spiky hair, and a nose ring. She wasn't my usual type at all, but her skin was flawless and her green eyes were hypnotic. The sexy, womanly voice didn't match her exterior at all, either, which I found captivating. I love a paradox.

"You see that woman standing there?" I pointed to Kat. "The one in the super-tight shirt."

The bartender nodded, appreciating the view.

"I need a fancy drink to impress the shit out of her."

The butch bartender gave me a glance that said, "You have no chance in hell."

I wanted to inform her that Kat was indeed already my girlfriend, but I didn't. I wanted a drink to impress Kat so she wouldn't get too flustered about Samantha.

I returned with the drinks as soon as possible, worried that in my absence Harold might say something insulting or Kat might act too bitchy toward Samantha.

Harold looked relieved when I set a glass of water in front

of him. He took several gulps, as though he'd just spent days in the Mojave Desert. Kat smiled when I handed her the exotic martini Butch had put together for her. The bartender told me what was in it, but I couldn't hear over the gay men behind me screeching because one had spilled a drink on another. Apparently, the drink ruined a three-hundred-dollar shirt.

Kat's drink looked sophisticated and fancy, which was all I cared about. She took a sip and smiled. I raised my glass to the female bartender, who couldn't stop staring at my girlfriend. The devil inside me screamed that I should give Kat a passionate kiss just to show the bartender that I was perfectly capable of getting the hot chick. Then again, she might think her concoction had worked and make a play herself.

Luckily, the conversation was flowing between Kat and Sam. Kat, probing for dirt, asked Samantha what she did, where she lived, and about her family. Both Samantha and I are only children; I vaguely remembered that from high school.

Samantha had approached me after one of my games and said, "We have something in common."

I just stood there foolishly. At the time, my crush on Sam had been out of control. She was slightly sweaty from cheerleading, and it glistened on her skin, adding to her appeal. At the time, I had thought, *Don't say something idiotic!* It meant I allowed myself too few words.

"What?" was my brilliant response. Maybe that was the first clue that I'd have problems finishing my novel—I wasn't good with words under pressure.

"We are both only children."

I continued to stare at her. "Oh. That's neat." I had been

holding a basketball, and even though I never did so during a game, or during practice for that matter, I fumbled it and it rolled away from me pathetically.

Another cheerleader called Samantha's name, and the last thing I remember was Sam looking back over her shoulder and giving me a slight wave. I half waved back, since I wasn't entirely sure she was waving at me, and I didn't want to look like that nitwit on the sidewalk who waved foolishly at someone who was waving at someone else.

Kat's voice brought me back to the present. "Oh, you're an only child. It's good that Cori is really close with her family. We have dinner with them every week."

I started to say that it wasn't every week, because that sounded lame (even though we do), but Samantha beat me to the punch.

"Me too!" She turned to me and whacked me playfully on my shoulder.

Kat looked peeved. I think she was trying to convince Samantha I was a boring fuddy-duddy and not worth chasing after. Instead, she'd made a connection between the two of us. Maybe I didn't have to speak the entire night. I'd just let Kat make the moves for me. That is, if I was trying to make any moves—and I wasn't.

"So are you a dy … lesbian?" inquired Harold.

His boldness silenced even Kat. I thought it more than likely that Samantha was here with some gay guy friends, and that she was a fag hag. Not once did I think she was a lesbo. I'd never considered it in high school, and even after stumbling into her in a gay bar, I still didn't think so. She was just open-minded. Had to be.

Harold was the only one who didn't look uncomfortable at the question.

Then Samantha laughed it off. "Well, if you really want to know, Harold, I think bisexual is the most accurate description. However, I haven't dated a man in years."

I almost fell over. I think I even stopped breathing for a minute.

Kat wasn't happy, but she plastered a grin on her face. "Does that mean you're dating a woman?" She looked keen for the right answer.

"No. My girlfriend and I broke up last week."

She was on the rebound.

Dammit! Why did I have to be in a relationship?

*Wait a minute, Cori, you aren't looking! Knock it the fuck off.*

Kat put an arm around Samantha and gave her a good squeeze, her breasts almost bursting out of her top as she did so.

As a result, Harold's eyes almost popped out of his head.

Samantha either didn't notice or was very good at pretending.

Seeing the two of them together was odd. Kat wore tight jeans and a revealing top that was losing the battle of controlling her assets.

Samantha wore jeans, not too tight or loose, and a semi-tight Red Sox shirt. Many would find Kat the sexier of the two.

I was torn.

Kat looked hot, no doubt about it. But Samantha's outfit hinted there was more to see, and that it wouldn't be a disappointment. And, Samantha exuded confidence. Kat normally did, but this evening her vulnerable side was making a rare appearance. I wasn't sure what to make of it.

I needed a moment, so I excused myself, saying I needed to pee. I didn't put it like that, of course. Only Samantha noticed that I had said anything at all. Harold was too busy staring at Kat's boobs, and Kat was too busy sizing up Samantha.

The bathroom was so disgusting, I decided not to pee. I had to, but going anywhere near that toilet was too much for my delicate system. My family hired maids for all of my life. For years, I would never use a toilet outside of our home. When I went to school, I had to. Then I discovered the nurse's office had a semi-clean restroom, so I started using that one. My family gave a lot of money to my private school, so no one said a word to me about it. I feel somewhat bad about that now, because it was an abuse of my family's money. Then again, it was either that or dash home every few hours. Or, I suppose, pee in the woods behind the school. That still seemed more appealing than using the shared restrooms. Secretly, I wished there were some trees close to this dive for me to squat behind.

When I rejoined the group, Kat and Harold were still interrogating Samantha.

"I thought you were planning a wedding," said Harold.

This piqued Kat's interest. If it were true, Samantha might be too heart-broken to be interested in anyone for a long time?

"What made you think that?" Samantha crinkled her nose and sipped her skunk beer. She pulled the glass away from her lips, inspecting it, before taking another slug.

"I thought you were away on your honeymoon," explained Harold, who still hadn't taken his eyes off my girlfriend's boobs. If it were anyone else, I would be irritated and would have whacked the back of his head. But it was probably the closest Harold had ever come to a naked female, so I let it slide for now.

"Honeymoon!" Samantha chortled. "My family went to Italy for a few weeks to celebrate my parents' thirtieth wedding anniversary."

"I knew it had something to do with marriage." Harold smiled meekly.

I wanted to kick him in the shins. He had me convinced that Samantha was married. Again, not that it mattered. My crush was in high school. Years ago. It didn't matter now. Of course, I had also believed she was straight. Her being bisexual never crossed my mind. I still couldn't picture Samantha eating pussy.

"How long did you and your girlfriend date?" Kat steered the conversation back to her fact-finding mission.

"Five years."

Kat stifled a gleeful smile. "Oh wow, that's too bad. It will take a long time to get over that one." She was laying it on thick. She put her arm around Samantha's shoulder again, and once more Kat's tits almost spilled out of her top.

Harold looked like he needed CPR, but for someone who wasn't breathing or moving, he seemed blissful enough. We needed to get this boy laid. He would probably die from happiness if that happened, but it would be a happy death, at least.

"Not really. We're still friends. The breakup was a long time coming, really." Not a trace of sadness flickered in Samantha's eyes, but I sensed a cheerless air. Was she putting on a brave face?

After she answered a few more questions from Kat the Inquisitor, Samantha excused herself to rejoin her friends. Before leaving, she said, "See you two Monday morning."

When she was out of earshot, Kat asked, "Monday morning?"

"She's a regular at the coffee shop." I released my grip on Kat's waist and grabbed my beer.

"Oh, that's nice." Her voice said otherwise.

It was time for damage control. "Harold, what do you say, have you had enough for your first experience? How about we grab some grub next door?"

He looked around smugly and said, "Sure. Not much happening here tonight."

I loved his act. At first, it bugged the shit out of me when he pretended he was the coolest thing ever. Oh, sorry, Mr. Kool.

Now, I loved his bravado. It was fake, but I found it endearing. Not many men try to act suave while sporting a tan mock turtleneck sweater and black chinos.

During a late-night snack at the Last Drop, Kat grilled Harold about Samantha. Not once did she question me, even though we went to high school together. Truth be known, Harold knew more about Samantha than I did. It was surprising how much we learned about our customers. Kat asked him questions, and I paid close attention to what he said, without looking like I was interested.

Munching on a fried mozzarella stick smothered in ranch sauce, I listened to Harold say that Samantha had worked for the same company since graduating from college. Every seven or eight months, she would put a new business card into the raffle bowl, and Harold noticed that her title always changed.

Kat sniffed loudly. Harold didn't notice as he nibbled on a buffalo chicken wing, smearing sauce all over his cheeks and chin. Before I found Harold a girl, I decided I needed to work on his manners. Maybe I should call in the big guns: my mom and aunt. Both were paragons of grace.

Kat grunted, obviously still peeved that Samantha was a go-getter. Inwardly, I smiled. A woman after my own heart. All of a sudden, I had the urge to write. Instead, I grabbed another cheese stick, still thinking of my novel. Why couldn't I nail the ending?

# Chapter Six

My mom and I bickered a lot when we were around other family members. However, we upheld a tradition that started when I was just a kid. Twice a month, we got a manicure and pedicure together. Mom hated helping me out with my bills, but that didn't mean she didn't spoil me in other ways. This was one of her many ways.

It was our mother–daughter time, a time when she was usually much more relaxed since she wasn't competing with her sister, her husband, or Kat. This was when Mom and I had our heart-to-heart talks.

"I think I'm going to hire a private detective to catch your cheating father in the act," Mom stated bluntly as she sat in the chair, her eyes closed.

I glanced down at my nail tech, who didn't flinch. I bet they overheard a lot of crazy stories. No doubt they have been trained not to react or show any emotion. Each time, we had the same girls work on our nails. Over the years, I'm sure they've become accustomed to my mother's outrageous outbursts. Last month, she worried my father had cheated on his taxes and would be arrested. This month, she was obsessed with the suspicion my father was cheating on her. I had steeled myself for more chatter on the subject, but I didn't think she'd go as far as hiring a private dick.

"Oh, Mom! Dad is not having an affair. Look at the man. Who would—?"

"Go ahead, Cori. Say it. Who would sleep with the man?"

"That's not what I meant … Okay, it was. But that's because he's my *father*. I can't see him as a lover." I fidgeted in my seat and shook my head, trying to knock some sense into my pea-brain.

"What, do you think you're a product of Immaculate Conception? A miracle baby?" She sniggered. "Back in the day, your father was a magnificent lover. We couldn't keep our hands off each other."

If my fingers hadn't been recently painted, I would have shoved them deep into each ear until they made contact in the middle. "Mother, please! I don't want to hear about it."

"Kat is right. You *are* uptight when it comes to sex."

I whipped my head around to face her. "Stop talking to my girlfriend about sex. It's weird!"

"That's the problem with you, Cori. You can't talk about S. E. X. Kat and I are starting an erotica book club. I urge you to join. It'll be the best thing you've ever done. When you were a kid, you loved joining groups. Lord knows how many classes, lessons, and sporting events I drove you to before you got your license." She blew on her wet nails. "It would make Kat happier."

"What? Has she said anything to you?" I didn't want to know, but I really did want to at the same time. I knew Kat was freakier in bed than me, but I didn't think I was a bad lover. Was I a bad lay? Was Kat sexually frustrated? Good Lord, did my mom know this? I'd never hear the end of it.

"It's hard knowing that a daughter of mine is so uptight in bed. You must get it from your father. God knows it took me years to train him."

Once again I had the urge to shove my fingers in my ears.

"What did Kat say to you?"

Mom turned in her chair and the leather made an obnoxious farting sound. "Say? She didn't *say* anything. But a woman knows." She peered over her glasses at me, which always gave me the willies. Usually, my mother only wore her glasses at home and never in public. But today she had an eye infection so she couldn't wear her contacts. I was surprised she didn't cancel our appointment.

I let out a sigh. She was blowing smoke out of her ass, just to make me feel insecure. And I had fallen for it, hook, line, and sinker.

"Come on, you can't think people will want to join an erotica book club. People read that trash behind closed doors. They don't talk about it openly." I drummed my fingers on the arms of my chair.

"We already have seven members, including your aunt and your co-worker Harold."

"Harold! How did he find out about it?" To say I was flabbergasted would be an understatement. I was beyond flummoxed. And I was pissed off. My mother and Kat discussing erotica with Harold was just too much for me to handle.

"Kat invited him. She thinks he'd make a good candidate for our good deed this year."

I rolled my eyes. "Do I even want to know what that means?"

"He needs to learn about the birds and the bees. I haven't met him, but from what Kat told me he needs, how do I say this, tutoring." She winked at me, and my skin crawled. Not only was my mother talking to my girlfriend about sex, now she was getting her talons into Harold. I shuddered at the thought.

"Please, for the love of God, do not sink your claws into Harold. He's a nice kid, and he'll figure things out on his own." I didn't believe that one bit, but the thought of my mother and Kat teaching Harold about life made me more than uncomfortable. I had to work with the man, and we were becoming buddies outside of work. This project was no good. I had to put a stop to it—and fast.

"I don't want to talk about Harold." She shook hair out of her face dramatically, like a movie star on the red carpet. "Later today I have an appointment with a PI. I know for a fact your father is getting his jollies elsewhere."

"Mother, I'm telling you right now: you're wrong about Dad. He isn't having an affair. We all know Roger is a cheater, but that doesn't mean Dad is. He is not cheating on you. Stop being so competitive with your sister." I let out a long sigh, exasperated, and then stared at the mirror in front of us to see Mom's reaction.

It floored me.

She was crying. Actually crying. Her cold heart had felt something besides jealousy.

"Cori! I will not sit here and have you ridicule me. God you make me so angry!" All of the muscles in her body tensed.

Okay, they were angry tears. But that was a good sign, I hoped.

"I'm not ridiculing you, Mother. I'm trying to talk sense into you. Whoever you hire won't find a thing. Save your money."

"So I can give it to you." She dabbed her tears with a tissue.

I wanted to slap her. Instead, I said through clenched teeth, "Oh don't worry about me. Kat's father signed me up to do his billing in my free time." Both Kat and I had been keeping it a secret. I didn't want to admit that I needed the money, and Kat hated talking about her family, even with my mother.

"Why don't you just finish your book? I know you have it in you." Her words sounded heartfelt.

"I'm stuck on the ending."

Mom's encouraging tone had made me feel more comfortable talking to her as a writer. Hopefully she could help guide me. Goodness knows she was an expert in the field.

"You always did have a problem finishing things."

I guessed professional guidance was out of the question.

"Careful, Mother. Your claws are showing."

"That's better. I know there's a part of me inside you."

If we weren't in public, I would have let out a primal scream. She remained the most frustrating woman I've ever dealt with.

Neither of us spoke, but I could sense, from the way she gripped the chair's armrests, that my mother was trying to think of the right words to say. My mother took exceptional care of herself. Ate right, worked out, had facials—she even endured colonics to stay healthy. It all paid off. Few would guess she was nearing sixty. She looked like she was in her late forties—except for her hands. Everyone's hands give away their age. As Mom struggled for the right words, I studied her hands. Her veins bulged and the skin was speckled with age spots. The thing that troubled me most, though, was how fragile her skin looked—like crêpe paper. If I ran my finger along it, it would tear, I thought. I don't mind getting older, but I'm not okay with my mother and aunt advancing in life. They've always been there for me, and now that they are showing their age, I'm scared to death I may have to go it alone.

My mother slapped the armrest with her palms, indicating she had figured out just what to say. "Cori, I don't know how to sugarcoat this. Just sit your butt down in a chair and write the end. Don't stop until it's done. You and your editor can work on it after the first draft is complete. Stop whining, and just fucking do it."

What Mom said made sense, but I didn't like the way she said it. And I didn't like that she was right; that bugged the shit out of me. Just fucking write. It sounded so easy.

"Do you want to go to my appointment with me?" Mom's eyes looked hopeful.

"Nope. Leave me out of this. He's my father."

Mom started to say something, but then closed her trap.

"You're right."

That shocked the hell out of me.

After a few moments, she added, "Well at least come to the bookstore with me. I need to buy some porn."

I couldn't help but laugh. And I would never skip an opportunity to go to the bookstore with her; Mom loved buying me books.

Later that day, I headed to Beantown Café for an extra shift I had picked up. Kat's father wouldn't pay until after the first thirty days, and I needed the money now. I wasn't thrilled that I wouldn't receive any money for a month, but he wanted to ensure I knew what I was doing and wouldn't fuck up his billing. Luckily, I'm the type that doesn't need a lot of sleep. I filed his claims late at night, and truth be told, the job was a cinch. Why Dr. Finn even hired someone else to do it baffled me. It took me forty-five minutes a night. I don't think he was a popular or busy dentist. I suspected he and Margaret lived off the family money. I didn't even know how much he would actually pay me, because he never mentioned that part during our "business" meeting. But Phineas had me over a barrel, and the bastard knew it.

When I walked into the store, I was shocked to see that Harold was still working. I knew he'd had the early shift.

He didn't look pleased. "Philip called out, and Mark won't let me leave."

I didn't have to ask how he felt. Harold turned toward Mark's office and flipped him the bird, or at least I thought he did. He had such an elaborate method, which involved waving both arms above his head, flashing his middle fingers, and then slamming his hands into his pelvic bones. I wasn't sure if I should be impressed or get him an icepack, since I think he hit himself much harder than he intended. What type of moron injures himself while flipping someone off? Only Harold. And my mom wanted to help him get laid. Goodness knows how much damage he would do to himself—and the poor woman.

Maybe Mom and Kat should give Harold coolness lessons instead of Sex Ed. He needed them, and God knows I wouldn't be much help on that front. I thought I could teach him how to dance, but after seeing his "flipping the bird" routine, I had some serious doubts.

Harold wiped the grimace off his face and leaned against the counter like a gigolo on the prowl. He looked ridiculous. It took effort not to burst into laughter as I tied my apron strings around my waist.

"Got any big plans tonight, Harold?"

He looked overjoyed that I asked. "I sure do!"

As I began wiping down the counter, I quizzed Harold further, knowing that he wanted me to. "Really? What?" I stared at the countertop, fearful he would see my true feelings.

"I have a date!" His voice cracked with pride, like a fourteen-year-old boy's.

My head snapped up, eyes on his face.

There wasn't a trace of falsehood in his expression at all. Every pore exuded pure happiness.

"That's wonderful, Harold." I actually meant it. After getting to know him, I had started to cheer for the loser. "With whom?"

"Kat set it up."

Oh shit. The word *mayday* flashed before my eyes in

scarlet lettering. I saw nothing but disaster coming from Kat's experiment, and I couldn't think of one of her friends who would be interested in our Harold. He needed a special woman—not special needs, but kind of close—and Kat didn't hang out with anyone who fit that bill.

Swallowing my fear, I dove in. "What do you have planned?"

"Come on, Cori. Stop fooling around." He flashed me a goofy, know-it-all grin.

I was taken aback. Did he mean he didn't have a date? Not knowing what to say, I said nothing, just gave him a shy, questioning smile.

"All of us are going on a double date tonight." Mr. Kool giggled like a teenage girl and playfully swatted my shoulder.

"Oh, that. I wasn't sure if it was a surprise or not. Has Kat been by today?" I wanted to throttle her beautiful neck. Not only had she set up Harold to have his heart ripped out, she had signed me up to watch the fiasco. The woman needed to stop meddling in other people's lives. I knew she had a big heart, but come on, setting up Harold on a blind date! She crossed the Rubicon and damned us all.

A customer entered before I could fire off a nasty "what the fuck are you doing?" text to Kat. When I turned to take his order, I was stunned to see my father. He was wearing jeans and a polo in the middle of the work day. He usually wore a suit and tie.

"Hey, Dad. What's up?" I tried to control my voice so I didn't sound panicky.

He looked rattled, as if he had never been into a Beantown Café before. My father didn't drink coffee, so that may well have been the case. He claimed caffeine made his ears ring.

"Oh, I just thought I would pop in and see how my girl is doing." He patted his pocketbook nervously.

"Did you take the day off? Mom and I just got our nails done, and she didn't mention that you had the day off." I felt bad about the implied accusation, but his appearance and behavior made me nervous. Was my father having an affair? Was he killing time before meeting his floozy? Oh, if that were the case, I would never hear the end of it from my mother. I could just see her gloating that she was right and missing the big picture completely.

*Jesus, Cori, so are you.*

"No, I'm working." He paused. I was certain he was searching for the right words. "It's casual day."

Accountants don't do casual—at least not at his firm.

"Really? That's a first, isn't it?" I crossed my arms.

"Yeah, it is. The first Friday …" he mumbled and didn't finish his thought.

"Have they extended your time off for lunch as well?" I knew it wasn't right for me to interrogate my own father, but I couldn't help myself. Mom's accusations, and his behavior, had made me suspicious.

"No. They don't like to give me much of anything, lately." His tone was bitter, hate-filled, but then he smiled bashfully. "I just needed some time today. Besides, I wanted to ask you something." He stood up straighter.

Harold started sweeping the floor close to us, and it was obvious he wanted to hear the juicy gossip.

"Sure. What?" I still kept my arms crossed.

"Do you want to have lunch tomorrow and then catch a

game?" Dad looked nervous as hell, almost as if he were asking a girl on a date.

I pushed aside my suspicions and his weird behavior. My father had me at "catch a game."

"Of course! You know you never have to ask. I'm always here if you need anything."

His eyes glistened a little. I didn't know what to say.

"Great. I'll pick you up at eleven." He turned abruptly and waddled out of the store.

Harold immediately stopped sweeping the floor and came back behind the counter. "He seems nice."

He had only swept one-fifth of the store, confirming my suspicion that Harold had been eavesdropping.

I was too puzzled by my dad's appearance to care. When the excitement of an invitation to the game started to wear off, I wondered whether my parents really were heading for a divorce. Even though I was almost thirty, the thought scared the crap out of me. They weren't the most lovey-dovey couple I knew, but they were my parents. A unit.

I groaned as another customer came in. Not feeling overly cheerful, I managed to be semi-friendly while I took his order. The man didn't notice. He was too busy pounding away on his cell phone to notice anything going on around him. Suits, man. So self-involved.

After making the suit's drink, Harold announced, "Time for me to go and get ready for the date."

I glanced at the clock. It was only four. "What time are we meeting again?"

"Eight."

"Does it usually take you four hours to get ready?" I

teased him.

Harold blushed. "No, Miss Smarty-Pants. Kat is meeting me — to help."

"Kat's helping you? You should have started hours ago. That woman likes to preen." I patted Harold on the back, glad to see a sparkle in his normally vacant eyes. "See ya later, dater."

He waved foolishly and scurried out the door. I hoped Kat would go easy on the poor guy. I pictured her tweezing his unibrow, applying makeup, and gelling his hair. Then a thought hit me: I bet she buys him a new outfit. Correction, I bet *I'm* buying him a new outfit. At least it would be for a good cause, I told myself, trying to control my panic over Kat spending a fortune. Jesus, I couldn't catch a fucking break.

A stream of customers flooded the store, so I didn't have time to ponder the situation. Harold's relief arrived several minutes later, and then the two of us never stopped working, thankfully. Since I had befriended Harold, the rest of the staff had begun treating me differently. For the most part, I didn't mind, apart from the annoyance of finding myself still dealing with high school drama at my age. Granted, most of my coworkers were years younger, so I couldn't get too upset, but did they have to be so damn annoying and condescending? Teenagers were almost as bad as gay men when it came to moodiness and bitchiness.

Seven p.m. arrived, and I shot out the door like Usain Bolt. Kat texted me to meet them at Clammy's, and I had plenty of time to walk to the waterfront restaurant.

"Cori!" came a voice from behind me.

I turned to see who in the heck was shouting my name. I

didn't really mingle with many people in the Financial District. To be honest, I was never really popular, not even when I was a super jock. And when my writing career crashed and burned, the few friends I had slowly disappeared. Thank God for Kat and my family.

Samantha waved her arms excitedly in the air so I couldn't miss her even if I was trying to. Walking back in her direction, I did my best to mask my glee at seeing her again.

"Where are you off to in such a hurry?" She breathed heavily, and I averted my eyes from her heaving chest.

"Clammy's. I'm meeting Kat and Harold." I mumbled Harold's name and immediately felt guilty about it. Was I as bad as my Beantown coworkers? I offered more. "Kat set Harold up on a blind date tonight, and we're making it a double date. He's a little nervous, so they're already at the restaurant. Poor guy thinks he'll be stood up. He has convinced himself that if he shows up early it will somehow help his cause."

Samantha giggled. "Oh, that sounds like Harold. Can I join you? In the event he is stood up, I'll be his date for the night. And if she shows, I'll leave." A mischievous look crossed her face. "I may have to hide in the background and keep an eye on things, though."

I was touched that she had offered to be Harold's backup date. "Sure! I was going to walk there, but we can take a cab if you prefer." The T didn't have a stop near there, and there was no way in hell I was going to suggest we catch a bus.

"Let's walk. Who knows how much longer we'll be able to enjoy this nice weather? I can't believe it's almost October." She linked her arm through mine. I noticed I didn't feel a frisson of excitement. It just felt friendly—on my side, at least. I was starting to wonder if Sam had a crush on me; that wouldn't be good. I'm horrible at hurting people's feelings, and my girlfriend would not be pleased if I led Samantha on.

Nervous that Sam might have a crush, I chattered away to hide my embarrassment. "Kat spent the afternoon fixing Harold up. I'm curious to see how he turned out." *And how much she spent,* I thought, but I kept that to myself.

"If I had known, I would have taken the afternoon off to help. I've always liked Harold. No offence, but the other workers in your shop are hideous snobs."

My esteem for Sam skyrocketed. "I know! And they work in Beantown Café, for Christ's sake." The words bubbled out of me before I could stop them.

"They're snottier than my coworkers—and most of them manage millions of dollars." Samantha either didn't notice my blunder or decided to help me through it. As I got to know her more, I was inclined to think she just didn't notice. Being friends with two people who worked at Beantown didn't seem to bother her, even if she was super successful.

"When you two aren't working, I won't leave a tip. A year ago, I learned all of you split the tips, so I started slipping Harold a buck each time he hands me my coffee." Sam's eyes beamed at her way of beating the system. "I can't stand how they treat him. He acts like it doesn't bother him, but it has to. I don't know many grown men who would enjoy being called Harry Pooper, even if they are huge Potter fans." Sam's crinkled face showed her contempt for my colleagues.

"Oh, I don't know. I think Harold has a way of getting even."

Sam eyed me curiously, so I explained about the doctor's note. "Hopefully, Harold knows he's better than the rest of them. He's the only one I get along with, actually. Thank God I don't work there a lot."

"I ran into Kat recently, and she mentioned that you do her father's dental billing. How do you like that?" Samantha faced forward, her eyes focused on something across the street.

I couldn't discern what was commanding her complete attention. Was she staring at the gigantic Hood Milk bottle, which is actually a snack shop, in front of the Children's Museum?

I wondered if Kat had "accidentally" bumped into Sam. Actually, there wasn't a doubt in my mind that she had. As a way to suss out her competition, it was both cute and frustrating.

"I wasn't thrilled with the idea when her father proposed it. I guess I felt pushed into it." I wasn't sure why I had answered her honestly. "But it's easy money. I'm actually getting caught up on my bills with the money I make from Beantown, so this will only help. I mean, I can't quit any of my jobs just yet. That will take some time, but I can breathe a little easier." Saying this out loud to a friend was a relief. Money trouble was such a burden. It weighed on me all the time.

"Times are tough. My company announced they are laying off five hundred people next week. I'm terrified." We still walked arm-in-arm and Sam patted my arm with her free hand. "I would be able to last a few months without a job, but not much longer than that."

The confession shocked the hell out of me. Here I thought Samantha had it made. Now I knew the truth.

"I'm so sorry. When will you know?"

"All next week will be a nightmare. My company has devised this brilliant method of informing people. When entering our building, we have to swipe our ID to get in. Each day, they will deactivate the badges of the employees they are laying off, and someone from HR will be standing by when an employee's ID doesn't work to talk to them in a private room downstairs. Next week is going to be hell."

"Jesus! That sounds barbaric. Is that even legal? It's not just the fear, what about the embarrassment?" I couldn't believe what she was telling me. I was suddenly relieved to have my jobs; at least they felt secure. All of a sudden, I appreciated Beantown Café and dental billing.

"Oh, I'm sure they ran it by legal. The bastards!" For the first time, I heard venom in her voice. Then her body language softened. "But let's not talk about it. It's Friday, and Harold has a date. Let's focus on the good. Hey, I'm going to the Sox game tomorrow if you want to join me. I have an extra ticket."

Damn my father and his surprise visit. "Thanks, but my father invited me earlier today." I hoped my voice didn't register my disappointment at not going with her.

"Great! We can meet there."

"Well, we aren't sitting in a box. He has season tickets in the bleachers." During one of her visits to the coffee shop, Sam mentioned her company had box seats at Fenway.

"Same here. Not me, but my uncle. He hardly ever goes now, and I usually go several times a year. Our whole family, I mean aunts, uncles, cousins, second-cousins—we all fight over who can go and when."

"How do you think our chances are this year? Will we

win the series?" Both of us slowed our pace, eager to continue the conversation.

Excitement returned to Sam's face. Kat didn't get sports, or why people become such fanatic supporters, but here's what I got about sports:

(a) Sports bring people together.

(b) When life is tough, a person still has their team.

(c) They always provide distraction from what's going on in life. [I know this sounds a lot like B, but it isn't completely, so I'm sticking with it.]

(d) Teams always give people something to talk about with another fan. It's an instant bond that only fans can possess. Red Sox fans rarely discuss the weather when there's a lull in the conversation.

"I have my fingers crossed. At least this season is better than last. They were dreadful last year, just dreadful." The color drained from her face.

The restaurant was in sight, and Samantha pulled on my arm to get me to stop walking.

"Before we go in, I have something to say."

I wasn't sure where she was going, and I was a little unnerved. Was she going to confess she liked me?

"Sure. What's up?" I said in a voice filled with dread.

"My cousin is a dentist, and he's looking for someone to do his billing. Would you be interested?"

Relief flooded through me. I thought for sure she had been going to say, "Hey, you know I like you, right? Leave Kat, and we'll be happy together."

"Really?" How could I say no? It was easy money, and it was awfully sweet of her to ask around for me. Minutes ago she had been talking about her company's layoffs, and now she was helping me with my money woes. "Yeah, that sounds great."

"Cool. I wasn't sure if you'd be offended." She handed me her cousin's card. "Call him on Monday. He's ready for you to start."

"Why did you think I would be offended?"

"I know your passion is teaching and writing. I didn't want you to think I was implying you should give it up. I can't wait to read your book when you finish it. I'll be your number one fan. Not in the *Misery*, Kathy Bates, way." She let out a girlish giggle. "I understand the billing thing is just until you get back on your feet. Who knows, maybe next week I'll become your partner."

"What should our company name be?"

"Red Sox Billing, of course."

"Can you do me a favor?"

"Of course. What?" It was Samantha's turn to look hesitant.

"Don't tell Kat about the extra billing. I don't want to ruffle her father's feathers, and I would hate to put her in a position to lie. Phineas supplied me with the billing software, and I'm sure if he found out, he would charge me to use it or take it all back."

Understanding gleamed in her eyes. "Your secret is safe with me. Now, let's go check out Harold." She waltzed ahead of me, as excited as a child on Christmas morning.

We strolled into Clammy's. Although I had been there many times, I always stopped to take in the bric-a-brac on the walls. I had heard that all the junk adorning the walls—ship wheels, barrels, buoys, and half-naked mermaid statues—came from ships or flotsam washed up on the shoreline. I'm not sure I believed it, but the odds and ends added to the ambience, at least. The outside resembled a clam shack; inside was anything but. Located on the Fort Point Channel, the restaurant was next to a marina, and it was still nice enough outside to dine alfresco on the patio. As usual, the place was packed. It was typically a hotspot for tourists, so I wondered why Kat had chosen it for Harold's date. Wouldn't it be better for Harold to meet someone in a café bookshop, like Neptune's on Newbury?

We located them in the back, on the patio side. It wasn't that hard to spot them, since Harold leaped out of his seat and waved his hands over his head to get our attention. One look at Harold made me realize Kat was serious about his makeover. His floppy, bowl-cut hairdo was gone. In its place he sported short hair that Kat had teased at the front to make it stand up a little. She had remained true to his nerdy side, so the haircut suited him. So did his clothes: dark blue jeans with a lightweight black sweater—not a mock turtleneck, thank goodness. It looked soft. Cashmere soft. It was a V-neck and he wore a white undershirt. I wanted to peek under the table to see if he was wearing white socks with his dark jeans. I groaned, hoping Samantha didn't hear it.

A wrapped gift sat on the table in front of Harold. Kat laughed and tilted her head towards it. I waved at them, noticing daggers shoot from Kat's eyes when she saw that I wasn't alone. It took some effort to make our way through the crowd, most of which congregated around the TV that hung above the bar. The Sox game was on. September always brought with it anxiety over the playoffs. Sox fans were hungry for another pennant but were cautious not to get their hopes up.

"Look who I bumped into." I motioned to Samantha, praying Sam would pick up on the fact that I didn't want to tell Kat we had strolled here together.

She did. "I'm meeting a buddy here." She gave Kat a quick hug and then turned to Harold. "I'm sorry, we haven't met." Smiling, she put her hand out to shake.

This pleased Harold to no end. "Oh, come on, Sam. It's me, Harold." He blushed. I thought he might throw in, "Aw-shucks," but he didn't.

"Harold, you look so handsome!" Samantha did not let on that I had told her about the blind date. "What's the occasion?"

Kat couldn't contain herself any longer. She had to jump in. "Harold has a hot date tonight. Actually, we're doing a *double* date." I think she thought Samantha might immediately disappear, like magic, if she emphasized the word "double."

Samantha had to have recognized Kat's meaning, but she chose to ignore it completely. "Oooh! Do I know this girl, Harold?"

I liked that she hadn't addressed the question to Kat. If Kat wanted Harold to stand on his own two feet, she had to learn to back off some. Setting him up on a date, dressing him up, and offering to go on a double date was all well and good, but eventually Harold would be on his own. Maybe I would have to play interference a lot this evening and steer the conversation back to Harold and his mystery date. I couldn't wait to see her. Please, mystery date, show up.

"Her name's Amber," Harold said, failing to mention that he'd never met her. I hadn't either.

Kat didn't have any friends named Amber. Then it hit me. I had seen Kat fooling around on Match.com last week. She said one of her friends had recently joined up and she wanted to check out her profile. My suspicion was that Kat had set up an account for Harold. I didn't see much good coming from this. Red lights flashed in my head.

"What's the gift?" I asked.

Harold stared at me seriously. "A book."

I tried not to laugh at his serious tone. "What book?"

"*Neverwhere.*"

Kat rolled her eyes, making it clear she didn't approve of the gift. "I told him it was too soon, but he wants to test the waters."

"If she's not a fan, or can't become a fan, of Gaiman, I don't see how we'll work out." Harold wasn't playing a game, even if the book was a test.

Samantha nodded, but I detected a hint of laughter in her eyes.

The book was so Harold. I felt relieved he wouldn't let Kat push him into anything he wasn't comfortable with. Score one for Harold. Maybe he would be able to stand on his own two feet after all.

Samantha and I sat down, and miraculously, the waitress appeared immediately.

"How much time until she shows, Harold?" asked Samantha.

Harold checked his Timex. I was relieved Kat hadn't also tried to buy him a cooler watch. "T-minus twenty."

"Great. I have time for a beer while I wait for my friend." Samantha ordered a Sam Adams, and I said ditto to the waitress.

Kat's facial muscles tightened around her intimidating grin. I wanted to tell her to get off her high horse. I was allowed to have female friends. Of course, I didn't plan on telling her that I had a crush on Samantha back in the day, and that I suspected Samantha might have a crush on me now. Crushes were innocent—completely innocent. No reason for anyone to get their feathers ruffled.

I steered the conversation back to Gaiman. "All right, Harold. You have piqued my curiosity. I'm going to the library tomorrow to check out *Neverwhere*."

"You won't regret it." Again, his tone was serious. I started to worry he might terrify the shit out of his date.

"Hey, why don't you just borrow my copy? I'll drop it off on Monday on my way to work," said Sam. The waitress placed our beers on the table, and Samantha raised her glass. "To Harold, and his date."

We all clinked glasses, even Kat, who I sensed wanted nothing more than to push Samantha off her chair and into the water. I had to do something.

"Whatcha drinking, sweetheart? Looks tasty." I winked at her, feeling silly that I had to try so hard to convince Kat she had nothing to worry about.

"A mint julep." She gestured for me to try it. I hated bourbon, and immediately regretted asking, but I knew Kat would be upset if I refused.

"A mint julep! Well, how very southern of you." Kat had started reading *Gone with the Wind* the other day, so I thought her ordering a mint julep was cute. I lifted the glass. The smell of bourbon made me gag involuntarily

Ignoring it, I took the tiniest of sips and quickly set the glass down far away from me, so I couldn't smell it.

"Not what I imagined … it's much … stronger than I thought it would be." I felt my eyes water.

Harold checked his watch again. Sam remained quiet but wore a wry smile.

"Don't worry, Harold, she'll show." Kat tried to sooth Harold's nerves, but it wasn't working. Quiet, expressionless Harold had been replaced by a nervous, jumpy little man who looked like he wanted to hurl. I felt for the guy.

Samantha shot a text on her phone. Seconds later, her phone chirped. I glanced at the screen: *"I'll see you there."*

Sam looked at me slyly. I understood she had arranged to have a friend meet her here, to keep an eye on the big date.

With all the excitement surrounding this Amber, I was starting to get jittery myself. Grabbing my beer, I almost upset my glass.

"Steady, big fella," Samantha teased.

My grin was a bit too wide, and Kat "accidentally" kicked me under the table. Not letting on about the kick to my shin, I said, "Geez, one beer and I'm already acting tipsy. Good thing I have my lovely Kat here to take care of me."

It appeased her some, and she placed a hand on mine lovingly—or possessively. "Always." Her voice was too cheery, her smile so forced it was silly looking. But I found it endearing anyway and raised Kat's hand to my lips, fearful she might take the opportunity to throttle me otherwise. Just because Uncle Roger was a cheater and Mom thought Dad was one as well, didn't mean I was.

"I better snag those two seats at the bar, so my friend and I don't have to stand all night." Samantha grabbed her purse from the hook under the table. "Harold, I'll be keeping an eye on you so I can learn some of your moves." She winked. Harold's aw-shucks demeanor returned. Samantha's tone and body language didn't indicate she was mocking him. I admired her ability to be heartfelt, even when Kat was staring at her like a lioness stalking her dinner.

The two barstools were right in front of the television. I was jealous. From there, Samantha would be able to watch the rest of the game. My sole entertainment was Harold and his date, and I cringed at the thought of watching him crash and burn.

Kat rose and sat next to me, so Harold's date could sit next to him. D-Day was just a few minutes away. I sucked in a long breath. God I hoped Amber would show.

Five minutes ticked by. Kat did her best to keep the conversation going, but after ten minutes, I glanced over my shoulder at the worried look on Samantha's face. Was it possible Amber wouldn't show?

Beads of perspiration appeared on Harold's brow. Poor guy. I tried to think of something to say to ease his suffering, but drew blanks. Even Kat looked concerned and wasn't her chatty self. Harold fiddled with the wrapped book, accidently tearing the corner off.

"Um, are you Harold?" a timid voice came from directly behind me.

Harold glanced up, but didn't speak.

Kat bounced out of her chair, "Are you Amber?"

"Yeah. I'm so sorry I'm late. Got held up at work." She continued to stand behind me.

Harold was gaping at her, his eyes bugged. I didn't want to turn and make the girl feel even more awkward. If I were her, I would be running for the exit.

"Oh, no apologies needed. You're here, and that's all that matters." Kat led Amber to the seat next to the bug-eyed Gaiman fan.

I nudged Harold's foot under the table, pleading for him to stop gawking. He either ignored me completely or didn't understand my meaning.

"Let me get the ball rolling. Amber, this is Harold." Kat motioned to Harold, who finally smiled bashfully and took his eyes off Amber. At least he wasn't ogling her like she was a science project gone awry. "And this is my girlfriend, Cori."

I shook Amber's hand across the table. "Very nice to meet you."

Harold still said nothing.

"Where do you work, Amber?" asked Kat.

"I'm a paralegal at a law firm." Amber fidgeted with the purse on her lap and looked miserable.

One minute in, and already I wanted to pull the ripcord.

"Harold and Cori work at Beantown Café together. That's how we all know each other." Kat was grasping at straws.

"Oh, that's nice." Amber didn't sound impressed.

"I also teach at Adams University. British lit," I added, and then kicked myself. She wasn't my date to impress and I made Harold look even more like a loser. *Dammit, Cori, you and your ego.*

"Really?" Finally, her face had some expression:

excitement. "I love to read."

Her statement kindled an ounce of life in Harold's body language. He nodded and peeked at her from the corner of his eyes. Then he stared at the water again. Baby steps, Harold, baby steps.

"Who's your favorite author?" I held my breath after my query. *Please say Neil Gaiman. Please, please.*

I felt Kat squeeze my leg in anticipation, digging all five nails deep into my thigh.

"J.K. Rowling."

*Dammit!*

"Which Potter book is your favorite?"

I was stunned to note that the question came from Harold. Seriously, I almost fell out of my chair. Kat slapped my thigh victoriously. A connection had been made. Halle-fucking-lujah.

Amber turned to Harold, a stern look on her face. "*Half-Blood Prince.* You?" Her tone implied she was ready for a duel—or a quidditch match.

"*Order of the Phoenix*, but *Half-Blood* is my second favorite." Harold was just as serious.

"Thank goodness. I can't be friends with someone who thinks *Azkaban* is the best."

"True, but you can't have the rest of the series without the foundation of *Azkaban*."

And they were off, ladies and gentlemen. For the next twenty minutes, Amber and Harold immersed themselves in the world of Harry Potter. Kat and I stayed mute. In fact, I was in awe. The two nerds didn't notice anyone or anything going on around them. Even when the bar erupted into cheers when

David Ortiz hit a homer, they didn't stop talking. All that mattered was Harry Potter.

The waitress came by and Amber took a breather from Pottermania to order a glass of water. The poor girl must have been parched. Kat and I ordered another round: mint julep for her, and a beer for me. Harold ordered a Coke. He hadn't touched his whiskey. Why he had ordered that again perplexed me. He had hated it at the gay bar. Thank goodness his date hadn't ordered an alcoholic drink or poor Harold would have had to try his best to choke down the firewater.

"How do you feel about Neil Gaiman?"

It was only a matter of time before Harold introduced the subject. I had hoped he'd ride the Potter bus a tad longer, build a little more rapport before he hit his make-or-break topic.

Amber tapped her fork on the table. "I tried reading *American Gods*, but I couldn't get into it."

*Mayday! Mayday!*

Kat's fingers dug into my thigh again. Both of us stifled gasps, our mouths open. I sensed Samantha knew trouble was brewing; I don't know how. I could just feel her observing and praying.

Harold was the only one who remained calm. "I see." He sipped his Coke, which the waitress had just set down. "That is one of the tougher ones to get into if you're not used to his writing. Have you read *Neverwhere*?"

"*Neverwhere* … never even heard of it."

I'm pretty sure Amber didn't mean it as a joke. Her face flushed, and her eyes filled with panic.

Harold thought the joke was hysterical. "Never even heard of it … that's a good one." Harold guffawed, dabbing his eyes with his sleeve.

I really hoped the sweater wasn't cashmere. I couldn't believe my eyes. Harold was acting somewhat cool; maybe even a little flirtatious.

He pushed the wrapped book across the table to Amber. "I got you this. I'm not saying you have to love it, but if you want us to be friends, you have to give it a chance."

Did I say he was being flirtatious? Now he was giving her an ultimatum—on the first date.

*Oh, Harold. I love you man, but sometimes you are too much.*

"Really?" Amber raised her eyebrows. Picking up the gift, she hesitated a minute before quickly tearing off the paper.

"Ha! I had a feeling."

Harold remained silent.

Kat and I stared at the poor girl.

Amber stayed calm. "I'll make you a deal. I'll read this, but you have to read my favorite book."

"Which is?" asked Mr. Debonair.

"*Pride and Prejudice.*"

"The chick book!" Harold's voice cracked, bringing a rush of color to his face.

"Yup! The chick book." Amber nodded confidently.

I liked her style. The first few moments of the date had been awkward, but once she settled in, Amber had shown herself to be self-assured, playful, and nerdy. For the first time, I was starting to appreciate Kat's efforts in finding Harold a date. I owed her an apology. I smiled, relishing that thought of thanking her later this evening maybe with a kiss or more.

"Oh, all right. But I'm not buying it. I bet I can find a free copy for my Kindle."

"Of course. I wouldn't want to endanger your machismo." Amber batted her eyelids at him.

Machismo and Harold: who would have ever put those two words together?

The waitress returned and we decided to start with a bucket of peel-n-eat shrimp. Not my preferred food choice for a first date—there isn't a neat way to eat them—but the two of them dug in as soon as the bucket hit the table. Gotta love nerds. They'll go crazy about books, but table manners don't matter.

While she ate, I took a moment to study Amber. Blue eyes sparkled behind black-framed glasses, which she was forever pushing higher up on her nose. Her skirt and baggy sweater screamed nerdy librarian. I didn't know much about paralegals, but I assumed she had to dress like that for work, or maybe she had changed and this really was her date attire.

Either way, it was perfect for Harold. I bet he's had a million wet dreams about a nerdy librarian.

Kat eased them into a conversation about movies, and it didn't take long for the nerds to launch into Peter Jackson's *Lord of the Rings* and *The Hobbit*. Luckily, Kat and I had seen the movies so we could join the conversation this time.

Before I knew it, the night was drawing to a close. I think Kat realized it was time to call it good while things were still on the up and up. Amber decided to call for a cab, and Harold offered to share it with her and split the fare. I was so proud I wanted to hug him. The lovebirds left, still jabbering on, this time about the Harry Potter films.

Samantha and her friend showed up as soon as Harold and Amber had left.

"So, that seemed to go well." Samantha sat down opposite me.

Her friend, a skinny brunette, sat opposite Kat. Besides being way too skinny for my liking, the woman was attractive. I wondered if she were gay. Was this the ex?

Apparently, Kat wondered the same thing. "Are you two on a date as well?" Her tone was playfully snarky.

I almost choked on my beer.

"You don't mess around do you, Kat." Samantha looked to her friend. "Cori, Kat, I would like you to meet my *friend*, Lucy."

I shook Lucy's hand. "Pleasure, Lucy. You'll have to forgive Kat. She loves to play matchmaker. If you aren't careful, she'll try to set you two up."

Lucy looked like a tax attorney. My first thought when I saw her was, "I bet she could add one hundred and twenty-seven digits together without using a calculator." Not once did I try to imagine her naked. Yes, I did that with most people.

Lucy's smile showed there were no hard feelings. "Too late, Kat. Been there, done that." Lucy wore little makeup and her clothes looked expensive, especially her jeans.

Kat tilted her head, obviously not understanding.

"We broke up recently and decided we're better at the friend thing than the girlfriend thing," explained Samantha. She took a sip of her beer, casually lowering her eyes. "It seems I'm always better at the friend bit." She stared directly at me, and I wondered what she was implying. Then Samantha looked back at Lucy, and I suddenly realized … she was still in love with her ex.

Thank goodness Kat was distracted and didn't notice.

Lucy gave Sam a quick glance, and then asked Kat, "So you set up the date tonight?"

"I sure did." Kat's face lit up. "And he may have another date on Sunday."

I was in the midst of raising my glass to my lips, but when I heard that I set my drink down heavily. "What? Why?"

"What do you mean, why?" Kat turned to eye me.

"He seems to really like this girl, and vice versa. Call this a success, Kat. No need to muddy the waters."

"Muddy the waters. Harold hasn't been on enough dates to know what he likes and what he doesn't. I don't want him to settle," she defended herself.

"Settle? No offense, but he's no Don Juan. And this girl was cute and perfect for him. It wouldn't be like he was settling." I sipped my drink, wondering how to proceed. "I know you; once you start a project like this, you don't know how to stop. Please, stop."

Kat crossed her arms. The mood at the table fell.

"Hey now, if you need to help someone, help me. I haven't had a first date in years." Lucy giggled. "The last one before Sam was such a disaster that I can't even count it ... so that makes it even longer."

Kat perked up in her seat. "Really? What type of women do you like?"

Samantha piped up, "Like me, but not so career-driven."

Lucy slapped her arm playfully. "Oh, stop. It wasn't your career. It was ..." Flames shot across Lucy's cheeks as she realized she probably shouldn't reveal the problem in their relationship to two strangers.

"Was what?" asked Samantha, who obviously didn't

know the real reason or wanted to confirm her suspicions.

Lucy leaned over and whispered in her ear.

It was Samantha's turn to blush. She slapped Lucy's thigh, somewhat hard. "I can't believe you!"

I so wanted to know. One look at Kat informed me she'd get the answer out of Lucy eventually.

Samantha feigned hurt. She stood. "I'm going to the bathroom." As she left, she mussed Lucy's hair, letting her know she wasn't upset.

Once Sam had disappeared into the crowd, I studied her ex. Lucy put out zero sexual vibes. In fact, if I hadn't known she had slept with Samantha, I would put money on her being a virgin. "Asexual" was the word that sprang to mind.

It didn't mean she wasn't attractive. Her face was pleasant, her smile sweet. She wore glasses, somewhat cooler glasses than I would have thought she'd wear. I wondered if Sam picked them out for her. Lucy's figure didn't shout look at me, but it suggested she stayed in shape and took care of herself. She smelled of rose petals—not a scent that attracted me. It made me think of a sweet old grandmother who liked to bake cake for afternoon tea. That was it. Lucy gave off a grandmother vibe.

Kat got right to business. "Lucy, do you have a Match.com account?"

"What? Online dating? No way." She pushed her chair away from the table.

"Oh, come on. That's how I found a girl for Harold. It's the twenty-first century. Loosen up. One in four relationships start online these days."

"Twenty-five percent! No way," I said a little too loudly.

"I'm telling you. It's the truth." Kat placed a hand on her heart like a schoolgirl reciting the pledge of allegiance.

"One in four …" Lucy sounded impressed by the stat. She looked like the type who loved stats. "I still don't know, Kat. I don't have time to check my profile and stuff."

"No worries. You can help me set up the profile and then I'll take care of it."

"What do you mean, you'll take care of it? Didn't Harold chat with Amber before this date?" I pinned her with a look.

"Harold! Are you kidding? No it was all me." She ignored my disgust.

"Katharine, that's deceitful—and dangerous." I didn't back down. "You have to let Harold take over now."

"Oh, Cori, stop acting so stuffy. I just acted like his secretary—there was no deceit." She threw me a glare meant to silence me. "So, Lucy, when can we start?"

"Start what?" Samantha returned and took her seat.

"Kat's going to help me set up a Match.com account and find a date." Lucy's hesitation was gone. The stats had won her over completely.

"Really? Online dating?" Samantha looked to Lucy, and then to me, shocked by the direction of the conversation.

"Oh, you're a stick-in-the-mud like Cori." Kat grabbed her purse from the back of her chair and pulled out her cell phone. "What's your number, Lucy?"

While they worked out the details, Samantha studied my face. I was having a hard time reading what she was trying to communicate to me.

"What about you, Samantha?" Kat held her phone, waiting for Sam's digits.

"I'm not looking for anyone."

"Are you sure? I'm good at this." Kat looked like a child waiting to open a present.

"Kat, I think you might be addicted. You should see your face." I put my hand on hers and lowered the phone.

Kat giggled drunkenly. "I may be a little addicted, but it's for a good cause. I like seeing people happy and in a *relationship*." She made direct eye contact with Samantha as she uttered the last word.

Desperate to save Sam from Kat's clutches, I asked, "Did you and Harold go shopping today? He looked nice."

The mention of shopping caught her attention, just as I knew it would. "Yes! You should have seen the outfit he wanted to wear." She rolled her eyes and waved a hand dramatically in the air. "His mother and I took one look at him and decided the only thing to do was to buy him some new clothes."

"Did you just get the one outfit?" I dreaded hearing the answer. Samantha seemed to catch my meaning.

"No, we picked out a few things. His mother was so excited about his date that she let Harold use her credit card."

I let out a silent sigh of relief.

## Chapter Seven

The sun shone, the grass was a vibrant green, the fans were merry, and the smell of popcorn and Fenway Franks hung in the air. It was a glorious day for a baseball game, and I was delighted to be at the Red Sox game with my father. In the third inning, standing in line for more beer, I felt a tap on my shoulder. I turned to find Samantha smirking at me.

"There you are. I thought you went to the other beer line." She casually popped into the line next to me. The line was twenty deep, and Ortiz was up to bat soon. I bet she didn't want to miss it, so she'd pretended we were together to avoid going to the back of the line. Lucy stood right next to her, looking uncomfortable about jumping ahead of all the drunk fans.

Some of the guys behind us grumbled. Wanting to squash any bickering, I said, "Sorry. I hopped in this line because it was closer to the bathroom. Glad you found me. You can help me carry the beer back to Dad."

It did the job. The two dudes right behind us settled down and turned their attention to their buddy, who had just spilled the beer he had left. It was only the third inning, but the guy was completely sloshed. I doubted he'd make it to the seventh-inning stretch.

We ordered two beers each and headed back to my section.

"Where are your seats?" I asked, confused as to why they were following me.

"A few rows up from you. I didn't see you until you made your beer run." Samantha did her best not to drop her beers when a couple of kids ran past, bumping her arm. "Kids today," Sam grumbled. "They need to learn some respect."

A person we assumed was their mother gave Sam a snarky look and bumped her arm again vigorously—and intentionally.

I opened my mouth to say something, but Lucy shook her head and hurried us along so we wouldn't miss Ortiz.

"Ah, that was sweet, though." Samantha flashed me a flirtatious smile that drew a rush of color to my face.

Thank goodness Lucy had stopped me, or I would have made a bigger ass out of myself. If the woman had turned around and challenged me, I'm pretty sure I would have dropped my beers and run screaming like a girl in the opposite direction. Confrontation was not my thing, even growing up around my mom.

"Mind if we sit with you guys until we get kicked out of the seats. You are so much closer."

Dad nodded his consent.

"Oh you can see the bullpen from here." Samantha gestured to her left. "Right on!" She sat down next to me.

I handed my father his beer, and asked. "What did I miss?"

He grunted in disgust. "Ground out."

I wanted to chuckle. My father was many things, but verbose was not one of them.

Samantha pulled out her phone and snapped a picture of the field. "Updating my Facebook and Twitter status," she explained,

Really? I didn't pin her as a social media person. I'd never bothered to get an account with either—weren't they both just for high school kids?

"Holy shit!" she exclaimed.

I turned to her to see if everything was okay. Several other fans turned in their chairs, too, wondering whether there was a fire or whether Ben Affleck was standing nearby or something.

Samantha whispered, "Sorry!" and covered her mouth. Leaning closer, she whispered, "Harold just tweeted that Mr. Darcy is an ass."

I wasn't sure what shocked me more: that Samantha followed Harold's tweets, or that Harold had a Twitter account.

"He must really like that girl." I leaned closer, so we wouldn't annoy anyone around us. Most people didn't care if you talked at the game, as long as you were polite about it.

"The one from last night?"

I gave her the *duh* look. How many girls did Harold have

in his life?

"Sorry. Stupid question." She sipped her beer.

"Amber said she'd read *Neverwhere* if Harold read *Pride and Prejudice*. I didn't think he would. Maybe the zombie version. Can you tell if he's reading the zombie version?"

"I'm a little surprised you know about the zombie version." Samantha tapped the keypad on her phone.

"Why's that?" I didn't attempt to hide my confusion.

"You seem a little too straight-laced for that."

"Seriously. I don't just read 'literature.'" I made quote marks in the air.

"What are you reading right now?"

"Your phone."

She smiled at my wit. "Ha! Nice try."

"This isn't a fair question. I'm teaching two British lit courses, so of course I'm reading a classic. And to answer your question: *Middlemarch* by George Eliot."

"Okay, what books did you read this summer?"

I thought back. The only book I had read for fun was massive. "*The Way of Kings.*"

"Sanderson." She looked astonished. "Have you read his Mistborn series?"

I shook my head.

"You need to read them. They're fantastic." Sam nudged my arm enthusiastically.

I tapped her phone. "Has Harold said anything about the date?"

"Oh no. Harold takes his tweeting seriously. It's only about books."

"Really? He must not have many followers then."

"He has thousands more than me. He's actually quite popular in the social media world. His blog has more than 5,000 readers."

I sat back in my chair, stunned. "Harold blogs?"

"Yep!" She patted my thigh. "You should start blogging. It would be good for your career."

"I doubt the university would want me to dis my students on a blog."

"Not about teaching. About your writing. Have you thought about self-publishing? Lucy does."

I leaned forward in my seat and looked to Lucy for confirmation. She took her eyes off the field briefly and said, "Yep. Two years now. I love it. Best decision I ever made." Then she turned her attention back to the game.

Samantha laughed. "Don't worry. She'll tell you more about it later. But you should start blogging to build your platform."

"Platform," I mumbled, confused.

My father handed me his phone. He tapped the screen. "Here's your mom's writing blog."

"Mom blogs?" I hollered.

Several rows of people turned to gawk at me. My face felt so hot I thought my forehead would pop off completely and smoke and lava would pour out of my skull like a volcano. Samantha and Lucy laughed like maniacs and even Dad guffawed—and he wasn't the guffawing type.

After she settled down, Samantha patted my arm. "You see, everyone's doing it." She followed it with another round of uncontrollable giggles—solo this time, because Lucy and my father were again focused on the game.

I sat back in my chair, baffled by this revelation. My eyes were on the commotion on the field, but I was too stunned to take it in; that is, until I heard the crack of the bat, and everyone jumped up from their seats. I rose, too, for a better view—thank goodness, because the ball was heading right for Dad's head. Instinctively, I put my hand out and caught the ball before it crashed into Dad's face. Everyone cheered.

*Damn that stung!* I grinned, not letting on how much my hand hurt. I had been to hundreds of games, and not once had I come close to catching a ball. It was Ortiz, I realized, who had hit the homer. Dad hugged me, and then Samantha, Lucy, and some random fans did the same. Not only was this a homerun, but if the Sox won today, more than likely they'd have home field advantage in the playoffs. This homer was a big deal—and I caught the ball! I was part of Red Sox history.

I sat back down, holding the ball in my hand.

"That has to be a lucky sign for your writing career," Samantha whispered in my ear. "Finish your book, Cori."

As soon as my father and I entered the kitchen, he said, "Guess who caught an Ortiz home run?" and giggled like a schoolgirl.

Uncle Roger looked pissed, his eyes on the ball I waved in the air. He had turned down Dad's invite to today's game to help my aunt hang artwork in the gallery. I was helping her finish up tomorrow afternoon.

Even Mom, the rabid Red Sox hater, seemed impressed. Kat sauntered up to me like a Manx cat on the prowl and gave me a peck on the cheek. Then she ripped the ball out of my hand. I flexed and wiggled my fingers. I still didn't have much feeling in my hand.

"Want an ice pack?" asked my aunt.

"Yes, please. It's killing me." I shook my hand vigorously.

Dad relayed the story, omitting that the ball was zooming toward his head and he was frozen in terror. I decided to tell Kat that bit later on. Leave the poor man alone in front of my mother.

"One of Cori's friends snapped a photo," Dad said, to my surprise. He passed around his cell phone for everyone to look.

Kat's smile vanished instantly.

When I saw the photo, I knew why. I hadn't planned on telling Kat that Sam happened to be at the game. From the photo, it looked like it was just Sam. Lucy wasn't in the picture at all. Damn, this was bad.

Turning to Mom, I asked, "You blog?"

It was enough to distract Kat, which was my intention.

"I'm sorry, Cori, is that English?" Mom readjusted the silk scarf she wore to hide the age lines around her neck. She had started the habit several years ago, and I couldn't remember the last time I had seen her without one, even in summer.

"You know what I mean." I almost ratted Dad out but changed tack at the last minute. "I found your blog today. How long have you had a blog?"

"Since my publisher told me to start one." Her look informed me I was an idiot. "A lot of authors have blogs these days."

"I don't."

Mom opened her mouth, closed it, and then said diplomatically, "You should start one."

I was blown away. I had been expecting her to make a crack that I hadn't finished my novel.

Aunt Barbara slipped an ice pack into my hand. "I have a blog for the gallery. I can help you set one up, if you'd like."

"Am I the only one in this kitchen who doesn't have a blog, Facebook, or Twitter account?"

"I believe you are. You never were very good with technology. Basketball yes. Computers, no. Remember when you had to write a computer program in the fourth grade? You came home in tears and said you never wanted to touch a computer again." Aunt Barbara patted my head. "Blogging isn't that hard. And I think you should start a Goodreads account."

"What in the hell is that?"

"A website for readers."

I groaned. How in the world was I going to keep up with my jobs, writing, and all this shit?

Kat handed the ball back to me, bringing me back to reality. "What do you think about self-publishing?" I directed the question to my aunt, but Mom answered.

"I'm thinking of going that route."

"Really?"

"Yeah. Cut out the middle man completely and make more money." She sipped her wine. "But, Cori, I want you to promise me one thing: don't get bogged down by all the social media. You need to finish your book."

Again, her tone shocked me. She really meant it. My mother was even giving me the "you can do it" look.

Before I could tell Mom that the ending was still percolating in my head, Mom changed the subject, asking about Kat's success at matchmaking Harold. I didn't mind, because right then a new idea for my novel's ending entered my mind. I excused myself to Aunt Barbara's office to jot down some notes.

I was sitting at my aunt's desk when I heard a click.

"Ah, my daughter at work." I turned to see Mom had snapped a photo.

A second click captured another.

Why was she being so nice? Why had Dad invited me to the game today?

Then it hit me: they were getting a divorce.

It was the only rational explanation for Mom's behavior. They were preparing me for big news. Had her private eye found something after all?

## Chapter Eight

On Thursday morning, I received a text from Samantha. *"Can you do lunch?"*

*"Where and when?"* I quickly responded.

*"Wherever you like. My day is wide open,"* she replied, which clued me in immediately.

Whenever I walked into Beantown Café in the morning, my mind briefly flew to Samantha and her company's layoffs. The bastards waited until Thursday to deactivate her badge and pull her aside in front of everyone. What a degrading way to let someone go.

My shift ended at ten, so I asked if Sam wanted to meet then. If I could have, I would have walked out right then and there, except that I needed the money.

The three hours following Sam's text were hell. Fortunately, customers came and went, which kept me busy, but it didn't stop my mind from wandering to how Sam must feel. As soon as my shift ended, I ran all the way to the Last Drop on Boylston Street. Samantha sat at the bar, nursing a beer. She gazed absently at the TV, which was replaying last night's Sox game.

"Hey there." I slid into the barstool next to her. "Can I buy you another?"

"Jesus! You scared the shit out of me." She placed a hand on her chest, sucking in a deep breath.

"Sorry. I didn't mean to startle you." I put a hand on her back to comfort her. "Are you okay?"

"Yeah, I was just thinking …" She stared at the TV and lifted her glass for a generous swig.

At first, I thought she just wanted me to hang out at the bar with her and drink, to keep her company. Then I noticed she was barely in control of her emotions. It was only a matter of seconds before she broke down.

"There's a table in the back. No one's there." I rose, gently pulling her arm.

She nodded, and started to motion to the bartender, but I lowered her hand. "Don't worry. I got this. Head on back, and I'll be there in a minute."

She didn't even look at me, just slunk to the back table dejectedly.

I asked the bartender what Sam was drinking, and ordered two of the same. Tattoos ran up and down both of his arms and neck, and two metal spikes stuck out of each ear. He nodded in Samantha's direction. "I'll bring them back there if you want to join her."

"Thanks," I said, and hotfooted to the back of the

restaurant, taking a seat opposite her.

"I really thought I was safe," Samantha confessed. "Yes, I was stressed, but deep down I thought it would be okay." She stared at the brick wall behind me.

I reached across to place my hand on hers. What could I say?

"All week they had been picking people off my team. I thought, 'Hey, they need me now. Who else will do all the work?'" She rubbed her face with both hands. "God! I feel so stupid now. I don't even have my resume updated. I thought that if I did, it would curse me for sure. They've wiped out my contacts and didn't hand over my Rolodex. And my email access—gone." She laughed bitterly. "They were kind enough to box up all my photos and knickknacks from my desk. Isn't that sweet of the assholes?" She raised her near-empty beer glass to her lips and slurped angrily, draining it.

The bartender placed fresh beers down in front of us almost immediately, and we both took generous swallows.

"I was in shock when the HR person told me to inspect my boxes to see if all of my stuff was there. One of my shoes was missing. He said I could make an appointment to get it after hours. God, I feel like such a shit now. All those hours I put in. All the sacrifices, my blown relationship—everything for a company that won't even let me in to get my shoe. And it's an expensive shoe!" She slammed a hand down on the table.

I processed the information. So it had been work. When Lucy said it wasn't Samantha's job that ruined their relationship, she'd fibbed.

"What am I going to tell my family?" The shame in her

voice was hard to take. "Plus, I'm supposed to be having dinner with Lucy tonight to celebrate surviving the cuts, because they announced yesterday that it would all be over before Friday. How do I face her, Cori?" Tears streamed from her eyes and I rushed from my side of the table to hers.

She put her head on my shoulder, one arm wrapped around my stomach. I let her cry it out.

"Trust me, Sam, no one is going to say anything when they see you. They'll just want to be there for you." I hesitated, and then added, "Even Lucy."

"But I let that job ruin our relationship." Sam pulled away from me, wiping her eyes with her sleeve. "I was going to tell Lucy tonight that I'm still in love with her, ask her to give me another chance." She sniffled. "Now look at me! I'm unemployed—I'm a wreck. Fuck! I feel like such a loser." She slapped her hand down on the table again, causing the beer glasses to jump half an inch.

"I don't know Lucy all that well. But I know you, and I can't believe for one minute that you'd love someone shallow enough to run for the hills when the going got tough. Maybe it's not the time for the relationship talk, but I'm betting Lucy will be there for you tonight, as a friend at least. There's no need to rush things. See where the chips fall."

Sam nodded and looked away. "Well, I can always go work for my father. Manage one of his stores. Need any carpet?" She tried to laugh it off, but a string of snot blew out of her nose at her snort, and she started crying again.

I fished in my backpack for some Kleenex and handed them to her.

"Thanks," she mumbled, wiping her eyes. She blew her

nose viciously, sounding like a goose honking at a passerby.

"I bet if you do that in front of Lucy, her heart will melt," I joked.

Sam pinched my arm and smiled sadly. "This is the moment you show your true colors, you jerk." She set the wadded-up tissues on the table. "Thanks for coming today."

"No worries, Sam. Would you like another?" I motioned to her nearly empty glass. She nodded, and I left to order another round.

"Can you please keep an eye on us and refill our drinks if they get low?" I asked the barkeep.

He nodded his assent. "Looks like she's having a rough one. Did her husband leave her or something?" His concerned look told me he wasn't just fishing for gossip.

"Something like that."

"Who in their right mind would leave a hottie like her?" He shook his head, but his greasy hair didn't budge.

I shrugged, and thought of Lucy. What had really gone wrong in their relationship? If Kat wasn't such a busybody, I'd have enlisted her help, but my gut told me to back off that plan. My best bet was to get closer to Lucy—to see if I could get those two back together. It was obvious they both still had tender feelings for each other. Then I remembered Kat was helping Lucy find dates on Match.com. Shit. I needed to get her to back off and quick. How, though, without letting the cat out of the bag?

Samantha blew her nose again as I sat back down. Even red-nosed and with puffy eyes, she looked damn sexy to me—in a pathetic way. Would Lucy think the same when she saw her tonight? Hopefully.

"I must look lovely right now." She dabbed at her eyes, streaking her mascara even further.

"I happen to find raccoons very attractive," I teased.

"Very funny, wise guy." She pulled a compact out of her purse and tried to wipe away the smudges. "What do you have planned today?"

I sucked in some air and then bit my lower lip, deep in thought. "Not much, just hang out with an old friend and get shitfaced. You?"

"Oddly enough, I have the same plan." She flashed a cheerless smile.

The bartender delivered the next round. I raised my glass. "To getting shitfaced."

We clinked glasses and downed a third of our beers. Thank God I didn't have to teach later that day. My students had the night off to complete a take-home exam. I had planned on writing, but there was no way I could leave Samantha to dwell on getting fired alone. Yep, it was an excuse, but a decent one.

"What time are you meeting Lucy tonight?"

"Around seven."

"Shall I get us a pitcher of water, so you aren't too drunk?" I started to rise, chastising myself for not thinking of it sooner.

Samantha waved the idea away. "No water. Let's order a bunch of greasy food and try to stay sober that way. I can't remember the last time I binged on junk food and beer all day." She thought for a moment. "Maybe in college."

With her figure, it didn't look like she ever binged on anything, but I wasn't going to put a damper on her mood.

Sam grabbed a menu from behind the metal bucket that held paper towels and condiments and browsed her options.

She tapped a finger on the appetizer sampler: onion rings, fried mozzarella, chicken fingers, and buffalo wings. "That's the one." Then she hopped up to place the order with the bartender.

It took longer than I had expected, which gave me the chance to check my texts. Nothing from Kat. Good. Usually we hung out on Thursdays, my afternoon off, but lately she'd been busy. Doing what, God knows. Actually, I feared she was out shopping with Mom.

Samantha returned with two shot glasses. "Care for a little whiskey chaser?"

I rolled my eyes playfully, hiding my fear. "Sure, why not?" I raised the glass with her and we both tossed them back. Tears sprang to my eyes. God, I hate whiskey: the taste, the smell, and the burn! My vision was growing fuzzy.

"I better order more food if we keep this up."

"What do you want? I'll get it." She was out of her seat before I could stop her.

"Veggie burger."

Samantha whacked her head. "That's right. You're vegetarian!"

She took her time again, and I feared she was getting more shots.

I was right.

After the second round, she giggled. "You know, Lucy may love the fact that I got canned today. Canned—that's a funny word." She swayed in her seat to the song "Buffalo Soldier," which played over the loudspeakers. I knew she had started drinking before me, but she was already beyond wasted.

"Really, why's that?"

"That's why we broke up."

"I thought Lucy said work wasn't the reason."

She giggled. "Do you know what she whispered in my ear?"

I shook my head.

With a hiccup, Samantha said, "That I was the devil's spawn."

I must have looked befuddled, because she pointed at my face and laughed. "You see, I have three freckles on my left tit." She grabbed her boob, and for a brief moment, I thought she was going to whip it out. "Been there ever since I was a kid. Mom tried to convince me to have them removed because she said people would think I was the devil or something." Sam rubbed her eyes, trying to focus on my face. "I'm not sure why she thought that. It's not three sixes or anything. It looks more like a smile."

I still wasn't following.

"I told Lucy how Mom thought it was the sign of the devil. It was our inside joke." She turned serious. "But it was my job that broke us up."

"I thought Lucy was just as successful and busy."

"Oh, she didn't care about my long hours. She cared that I wasn't out at work."

"Really?" That shocked me. Boston was a fairly gay-friendly place.

"I work in finance. It's still a good ol' boys club. Announcing I'm a lesbian would have been catastrophic."

"And that bothered Lucy?" It seemed petty. I mean, Sam was in the closet just to keep her job, which was understandable. I would have been supportive.

"It was the way I handled it. One night I invited Lucy out with some coworkers. I hadn't told Lucy I wasn't out at work, and when she showed up, one of my coworkers asked how she knew me. I panicked, jumped in, and said, 'We've been friends since grade school.' It was a lie, of course. For the rest of the night, this one dude kept hitting on me right in front of Lucy. I didn't say anything. Oh boy, was she pissed. I don't think she ever got over it. Then, when I started working longer and longer hours, well, everything fell apart."

I bit my lip, wondering how I would have handled it if Kat had done something like that to me. I don't think I would have been all that happy, to be honest.

"I see." It was all I could think to say.

Samantha raised her beer glass, cradling it against her cheek. "I really can't blame Lucy. I would have been pissed as well. I don't think she thought I would cheat on her, but she didn't like me allowing men to hit on me without informing them I was in a relationship or without giving them the cold shoulder." Her expression grew sad again. "Guess I don't have to worry about that anymore … on both fronts."

"You don't think Lucy can get past it?"

"Sometimes yes, and sometimes no. That woman is the most stubborn woman I know. That's one of the things I love most about her, even though it bugs the shit out of me." Sam laughed, and then burped. "How are things with Kat?"

"Good." Taken aback by the abrupt change of subject, I looked away from her and added, "I guess."

"Uh-oh. Trouble in paradise?"

"How do I put this?" I rubbed my hands together nervously. "I love the woman to pieces. She's beautiful, smart, funny, and loving. But for the life of me, I can't understand why she has no ambition. She can dance, sing … and she's an artist … but she does nothing with her talents. I don't expect her to go out and make millions, but I want her to do *something*. Anything. Anything other than just go shopping with my mom."

The bartender approached with two more beers.

"Thanks," I said, not all that thrilled about it. I didn't take a sip, just continued my story. "The other day, I came home and she was super excited. She said she had a solution to our money woes."

Samantha leaned in closer to hear it.

"Kat and her friends were all going to listen to a call-in radio show and try to win fifty grand by being the first caller in some crazy contest. That was her solution." I shook my head. "And I think she really thought she'd succeed."

Samantha let out a laugh, and then quickly covered her mouth.

"You can laugh. I know it's crazy. She gets in these really strange moods, and I just don't know how to react. And then there's her shopping …" I let my words die.

"Do you think she's a shopaholic?" Samantha's tone was serious.

"You mean, like in that book?"

"Yeah. If she shops as much as you're insinuating, and you two are broke, I think there's a major issue going on."

"Huh. I just thought she was a spoiled brat." I worried

Samantha would think I was an ass for saying that about my girlfriend.

"Well, that could be the case."

I slumped back against the booth and looked at the ceiling. "I just wish she'd show some passion … besides … in the bedroom." That I'd actually uttered the last bit shocked the hell out of me. The booze was going to my head.

Samantha shouted, "I knew it!"

I felt my face flood with heat and color. I wished I had some ice water to cool it off.

"The first time I saw her, I knew she was a vixen in bed. Score, Cori!" She high-fived me.

"A vixen at night. A spendthrift by day. Not a great combo."

"Have her hang out with Lucy. That woman hasn't bought any new clothes in the last decade."

"Are you kidding? I would love that. Kat buys new clothes all the time, and she doesn't even wear them. Soon I might have to rent a storage unit for all the clothes she buys. But when I get home at night, she's wearing one of my T-shirts and a pair of Victoria's Secret sweats she's had for years. I just don't get it, at all."

"She likes to show off her ta-tas in public." Samantha chuckled.

"Oh, I'm aware. And do you know who helps her buy those tops? My mother!"

"Get out!"

"I'm not kidding. My mother is a sex-crazed maniac. Do you know the two of them started an erotica book club?"

Samantha couldn't stop laughing for several seconds.

"Maybe I should join. Lucy always teased me about being too vanilla."

Outwardly, I smiled, but inwardly, I was disappointed. I always thought Sam had a naughty side, but then again, I always thought she was straight as well. I really didn't know her at all back then.

"Kat says the same thing about me." Again, my frankness surprised me. But it felt good to have someone to talk to. For months I had been holding all of this in and pretending everything was great. "Do you know what Mom did to me when I was little?"

Worry marred Samantha's beautiful face for a moment.

"Oh, no! Nothing like that."

Curiosity immediately replaced her anxiety.

"Once, when I was about twelve or thirteen, I had some friends over at the house. I can't even remember how the conversation started, but Mom, who always had to be the funniest and coolest in any group, asked if we knew what oral sex was. I nodded, along with the rest of my friends, and Mom pounced.

"'Really, Cori. What is it?' she asked.

"I didn't actually know. I mean I knew about blow jobs and such, but didn't know the technical term, so I sputtered 'Talking about sex.'"

"No! You didn't!"

"I did! Some of my friends have never let me live that one down. God knows Mom didn't. The first time I invited Kat to a family dinner, Mom mentioned it. Kat teased me the rest of the night. That was how she and my mother first bonded. Now, the erotic book club. I know Kat doesn't read smut. She may not look like it, since her boobies are always spilling out of her shirt, but she loves classics and historical fiction. You should see how sexy she looks in bed, glasses on, wearing a tank top and lingerie, reading *Oliver Twist*. Smart women turn me on."

Samantha bolted upright in her seat, both palms on the table. "I'm the same way. The first time I saw Lucy wear her glasses, I think I fell madly in love. And the fact that she's a writer; well, that's sexy as hell."

I raised my glass. "To sexy intellectuals!"

Our food arrived, and Samantha dug in right away. After she had finished her first buffalo wing, she asked, "How come you never talked to me in high school?"

"I had a major crush on you." I covered my mouth, but it was too late to curb my candor.

She smiled. "Maybe I should tell Kat whiskey is your truth serum." Samantha dipped another wing into the blue cheese sauce. "I had a crush on you as well."

"Really?" My voice cracked.

Samantha giggled. "Yeah. You were the top jock in the school, but you had a sensitive side. You always had your nose in a book. I remember the day I discovered you in the back of the gym reading *Wuthering Heights*. I think I fell in love instantly … I at least swooned." She winked at me.

"It's a good book." I bit into my veggie burger, smearing ranch sauce and Frank's Red Hot Sauce all over my face. "How come you never told me?"

"How come you didn't tell me?"

"Are you serious?" I cringed at the thought. "Every time you tried to talk to me, I couldn't form a complete sentence."

"I always thought that was cute." Sam sipped her beer and followed it with a bite of onion ring.

"Well, *now* you tell me." I winked at her.

"It's a good thing we didn't pursue it. Can you imagine: two vanillas trying to figure out lesbian sex together?"

I laughed. "We'd just dry hump each other's legs until the cows came home."

She laughed, spraying chunks of onion ring across the table. "I can't believe Cori Tisdale just said 'dry hump!'"

"Maybe I should get us another round of that whiskey truth serum, and I'll start using words like vagina, vulva, tribadism, G-spots, dildos, rimming, clitoris, erogenous zones, post-coital bliss …" I motioned with my hand, implying etcetera.

"Goodness! Did Kat teach you all that, or is there more to the Brontë sisters than I thought?"

"I would love it if they mentioned rimming in their novels. Might make my students like them more. It's like pulling teeth to get some of those shits to talk about the novels in class. There are days when I feel no one hears me, not even when I'm lecturing."

Samantha nodded her understanding as she watched several customers stream in for the lunch rush.

"We could have attended prom together," she said, finally.

"Oh, good Lord. My mother would have had a field day if the school refused to sell us tickets. I can see her now, marching in front of the school protesting homophobia in the education system. I bet she would have got the governor involved. Such a shame we didn't let her."

Samantha smiled. "My parents have always been cool with it as well. Of course, I'm bi, so they think there's a glimmer of hope I'll settle down with a man and have kids."

"Do you think you would?" I nibbled on a French fry.

"Nah. I just like to have sex with men, not to be in a relationship with one. Women aren't that much easier, but at least they talk. Of course, when Lucy used to sit me down for one of our talks, they would last forever. I would always think, 'If she were a man, this would have been over in less than a minute.'"

"I totally get the 'chats.' When Kat starts one, I make sure I'm close to food and water. Who knows how long I'll be held prisoner?"

"So what was it that attracted you to Kat—besides the obvious?"

"What do you mean, the obvious?" I fished for compliments.

Samantha saw right through me. "Hey, I thought we were here to help stroke my wounded ego, not yours! Besides, I don't need to tell you your girlfriend is hot. After Lucy met her, she said, 'That's the most beautiful person I've met in real life.' I was jealous as hell. I let Lucy have it." Samantha snatched a chicken strip from the platter, as if someone else was going to nab it first.

"So, tell me," she continued, "is her body as great as I think it is?" Her face turned crimson at the question, but she leaned forward, eager to hear the answer.

"Let me put it this way. If Michelangelo had seen Kat naked, he wouldn't have messed with his David statue. Instead, there would just be one of Kat."

Samantha set her beer glass down on the table. "I knew it! Man, I hate her."

I thought I saw a fleeting look of panic cross her face.

"I mean, I'm jealous. I don't really hate her," she added quickly.

I waved her fears away. "Don't worry about it. I hear things like that all the time. At first, I admit it was her looks. When I asked her out on the first date, all I could think of was getting Kat into bed. But then, when we started talking, she could carry on a conversation about Charles Dickens vs. Wilkie Collins—I know, not the sexiest conversation, but for me it was … A woman with a body to die for and brains. I … what did you say earlier … swooned."

"Wilkie Collins! That's a new one."

I grinned at the absurdity. "There's one other thing. Every morning when we wake up, Kat smiles like she's actually happy to see me. No one has ever made me feel that way. Every morning, for more than two years. Thank God she's not tired of me yet."

*Or ashamed of my failure,* I added mentally.

The bartender arrived with two more whiskey shots. I stifled a groan. I needed to go to the bathroom, but I was worried I might not make it there on my own without resembling a fall-down drunk. I asked him for a grilled cheese, hoping the bread would help soak up the alcohol. Samantha requested a pitcher of water. He smiled, understanding our dilemma. I was relieved that Sam had finally caved on the "no water" thing.

Once he had retreated behind the bar, I said, "All right, I spilled the beans. Now what about Lucy gets you all hot and bothered?"

"Everything," she said in a breathy voice.

"Oh, come on! She must have some faults."

"Yes! She has faults coming out the ying-yang, yet somehow I can never stop thinking about her. I feel like a teenage girl. Call me Bella Swan."

"Who?" I felt my brow crinkle. The name sounded vaguely familiar.

"Oh my, you haven't read *Twilight*?"

"The vampire book—the vampires who sparkle?" I was floored that Sam had read it, and that she even referenced it.

"Yes, that one. You have to read it. Promise me you will." Her swollen eyes pleaded for me to agree.

"Okay, I promise. I have to admit it's a better name for a love interest than Bathsheba Everdene?"

"Who's named that? That name is hideous." Her scrunched face conveyed her distaste.

"Oh my! You have to read Thomas Hardy's *Far From the Madding Crowd* if you want me to read your sparkly vampire book."

We raised our shot glasses. Neither of us looked very comfortable.

"You sure you want to?" Samantha's eyes implored me to say no.

"Only if you do."

She shrugged and tossed it back. I did too—reluctantly.

# Chapter Nine

Hours later, I stumbled through my front door. Kat was sitting on the leather sofa, and so was my mother.

"Cori! Are you wasted?" Kat's tone wasn't pleasant.

"Um, I may be." It was hard to suppress a nervous laugh, but I managed.

"I thought you were working on your novel today. What in the hell happened?" Kat raised one eyebrow. I think. I couldn't actually see straight, but she always did that when she used that tone of voice. It punctuated her sternness.

I narrowed my eyes, trying to focus on her face. "A friend called and needed someone to talk to."

I'm pretty sure she crossed her arms, but I couldn't really tell.

"Let me guess. Sam?"

"Yeah. She got some bad news … about her family and

she didn't want to be alone." I sounded like a babbling idiot and a liar. But I had promised I wouldn't tell anyone Sam had been laid off. I was sworn to secrecy about the Lucy bit, as well.

"Kat, would you mind making my daughter a strong cup of coffee?" Mom's voice was firm, bordering on commanding.

"Hi, Mom!" I waved. I knew it wasn't the right response, but my brain wasn't functioning fully. Actually, it felt as if it were swelling up in my head.

"Cori, why don't you have a seat before you topple over?" She actually used her motherly tone, which was highly unusual. I wondered what was up. Normally, she would find this kind of thing hysterical, since it was so unlike me.

I could hear Kat making coffee in the kitchen. From the sound of it, she was throwing some stuff around.

I whispered, "She's mad."

Mom harrumphed.

"I think you're mad too … mad as a hatter!" I broke into hysterical drunken laughter.

"Oh, Cori. I'm not mad. I'm shocked. Totally taken aback by this. Who's Sam?"

I sensed she was nervous.

"Don't you remember Sam? The hot cheerleader when I played ball in high school." I tried to rest my shoe on the edge of the glass coffee table, but misjudged the distance and my foot crashed to the floor.

Mom grabbed my chin with her hand. "Cori, you need to shut up—now. One more word like that, and I won't be able to protect you from Kat."

I wiggled my chin free and rubbed it. "Don't manhandle me."

"Be glad I'm not putting you over my knee. Kat has been worried sick about you. She's called and texted at least fifty times since four o'clock. And you were out getting drunk with a hot cheerleader." Disdain dripped from every syllable.

"She's not a cheerleader anymore. Finance. She's a finance person." I babbled. "And she's in love with Lucy."

"Are you in love with Sam?"

I shook my head slowly. I could feel my brain swishing back and forth in my head. Holding my head with both hands to stop the pain, I said, "No. I'm in love with Kat, but she's mad at me."

"Then, for the love of God, stay quiet. You obviously can't handle your liquor."

"Whiskey. Tastes like shit and burns. It's truth serum."

Mom couldn't help laughing. "I wish Barbara could see you."

"Where is she? She wouldn't be mad at me." I pouted.

"No. She might challenge you to strip down and run through the neighborhood, though."

"Need more whiskey for that. You know who would? Kat! She's the sexiest thing."

Kat walked in at that moment. "Who's the sexiest thing?"

Unfortunately, she only heard the last sentence. I was sure she thought I meant Samantha. I ducked, expecting her to throw the coffee cup at my head, which made me look even guiltier.

"You, Kat, according to my inebriated daughter." Mom came to my defense.

"You don't have to cover for her." Kat set the cup down angrily, slopping coffee on the glass table.

"I'm not covering for her. You know I don't lie. Apparently, if you get Cori drunk on whiskey, she loosens up some. Let's get her somewhat sober and take her along tonight."

"Take me along where?" I slurped the coffee, knowing I had to sober up fast to avoid losing Kat. At the very least, I would otherwise be in for one hell of a night of fighting and reassuring. My head wasn't in the mood for that, and my tongue felt swollen and slime-covered.

"I have an appointment with a psychic," said Mom.

"A psychic? What in the hell for?"

"My private investigator didn't find any proof of your father's affair, so I'm hoping a medium will be able to help." She made it sound like the logical next step.

God damn! I had picked the wrong day to drink so much whiskey and beer. The invective that almost flew out of my mouth would have not only pissed off my mother but possibly also permanently damaged our relationship. I bit down hard on my lip to stop myself from saying anything.

Kat sat next to me, and I nestled my head on her shoulder, half-expecting her to push me away; she didn't.

"How are you feeling?" She ran her fingers through my hair.

"I'm so sorry!" I blubbered.

Her body tensed. "For what?" I didn't think she really wanted to know. I was positive she imagined Samantha and me indulging in an afternoon tryst.

"For being such a loser." I couldn't stem the tide of tears. "You deserve so much more. Someone who can provide for you ... better than I can. Someone who doesn't work at

Beantown Café."

"Honey, what are you talking about?" Kat lifted my chin and gazed into my eyes.

"I don't make millions of dollars like we thought I would. If I did, you could shop all of the time." I attempted to wave my hand in the air, but ended up whacking my chin.

Kat's expression saddened, and I felt responsible.

"Well, I think we need to get more coffee in her and a nice hot meal," Mom interrupted. "Or who knows if she'll ever stop feeling sorry for herself?"

I nestled my chin onto Kat's chest, ignoring my mother, even if I was grateful she had nipped my outburst in the bud.

"Cori, finish your drink, and we'll go to Pablo's Café." My mother is not a woman who can be ignored. "I think you'll need some greasy food, and lots of it. The psychic is just around the corner from the restaurant."

I did as I was told. All the while, Kat held me. The sadness never left her eyes, and I wanted to kiss it away, but I couldn't with my mother sitting there tapping her watch.

By the time we reached my mother's appointment, my head was starting to clear up. I wasn't in the best of shape, but I no longer felt like weeping every other second. Never again would I drink whiskey. It brought out all of my sadness. I kept thinking of that saying, "Loose lips sink ships."

When we entered the psychic's "office," which was actually her home, I had a hard time not laying into my mother about her stupidity. Seriously, it was bad enough that she had hired a PI who didn't find anything, but now she was seeing a shyster! What next? A tattoo on her forehead that read "I'm a fool. Take advantage of me"? Or maybe a computer hacker?

"Now, Cori, I want you to be on your best behavior." Mom flashed her best *Mommie Dearest* look.

"Oh, of course, Mother. Why would I misbehave here, of all places?" I looked away in disgust. The place reeked of incense: patchouli, my least favorite scent. The loony had a corkboard with testimonials attached to it. Seriously, someone came to her to find their cat, and miraculously, Fifi the cat was found. Or maybe it just got hungry and came home. I doubted it was a psychic miracle.

A dark-haired woman with olive skin rushed into the office, aka her entryway. Smiling, she shook my mother's hand, and then Kat's. She didn't offer to shake my hand. Instead, she said, "I don't want you here."

"What?" I replied, bewildered.

"You have a bad aura. I can't work with anyone while you're in the house. You have to leave." The loon's face and posture hardened.

I looked to Mom and Kat for support, not receiving any. "Are you serious?" I said to the woman.

"Deadly."

"You're deadly serious that I have a bad aura. Or do you just know I can see through your bullshit?" I couldn't hold my opinion in any longer.

"Cori!" Mom was not pleased. Her *Mommie Dearest* face turned into an "I will kill you if you embarrass me further" look. Kat seemed shell-shocked by the whole thing.

"Fine, Mother. I'll go back to Pablo's and have a drink. Kat would you like to join me?" I put my hand out.

"Kat also has an appointment." Mom informed me.

"What? Kat, you think I'm having an affair?" I was too

stunned to move.

"Ha! You have no faith in yourself. You'd never have an affair," sputtered the clairvoyant.

"Honey, it's not what you think. I'll tell you later." Kat turned her back on me.

Without another word, I stormed out of there and headed to Pablo's. I was beyond pissed. How could Kat think I was having an affair? True, I had just spent the day getting blotto with Samantha when I should have been writing, but Samantha needed a friend. How did that constitute cheating?

And how did that nutjob know I had no confidence in myself? I didn't like her to begin with, but now she was my archenemy. Why in the world did my girlfriend want to talk to a medium? Mom has always been crazy and attention-seeking, but Kat? Sure, she loved to be the center of attention and wore tops that make my eyes bulge out of my head, but this was a whole new level. I decided I needed her to stop hanging out with Mom. It was getting weird—insane, even.

Only two seats, side-by-side, remained vacant at the bar. I grabbed the one near the wall, placing my jacket on the seat next to me so no one would sit there. After ordering a margarita, I asked for some chips and salsa, hoping to soak up the alcohol. I had to be up at five the next morning for my shift at Beantown. I sat there sipping my marg, eating chips, watching the Red Sox on the tiny TV above the bar, and stewing.

Kat appeared after forty-five minutes. She slipped into the seat next to mine, not saying a word. I motioned to the bartender and ordered her a glass of red wine. Neither of us spoke. Kat nibbled at the chips nervously.

I couldn't stand the tension. "Seriously, Kat. You think I'm fucking someone else?"

The man standing behind us gave me a startled look before hurriedly placing his order at the bar.

I was too upset to care that I was causing a scene. The bartender overheard, too, although he was better at hiding it. A quick peek at me, out of the corner of his eye, was his only acknowledgment.

"Cori, your mother went there because she thinks your father is having an affair. I had a different reason."

"What?" I tried to erase all condescension from my face, hoping Kat would open up.

She never looked me in the eye. Staring at her purse in her lap, she muttered, "Just things."

"Does my mother know what these things are?" Once more, I tried to mask my frustration.

She looked so downcast and unsure of herself—not like my Kat at all.

"She knows some of it. Only because she's guessed."

That hurt. The insinuation was that my mother either paid more attention to Kat or knew my girlfriend better than I did. Probably both were true, which annoyed me.

I lifted Kat's face to stare into her eyes. "I know I'm not the easiest person to talk to, and I'm not completely in touch with my own feelings, but I want you to know one thing: I'm madly in love with you, and I'm always here for you."

She gave a half-laugh, half-cry. "Wow, I think that's the first time you've admitted it."

"That I love you? I say that to you all of the time."

"No, you don't. But I was referring to you being

emotionally detached. From yourself …" She paused, and then added, "And from me."

If she had punched me in the nose, I wouldn't have been more stunned.

"Is that why you went? To find some hocus-pocus way to get me to talk?" I tried to get Kat to smile. I failed.

"No. It was about me. But I might try to find a witch to cast a spell on you." The tiniest, most fleeting of smiles appeared on Kat's face for a moment.

I leaned over and kissed her cheek. "You don't need any spells. From now on, I'll try to open up more." I ordered another margarita, and Kat gave me a look. "I know I shouldn't. However, Mom will be back soon, and I want to be in my happy place to hear about her appointment." I pushed the empty glass away, noticing a paper cup sitting by Kat's wineglass. "What's that?"

She colored. "Oh, it's from Kay."

"Who's Kay?"

"The woman I just saw."

"Her name is Kay? Not some fancy East European name like Agnieszka?"

"Yep. Just Kay."

"Why'd she give you a paper cup?" I really was walking on eggshells, so I asked as innocently as possible.

"I'm supposed to pour the water over my head at midnight."

I reached for the cup, to see the magic potion, but Kat slapped my hand away. "She told me you shouldn't touch it. You'd ruin it."

Luckily, the bartender arrived with my drink. I sipped it

quickly so I wouldn't say anything stupid. "Oh, I understand." I said slowly. "What's the ceremony for?"

"To find answers." Her body tensed, and I knew she wouldn't tell me what answers she sought.

"That's cool," I mumbled.

"Cori, you're still drinking?" My mother had arrived. She didn't sound overly annoyed, and she even ordered a drink for herself.

"Yep." I wanted to add that I was looking for answers, but I didn't want to sleep on the couch, so I kept my mouth shut.

"Well, let's get a table. I want to pick your brains about something." Mom informed the bartender we were getting a table and instructed him to bring the drink to us.

"Good luck finding anything in here." Kat rubbed the top of my head somewhat lovingly; mostly, she looked lost.

I held her hand and we followed Mom to the hostess to request a table. I had eaten nothing but crap all day. I was starving.

"Well, that was informative," announced my mother as soon as the hostess left us alone.

I started to speak, but stopped when Kat dug her nails into my thigh.

"What did she say?" Kat asked.

That we were, once again, discussing whether or not my father was having an affair disgusted me. Yet I knew there was no way to stop my mother searching for an answer until she was completely satisfied one way or another. It annoyed the hell out of me that she didn't just ask the man.

"Nothing definitive, actually. But she gave me much to

think about." Mom fiddled with her fork, which was out of character for her.

"Where's your water?" I sniggered, and Kat whacked my leg under the table.

"In the car. I didn't want you, the vile non-believer, to touch it." Mom glared at me. "Are you going to play nice, or do I have to send you home so Kat and I can have an adult conversation."

Adult conversation. I was the only one at the table who hadn't lost my fucking mind.

I mimed locking my mouth shut, pretending to throw the invisible key over my shoulder.

"Good." Mom continued to speak non-stop for the next ten minutes. I tuned her out completely; otherwise, I wouldn't have been able to keep my trap shut.

When I heard her ask Kat about her appointment, I checked back in to the conversation. Laying a supportive hand on my girlfriend's thigh, I hoped Kat would give me a clue about what was bugging her—any clue.

"Oh, she gave me much to think about as well."

That was all she said. Great! Now I had much to think about.

Mom glanced in my direction briefly and looked sympathetic. Maybe I could fish for some information or hints at our next nail appointment.

"You won't believe this, Nell, but Cori actually admitted she's not good at opening up." A devious smile returned to Kat's face.

"Twenty-eight years and two degrees from Harvard and you've finally learned that, Cori." Mom lifted her marg glass to salute me.

"It seems like I'm not the only one having issues lately."

Kat's face fell. Trying, and failing, to hide a look of betrayal, she ran from the table.

"Jesus, Cori. You can be such a jackass when you want to be!"

"Why won't you tell me what's going on?" My voice was filled with accusation and guilt.

"Don't place the blame at my feet. Go after her. Now!" Mom pointed to the exit.

I threw my napkin down on the table and went to seek out Kat, who disappeared around the corner of the restaurant.

She was sitting on a stone bench opposite The Coop, Harvard's bookstore. Her hands covered her face, and her chest heaved slightly from crying. I sat down heavily beside Kat, wrapping my arms around her. She didn't fight me, thankfully.

"My mom's right. I can be a jackass."

Kat sniffled but didn't speak.

"I'm afraid I'm not scoring any points with you today, am I?"

She shook her head. Clutching the front of my shirt with one hand, she wiped her nose on my shoulder.

"I just don't know what's going on and that scares me," I whispered.

"Why were you with Sam all day?"

So it was about Samantha. Or was she deflecting? Damn, it was so hard to tell with her.

I inhaled. "Kat, you have nothing to worry about. Samantha needed a friend today. Just a friend. I would say more, but I promised I wouldn't. Look me in the eye"—I lifted her chin—"you need to trust me on this one. Please."

Kat nodded meekly but unconvincingly. Then, out of the blue, she said, "When I'm ready, I'll tell you why I went tonight. I need to work—to figure some stuff out."

"Can you at least tell me if I need to worry?" I pleaded.

"Not about us. You are a jackass, but you're my jackass." There was a hint of a twinkle in her eye, and I kissed her. I meant for it to be a reassuring kiss, but Kat had another idea in mind. Reaching around the back of my head, she pulled me in passionately and slid her tongue into my mouth. Her hands tugged me to her with frenzied desire. Despite not wanting to stop, I knew we had to, especially when catcalls floated from across the alley.

A voice more powerful than a cold shower said, "Get a room you two." My mother approached, carrying a takeout bag.

"Perfect timing," I said, mortified.

"I should have waited a few more seconds and seen how far you'd let it go."

I glowered at her, but she waved my disgust away. "I had them pack up your second dinner. I figured I should take you two home, so you could talk, but it looks like you might want to do the tango instead—the naked tango. Make-up sex is healthy for a relationship. God knows I try to piss off Dale as much as possible for the payoff."

"Mother!"

"Don't act indignant with me. I'm not the one putting on a sex show in the middle of Harvard Square." She mussed with her hair and checked her makeup in a shop window. "Are you two ready to go?"

As soon as Mom had dropped us off and we entered our front door, Kat grabbed me and forced me up against the door, dropping her water from crazy Kay. Her kiss was passionate, purposeful. I won't lie: it was fucking hot.

Her tongue explored my mouth, as if searching for something but never quite finding it. Usually, Kat wasn't into kissing that much, which was one of my laments. Tonight, however, she was all about it. I felt a tingling, warm sensation down below. Yet I wasn't in a rush. Sometimes, the simple act of kissing is more erotic than fucking.

Without stopping, Kat maneuvered us to the couch. The nights were getting chillier, and I noticed she was shivering. Stopping briefly, I located the fireplace remote and turned it on. When Mom had insisted we install it, I thought it was a waste of money; now I saw its benefit.

Kat brushed a few strands of hair off my face and stared deeply into my eyes. She didn't speak, but I sensed she wanted to.

"What, honey?"

"What, you?" She laughed and kissed me again. I didn't push her to speak. There was time for that later.

Unbuttoning my shirt, Kat continued kissing tenderly further and further down my chest. Her fingertips explored my skin, sending currents of desire coursing through me with each touch. A smile crossed her face, and then she said, "You know I love you, right?"

"Of course. And I love you." Her manner left me uneasy; that is, until she leaned down and removed my jeans completely.

Artificial firelight warmed the room, and Kat placed a blanket down in front of the fireplace. I wanted to feel her skin against mine, and seeing the flames reflecting in her eyes excited me all the more. I frantically grabbed her and stripped her naked, too.

"How come we don't make love in front of the fireplace more?" she asked. "You obviously like it." She ran her finger over my clit. "Yes, you really like it." She licked her finger.

I pulled her closer, kissing her again while rolling her onto her back. I wanted her immediately. Her body arched when I slipped a finger inside her, my tongue still exploring hers as we kissed. Slowly, I eased my finger in and out, keeping Kat in the moment but preventing her from climaxing. We had all night. I wanted to savor each and every moment.

Kat must have sensed my thoughts. She stopped me and reached for the stereo remote. Jazz filtered through the speakers.

I tilted my head to listen. "Is this a new CD?"

"Yeah, Ella Fitzgerald."

"I like it."

"How much?" she asked in a teasing voice.

"Let me show you."

I ran my hands over her body, then took one of her nipples in my mouth and bit it gently. Its sudden hardness inspired a surge of my own wetness down below.

Kat raised her hip against my crotch. "I love how wet I make you," she whispered breathily.

"Only you have ever made me feel this alive."

She pulled my head up to hers and gazed at me with such fervor that I felt somewhat stunned. "Tell me you'll never stop loving me, no matter what." Her voice was firm, desperate even.

"Never, Kat. I never want to be with another person."

Ella's song, "If You Should Ever Leave" started to play. I stroked Kat's cheek. "I love you, and only you."

That got her going. Before I knew it, I was on my back and Kat was inside me, her fingers thrusting in and out. Her smoldering look forced me to focus my eyes on her beautiful gray ones. She pushed in deeper. There was no fighting it; I was close to coming.

"Kiss me while I come," I pleaded.

"Anything you want, darling."

Light flashed, exploding behind my eyes, and Kat held her mouth to mine as my body writhed in ecstasy. Kat plunged her fingers in deeper, and stayed. Wrapping my legs around her, I felt my juices flooding out. I came not once, but twice—all the while savoring Kat's fervent kisses. It topped all of my other orgasms with her, or with anyone else, for that matter.

The sensations stilled after several minutes, but Kat still lay on top of me, exhausted.

"That was amazing." I breathed in her sensual fragrance.

Louis Armstrong's gravelly voice joined Ella's on the CD. "What song is this?" I asked.

She craned her neck, waiting for the lyrics. "'Gee, Baby, Ain't I Good To You.' Do you like it?"

"Yes."

She nestled her head back against my chest, and I ran my hand down her back.

"We should play it at our wedding," I said.

Kat sucked in a deep breath. So big that I thought for sure

she wasn't happy. We had never talked about getting married.

"Wedding?" The word sounded as if it had come from the other side of the room.

"Forget I said it," I murmured, not wanting to ruin the mood.

She rolled off me and propped herself up on one elbow.

"What if I don't want to forget it?" she whispered, casually playing with one of my nipples."

"What do you mean?" Nervousness seemed to crest within me.

"I didn't think you ever thought of it—getting married, I mean." Kat stilled her hand, resting it on my heart. I thought for sure she could hear it fluttering like mad. I imagined it looked like a bee trapped in a pop can, desperately seeking a way out.

I laughed, unsure what to say. "To be honest, I hadn't before. But, now … here … I want it."

Kat didn't speak for several seconds.

The pregnant pause stilled my breathing until, finally, she broke the uncomfortable silence.

"I do too," she said. "Just not yet."

I let out a relieved sigh. "Deal. Besides, I need some time to come up with a romantic way to ask."

Kat slapped my stomach. "Like you would ever do that."

I rolled over on my side and cradled her head in my hands. "Is that a challenge?"

"Maybe." She gave a sexy little laugh.

"Just you wait. I plan to sweep you off your feet."

"I'll believe it when I see it. The practical Cori Tisdale getting in touch with her inner romantic …" She threw me a disbelieving look.

"You forget, Kat, that I'm a British lit teacher. Romance abounds in those novels."

"What are you going to do, study *Pride and Prejudice* to come up with ideas? Then again, you are a lot like Mr. Darcy: opinionated, stuck-up, and stubborn." She grinned.

"I can't believe you said that." I pinned her down, and started to tickle her.

"Stop!" She squirmed under me.

"Take it back," I teased, not letting up.

"Never." Kat continued to wriggle. She had never looked more beautiful.

I stopped tickling and made love to her. And we didn't stop until I had to get up to shower for work.

By the time I was ready to leave for the coffee shop, Kat was sound asleep on the floor in front of the fire. I covered her with our comforter, kissed her forehead. Pausing to admire her exquisite face, I whispered, "I never want you to doubt me."

Her eyes flashed open. "Ditto."

"Not a chance in hell."

"Never forget you said that."

I sealed my promise with a kiss. "Get some rest, beautiful."

Work was painful. My head was throbbing and I felt nauseated, but it also seemed that everyone in the Financial District had called in sick—or maybe it was the shitty economy. Every once in a while, a customer would come in, but there was nothing else to make the time pass more quickly. Harold jibber-jabbered about Amber, and I did my best to act excited for him. He was quickly falling head over heels in love. Or was it lust? Mostly, I just wanted my shift to end.

I texted Mom, asking her to meet me for lunch in the café of Neptune's bookstore, on Newbury Street.

When I received a rapid "*yes,*" I wondered if her cell phone was permanently attached to her hand. Maybe she was blogging. Was that even the right word? It sounded so crass.

Arriving a few minutes early at Neptune's, I grabbed a table in the back. It would be harder for Mom to find me, but I was hoping it would be quieter. Those hopes were dashed when two giggling women sat at the table nearest to mine.

I glared at them.

They ignored me.

Maybe they were unable to see my eyes through my dark sunglasses. Why in the world had I consumed so much alcohol yesterday? I rubbed my throbbing temples.

"I'm surprised you're even out of bed," Mom said, taking a seat across from me.

"Had an early shift this morning," I grumbled.

"Did you invite me here to yell at me?" She crossed her arms.

"What? Why?" I poured some sugar into the coffee I had ordered, and the waitress waited for Mom's order, tapping her pencil on her notebook. Her hair was frizzled and matted into dreads, and from the looks of her, she hardly showered. I eyed her warily. How skuzzy people were able get jobs serving food always baffled me.

"Cappuccino," requested my mother, and the waitress shuffled back behind the counter.

"So, out with it, Cori."

"I don't know why you think I want to yell at you."

"Last night. The appointment with the psychic ... does that ring any bells in that dense head of yours?"

I massaged my temples again and then removed my shades gingerly. Squinting across the table, I responded, "I haven't forgotten about that. How did your water ceremony go?"

Mom waved her hand, and frustration flooded her face. "It was a waste. A complete waste."

"I'm sorry to hear that."

"What? You're sorry ..." Mom cupped a hand to her ear. "Are you okay, Cori, besides being hungover?" She leaned forward, peering into my haggard face.

The disgusting waitress returned with the cappuccino.

"Want food?" she asked.

How could we refuse? I ordered the tofu scramble, and Mom selected her norm: the classic Caesar salad. She always got that for lunch, no matter where we went.

After the waitress retreated, Mom drummed her fingers on the table, awaiting my answer to her earlier question.

"Why are you convinced Dad is having an affair?"

She sighed, flicking her hair back from her face. "He's not acting normal. What else could it be?"

"How's he acting?"

"Aloof, timid ... he hasn't touched me in weeks. I know you hate to hear it, but your father and I have always had an active sex life."

One of the women at the table next to us turned to get a good look at my mother. Mom's cold stare forced her to quickly avert her eyes.

"But it could be any number of things," I explained.

"Such as?" Mom sipped her cappuccino. It was too hot, and she made a sour face.

"Depression, illness, he's tired ... have you thought about just asking him? You're usually not shy about putting people on the spot."

Her eyes darted away from mine. "I—"

"You're scared to find out."

Her head snapped back around. "Is this why you asked me here today? To lecture me?"

"Partly."

"What's the other reason?"

"I'm not done talking about Dad."

"I am." Her tone suggested I better leave it alone.

Raising my coffee cup to my lips, I pondered how to proceed. I hesitated a little too long.

"You need money," she said bluntly.

I sighed. "Yes, but not for the normal reason."

"The normal reason. Ha!" My mother laughed. "What's the normal reason?"

"Not making ends meet ... bills, mortgage, Kat's ..."

"Kat's what?"

Her body language suggested she wanted me to finally say it out loud.

"It's no secret Kat loves to shop. Let's face it: I don't make enough for her tastes."

"A lot of people your age would have a hard time supporting a woman like Kat." Mom's sincerity flummoxed me. It was the first time my mother had said anything like that. I had no idea how to take it.

"Kat's wonderful in every other way … she just likes to shop." I could tell I was coming across as defensive.

Mom placed her hand on mine. "I know you love Kat, and I love her too. I'm not trying to bash her, I swear."

"That's good, because I'm going to ask her to marry me."

My mother stiffened in her seat, her mouth opening and closing. Not once had I seen my mom speechless. Not when I came out. Not the time I told her I might have leukemia. (The blood test had come back negative, thank goodness.)

I was suddenly nervous. What if Mom disapproved completely? It would be the first time I'd decided to go against her wishes. She may not always have believed I was making the best decisions in the past, but she always supported me. What if she didn't support me in this?

"Excuse me, I need to use the restroom," she said finally, leaving before I could stop her.

Our food arrived, and knowing Mom must have wanted some time, I dug in to mine so it wouldn't get cold.

She returned to the table ten minutes later, carrying a stack of magazines.

"Good thing you ordered a salad. It's supposed to be cold."

"You're full of surprises today. That joke was kinda funny."

The twinkle in her eye made me curious. "What's up with the magazines?"

"Wedding magazines, of course. My baby is getting married!"

I smiled, relieved. But I still needed clarification. "You approve?"

My mother drove me crazy, but I always wanted her support.

"Approve? Of course!" She cupped my chin with her hand. "I never thought this day would come. My independent child is actually getting married."

"Don't get ahead of yourself. I haven't proposed, yet."

"What, you need money for a ring?" Mom reached for her purse, and I thought she was going to whip out a wad of bills. Realizing what she was doing, she laughed. "I'm sorry. I'm just so excited."

I chuckled. "Thanks for the offer, but I want to give her grandmother's ring. Kat loves everything from the nineteen-twenties, and I think the ring is perfect."

"I don't believe it! That's perfect. Why didn't I think of that? And how did you come up with that on your own?" She slapped my hand playfully.

"All right, who are you and what did you do to my mother?" I joked.

"Oh, shut up."

"That's better. I was starting to get worried." I scooped more food into my mouth.

"So if you don't need money for a ring, what do you need it for?"

"I want to take Kat to Italy. She's always wanted see Michelangelo's *Pietà*."

"Is that where you're going to pop the question?" She forked up some salad and, to my astonishment, chewed with her mouth open. Clearly the shock still hadn't worn off.

"I would like to. Is that too cheesy?" I sat back in my seat.

"Don't worry about being cheesy. This is about you two,

not about what others will think."

Our conversation was interrupted by Aunt Barbara. Pulling out a chair next to my mother, she said, "Nell told me I had to come here quick. What's up?"

Aunt Barbara's gallery wasn't far away, and she had obviously come from there. Her shirt and hands were still speckled with paint. Although she never showcased her own work in the gallery, she did all of her own painting in the backroom.

Spying the magazines on the table, she put a hand over her mouth for a second, and then mouthed, "Get out!"

Mom nodded enthusiastically. "Cori wants to pop the question!"

"Get out!" was all my aunt could say.

I smiled shyly. "What do you think? Would Italy be a good spot to propose?"

"Oh, Kat was talking about Italy just the other day," said Barbara.

Mom must have kicked her under the table, since my aunt's knee immediately whacked into the tabletop.

I was too overwhelmed to give it much thought.

"You know, Phineas Finn will be your father-in-law." Aunt Barbara leveled her eyes on mine.

"It can't be helped. At least Kat hates hanging out with him as much as I do."

"What about when you have kids? He'll be their granddad." Mom chipped in.

"Are you two trying to talk me out of this?" The words trembled in my throat.

"No!" they shouted in unison.

"Good, because I'm set on it. I want to marry Kat."

"Does she have any inkling?" inquired my aunt.

"I think so. We talked about it briefly this morning."

"What did you say?" she continued.

"We were listening to a song, and I said we should play it at our wedding. Honestly, the words just slipped out. Until that moment, I hadn't thought of getting married."

"You two must have had some night last night, after I dropped you off." Mom nudged Barbara and winked.

"Mom, please. Don't ruin this moment."

My aunt motioned to my sunglasses, folded on the table, and then to the bags under my eyes. "Did you sleep at all last night?" she asked.

"No." I had tried using concealer, but there was no hiding my exhaustion.

"Oooo … Oh to be young again." Aunt Barbara looked past me, to the bookshelves beyond. I assumed she was daydreaming, maybe about former loves.

"When are you going to pop the question?" Mom got back down to business.

"Not for a while."

"Cori, don't overthink this."

I waved her off. "Kat said she wasn't ready."

"Well, that makes sense," proffered my aunt.

Mom kicked her again under the table and gave her the evil eye.

I sat there looking between the two of them, puzzled.

"I'm just saying, if you want to pop the question in Italy, you need to plan it." Barb turned to face my mother. "And stop kicking me. I'll be bruised from head to toe soon."

Mom ignored her. "I'm going to buy a fancy red dress."

"You will not!" threatened my aunt.

"Why not?" my mother shot back.

"You can't wear red to a wedding. It's gauche."

"I can't wear white."

"Or red. You aren't supposed to be the center of attention. You aren't one of the brides." My aunt waggled a finger in her face.

"I'm a mother of the bride. Besides, Cori won't want to be the center of attention."

"Kat will."

"Ladies, there's plenty of time to discuss this matter," I interjected, knowing the argument would otherwise last until one of them died. I tried to distract them with a random piece of trivia. "Did you know Mark Twain wore his Oxford robes to his daughter's wedding?"

My aunt looked at me, gave me a quick smile, and then laid into Mom again. "Red is out of the question!"

"How about purple?"

"Purple! A woman your age shouldn't wear purple."

"My age! You're eight years older, remember?"

I slipped away from the table and wandered to the bookstore. I could still hear them arguing, but decided it was best to stay out of it. Two sisters fighting—who knew what past sins they'd throw in each other's faces? It was a good thing they loved each other, or there would be blood on the walls.

As I searched the stacks for something to read, the cover of *Twilight* caught my eye. Hands holding an apple, like an offering. It didn't look like your typical vampire novel. I picked it up, remembering my promise to Samantha.

Next, I searched for a copy of *Confessions of a Shopaholic*. Maybe it had some answers for me. Relieved to find both books in this small shop, I headed to the cashier, paid for the books, and returned to our table.

Mom and Aunt Barbara were now bickering about what the other had worn to my grandfather's funeral.

I sat for several minutes, reading *Twilight*, before my aunt included me in the conversation. "Cori, what do you think?"

"Hmmm …" I peered over the book.

She harrumphed, knowing I wasn't paying attention, and returned to battle my mother on her own.

"Need anything more?" The scuzzy waitress returned and directed her question to me, since my dining companions were squabbling like children.

"Another coffee, please. And the check."

The hippie waitress refilled my coffee cup and tried to keep her eyes off the bickering women. She failed. It was like watching a train wreck.

I shook my head and went back to my book. All around us, I sensed that other patrons were eavesdropping. They might have wondered how I sat there calmly reading during the fracas.

Years of practice.

I loved my mom and my aunt, but boy could they act like idiots.

# Chapter Ten

The next Saturday night, Kat and I were back at Aunt Barbara's for dinner. I immediately grabbed a Sam Adams from the fridge and began to walk toward the deck, to join the men outside. Two years ago, my aunt had arranged for cable to be hooked up on the deck. She hated watching baseball, but my uncle was a devoted Red Sox fan. When Barb installed it, she had proclaimed she'd killed two birds with one stone. She got her TV back and she banished Roger outside like a dog. Roger, on the other hand, loved watching TV outside. He thought it was one of the sweetest things his wife had ever done for him. Even though fall had arrived, he still preferred bundling up and watching the game on the deck. Bostonians were hardy folk.

Before I could make it out there to join then, Kat tugged my arm. When I turned around to see what she wanted, she kissed me—not a peck on the cheek, but an "I want to fuck later" kiss.

I heard Mom and my aunt murmuring, and I felt blood rush to my face. That wasn't all that was flowing, either. I got a distinct sensation of moisture flowing down below. I broke away, embarrassed, and strode off to the deck.

"Cori." My uncle patted me on the back like I was a conquering hero. It made me cringe. My feelings about my uncle were constantly in flux. Roger screwed around all the time, and I hated him for that. Yet he was still my uncle, and he had been completely loyal to me since my birth. He had never missed a single one of my basketball games. Always showed up for my dance recitals. Once, when a rock severed a hose on my car at two in the morning, Uncle Roger had driven thirty miles to pick me up. The next day, he'd had my car towed for me. Roger was an asshole, but he had heart. Besides the infidelities, he loved my aunt completely, and she loved him. Not even my mother knows how they came to this arrangement. I'm pretty sure they never had sex. Maybe in the beginning they did, but not now. But they were together for every family function, and they always went on trips together. They were more like best friends than a married couple, I guessed, and that worked for them.

I patted my uncle's knee, and asked, "How they looking?" I motioned to the TV.

"I think we're going to win the series this year. Best of all, the Yankees didn't even make the playoffs." He grinned like a boy.

My father grunted his enthusiasm.

Knowing that would be the extent of the conversation, I

sat back and observed the women inside. My aunt and mom swarmed around Kat, all three of them whispering. Kat snuck a glance at me over her shoulder, and flashed me a sexy smile when she found I was watching. Ever since that night of fucking in front of the fire, Kat had seemed more confident. Or maybe it was my mention of a wedding.

If Mom and Aunt Barbara were clueing Kat in on my Italy plans, I was going to kill them. Kat wanted time, and I respected that. Plus, I wanted it to be a surprise.

Dad and Uncle Roger broke into a cheer, and I glanced at the TV. Napoli hit a homerun. All of us clinked our beer bottles in celebration.

"What's the ruckus?" Mom sat on the arm of the wicker couch.

"A homerun." Dad didn't even look in her direction. He was engrossed in the game, or he pretended to be.

I whispered, "What are you three talking about?"

"Sex," Mom whispered back.

Roger overheard, and sniggered, and Mom huffed and walked away in disgust.

I was able to see Roger's good points, but my mother wasn't. Of course, Aunt Barbara said that Mom never had liked him. When Roger was wooing my aunt, early in their courtship he had shown up for a date bearing flowers for my aunt and chocolates for my mother, to soften her up some.

It didn't work.

Mom had thrown the box on the ground and spat on it. My aunt laughed it off, explaining that Nell was just a spoiled brat. Mom was eleven at the time, and my aunt was nineteen. She had married Roger two years later, leaving Mom alone with their parents. My grandparents were solid people, but they were as loving as ice cubes. I was sad when they passed away, but not devastated. I think I was more saddened that I didn't really miss them.

My aunt appeared in the doorway. Sneering at the TV, she announced, "Dinner's on."

Uncle Roger paused the play-off game so we could watch the rest later. We took our seats at the large mahogany table that had been in the family for generations. People back then were much shorter. Even though we sat at this table all of the time, all of us struggled to get our long legs under it comfortably without severing a kneecap. I bumped my knee and almost upset all the water and wine glasses.

Mom steadied her wineglass and shot me an admonishing look. The tablecloth was another family heirloom, crocheted by my grandmother. Spilling red wine all over it would not be looked upon too kindly by my aunt, even if she usually was the most forgiving person I knew.

Kat patted my leg under the table, and then rested her hand in between my legs. Her touch found my clit immediately. The feeling was sensational and frustrating simultaneously. I coughed to stifle a groan.

No one else seemed to notice that my girlfriend was trying to get me to come at the dinner table. I placed her hand back on her own leg, thinking that she would never attempt such a thing around her own family.

She smiled guiltily. Part of me was tempted to put her hand back, but the perverts in my family would surely recognize if my eyes suddenly rolled back in my head. Actually, I thought even prudes would be able to put two and two together.

I hoped my eyes promised "later," but to distract Kat, I asked Aunt Barbara, "So when's the next big opening at the gallery?"

Mom dropped her salad fork, and Kat squeezed my hand hard.

"Uh … I need to check my calendar, but soon." She looked at Kat and repeated, "Soon."

"Is it a new artist, or one of your faves?" I let go of Kat's hand and started eating my salad.

"A new talent. I recently discovered her …" my aunt mumbled.

"So Warren, how was work this week?" Mom pounced on my father.

Both Kat and my aunt looked relieved. I wondered if the new artist was risqué. My aunt had once showed an artist that was anti-abortion, and the pro-choicers got up in arms. My aunt, a diehard pro-choice advocate, refused to close the show early. She believed just as firmly in the right to free speech. Kat hung out at the gallery with my aunt quite a bit, so I figured she would probably know more about the new artist. I made a mental note to ask her later if I didn't get distracted.

I peeked down at Kat's revealing shirt, catching her eye. She leaned forward to pick up her wineglass, obviously so I could get a better look.

"Work? It was fine." Dad tipped his beer into a pint glass. Beer bottles were not allowed at my aunt's table. On the deck, yes, but not here.

"Really? Because I stopped by yesterday and your secretary said she hadn't seen you for days."

My father set his beer down slowly. From the look on his face, I knew he was weighing his response carefully.

"Uh—"

My mother interrupted. "When you left yesterday, you said you had meetings all day. Why the lie?"

"What exactly are you accusing me of, Nell?" My father wasn't normally the combative type, but he had sure thrown the gauntlet down today.

"I think you're having an affair."

"Mother!" I interrupted.

"What, Cori? You told me yesterday to ask him. After I left you two"— she motioned to my aunt and me—"I went to ask him. He wasn't available."

"I didn't say ask him during our family dinner," I muttered through clenched teeth.

Kat placed a tender hand on my thigh to support me.

Mom harrumphed and ambushed him again. "Just be honest, Warren, are you fucking someone? Goodness knows you aren't fucking me."

"Who do you think I am?" Dad winced and looked at my aunt, who plonked the bowl of bread down angrily. "Bill Clinton?" asked Dad, trying to cover his blunder.

Roger stared down at his plate, his face betraying no emotion.

Mom wasn't deterred by the arctic atmosphere at the table. "Tell me! Who are you fucking?"

My father stood abruptly, and all of us reached for our glasses to spare the tablecloth. "I quit my fucking job, that's why I wasn't there!" He stormed from the room.

"Do you expect me to believe that?" shouted my mother.

Dad rushed back into the room. "Yes! Because it's the truth. I couldn't stand working there anymore. They don't respect me and … and I just got fed up. I left weeks ago, and I don't intend to go back. No matter what you say!"

Twice in two days, my mother was stunned into silence.

The two of them stared at each other. Dad's shoulders heaved up and down. Mom never blinked. The rest of us sat frozen in our chairs. Roger still stared at his plate.

Finally, my aunt broke the silence. "Would anyone like some bread?"

This rallied my uncle, who motioned for her to pass it to him. She handed the basket to Kat, who handed it to me, and I gave it to Roger. No one dared look at the warring couple.

"Are you telling me the truth?" my mother finally demanded.

"Yes," hissed my father.

"Good. You're too good for that company. I can't believe you stayed there for twenty years." Mom adjusted her shirt and clutched at her wineglass before taking a sip.

Dad took his seat, placing his napkin back over his lap.

"Well, now that we have that settled, I'll bring out the main course," said Aunt Barbara.

Kat and I followed her to the kitchen. "Are you okay?" I asked my aunt as she pulled the over-cooked roast from the oven.

"Me? Of course." Her stony face told me otherwise.

Kat took the ruined roast from her, and I gave my aunt a hug.

She patted my cheek tenderly. "Let's get back before your Mom finds some more dirty laundry to air. Goodness knows she won't rest until she dies."

Later that night, Kat and I lounged in the hot tub out back.

"Have your family dinners always been so entertaining?" Kat grabbed the champagne from the ice bucket and refilled her glass.

"Oh, you know the answer to that, although you did miss the Thanksgiving when Mom dumped an entire bottle of red wine in Dad's lap." I closed my eyes trying to remember why. "For the life of me, I don't remember the circumstances. My mother is very passionate."

"I nearly fell off my chair when your father said he wasn't like Roger. Why do you think your aunt puts up with his affairs?"

"Fear of being alone? She loves him? She adores him as a friend? I doubt any of us will ever know the true reason." I played with some bubbles on the surface of the water.

"Have you ever seen her nudes?"

I looked up at her in surprise. "Why in the world would I want to see my aunt in the nude?"

Kat splashed at my face playfully. "Not her in the nude. Her nude paintings."

I felt silly. "No, I thought she only did abstracts."

"She showed them to me once. They were all of the same young man. When I asked her if she knew him, her eyes clouded over, and she said, 'Yes, a very long time ago.' The way she said it broke my heart."

I sat up in the water. "Now that you mention it, Mom told me once, years ago, that Aunt Barbara had been madly in love with a poor boy she met a year into her relationship with

Roger. Her parents found out and put a stop to it. It was very Gatsby-like."

Kat pulled my foot out to massage it. "To be honest, I think your aunt idealizes love but doesn't really want to be in love. She can't let anyone too close to her. She's too independent—like someone else I know." She tickled my foot.

"Hey now, I let you in." I wiggled my foot free. "I think that's why my mom and my aunt are so supportive of me. They don't want to be like their parents: stiff-upper lips and showing no feelings. Mom takes it to an extreme. Aunt Barbra doesn't show her feelings a lot, but she's nothing like my grandfather. You could have stabbed him in the leg with a fork at the dinner table and he would have calmly asked someone to pass him the butter."

"How come he didn't leave you any money?"

I positioned a jet to blast at my lower back, to ease my pain. "He did. I'll have access to it when I'm fifty."

"Fifty!"

"Yep. He told me he wanted me to succeed on my own. So far I haven't lived up to his expectations."

"Will you stop that? You have more drive in your little finger than most people will ever have." Kat stood up in the tub and came to me, unconcerned about her nudity. "It's only a matter of time, Cori. We'll be fine, I promise you."

If any of our neighbors were awake and paying attention, they would have seen quite a show; however, most of them were in their sixties. My mother teased that it was perfect for me to live in a "retirement community" because I always acted like an old fogey anyway. When I saw this house, I didn't care that I would be the youngest person on the street. All of my neighbors had perfectly manicured lawns, never played loud music, and left me alone, for the most part. Mrs. Henderson does shake her head a lot when she spies Kat mowing the lawn in cut-off jeans and a bikini top. Her husband usually sits on the front porch and watches Kat mow, all the while stroking the top of his bald head. I'm pretty sure he'd stroke a different bald body part if he could get away with it. He's eighty years old. I fear he'll have a coronary one day while he's ogling my girlfriend. Still, I would never discourage Kat from wearing her "gardener's" uniform. If I'm home, I sit on the front porch in my rocking chair and pretend to read. You should see the outfit she wears to clean the shower! When she first proposed that she'd be like a housewife from the fifties, I scoffed. It didn't take me long to change my tune.

I sighed. "Sometimes I feel as though I have the perfect ending, and other times I just want to put a match to the entire thing and just be content with teaching. You know what they say, 'Those who can, do; those who can't, teach.' Maybe I should just accept it and stop torturing myself." I sipped some champagne.

Kat nestled her head on my shoulder.

"It doesn't help being Nell Tisdale's daughter. Her writing is brilliant, and I know I'll always be compared to her."

Leaning my head back on the lip of the hot tub, I stared at the dark sky. The moon was almost full, its brilliance muted by swiftly moving clouds that gave the illusion the moon was actually falling. I eyed Kat and gestured to the sky. "Look at that. It looks like it's falling." She tilted her head to watch, a curious expression on her face.

"Maybe that's the end to my story. Have the moon fall

from the sky and obliterate my characters and all of life. That would simplify things." I sighed, knowing I sounded like a fool.

Kat said nothing for a few moments. Turning me around, she started to massage my shoulders. "You carry all your tension here." Her fingers dug in, deep, and I whimpered with the pain and the relief.

"I know you put a lot of pressure on yourself," she continued, "but I want you to know that you are the only one who does. No matter what happens, I'll be proud of you." She leaned over my left shoulder and peered into my eyes. "And so will your mom and aunt. Stop thinking so much. I know that's like telling a rattlesnake not to rattle, but they only do that when alarmed. Calm down, and it will work out."

Leaning against her, I said, "Thank you. You may have to repeat that speech before I finish my novel. Now, in regards to getting my mind off things, care to help me?" I stood, revealing my nakedness, and reached for her hand to help her out of the tub.

"Do you have anything in particular in mind?" she asked seductively.

I stepped out of the tub and wrapped her up in her robe before putting mine on. "I was thinking of a game in front of the fire," I answered.

"A game? Hope you don't have strip poker in mind—we're already naked."

"I'm sure I can come up with something more entertaining."

## Chapter Eleven

Kat opened the shades in the bedroom and sunlight poured in, causing me to roll over in bed and hide my head under a pillow.

"Kat!" I felt the bed lurch to the side when she sat down next to me.

Stroking my back, she said, "Time to get up, sleepyhead."

"I don't want to," I mumbled.

"You have to. We have plans."

I lifted the pillow to peek at the alarm clock on the nightstand. "Plans? It's only seven a.m.—on a Sunday. Please tell me we aren't having breakfast with my family."

"We aren't having breakfast with your family." She paused and prepared me with a sweet smile. "We're having breakfast with mine."

I groaned. We usually had dinner with her parents once

a month. I wasn't in the mood to start a new tradition: Sunday brunch with the Finns.

"I'm not excited about it either, trust me. But my mom called yesterday and asked. How could I say no?"

I lifted the pillow off my head and watched Kat put on a diamond earring. She wore a long, flowing purple skirt and a plain white sweater. Diamond earrings replaced her usual funky, dangling earrings, and her makeup was nearly non-existent. She looked like she was going to church.

"I set out an outfit for you." She slipped the other earring into her ear. "You have time for a quick shower, and there's a cup of coffee waiting for you, too." She motioned to the nightstand, where my favorite Dorothy Parker mug was brimful of delicious hazelnut coffee. The vapors coming off it made my mouth water. The bed creaked again as she stood up. It might be time to get rid of this antique and buy a new one. The neighbors must hate it—except for Mr. Henderson.

Twenty minutes later, we sat on the subway heading to the Back Bay. Kat's parents lived in a house their ancestors had built over two hundred years ago. It was a creepy place. I was utterly convinced it was haunted by Silas Lapham. True, Lapham is a fictional character in a novel by William Dean Howells, but stranger things have happened.

The clouds looked heavy with rain, and I cursed myself for not bringing an umbrella. Normally, I didn't carry one, but Phineas Finn had admonished me once when I walked into a restaurant with a *Metro* newspaper over my head. He was so rude that I'd wanted to remind him that my family had arrived on the *Mayflower*, too—on both sides.

Kat, sensing my annoyance, placed a hand on my arm to

curb my outburst about the impending rain.

I was beyond grumpy. After several nights of not sleeping, I was ready to snap at anyone for no reason.

"Great, I forgot my umbrella," I grumbled through clenched teeth. "And I'm not in the mood for one of Phineas's lectures."

"My, you're cantankerous today." Kat patted my leg, setting her copy of *The Big Sleep* on her lap. Reaching into her purse, which was more like a piece of luggage, she pulled out an umbrella. "I don't want you going off on Phineas today. I promise you, I'll make it worth your while if you can pretend to be charming."

I nestled my head on her shoulder. "Deal. Wake me up when we get there."

Kat continued reading while I watched the rain splatter against the windows. Only three other people were on the train. When we rolled by Coolidge Corner, only a woman and a child stood on the platform. The child held a frog umbrella, and I secretly wished we could trade. Imagine what Phineas Finn would have to say about that! That Kat's parents wanted to have Sunday brunch before 10 a.m. annoyed the shit out of me. Thank goodness they weren't dragging us to church—or at least I hoped they weren't. Kat had made it clear to them years ago that she was agnostic. I wasn't sure what I was. For me, reconciling evolution with God was too complicated. I didn't take the time to think about it much. My family only went to church on Christmas, so my background in theology was hazy at best. I haven't ever read the Bible. As a literature teacher, I felt somewhat embarrassed about that, but not as guilty as I felt about not having read *War and Peace* or *Don*

*Quixote.*

We got off the subway and made our way to their house. They wanted us to stop by the house first, before heading to a posh restaurant. Kat's parents lived on Louisburg Square, the prime location in the area. Some of the other houses on the square had been converted into apartments, but the Finns kept their entire house to themselves, even though it was just the two of them. I wondered if the neighbors disliked the Finns and their creepy house as much as I did, Kat excluded, of course.

On our way, we passed Acorn Street, a narrow, cobblestone lane tourists loved to photograph. I'd read it was one of the most photographed streets in America. Even I couldn't resist its charm. I paused, pulled out my cell phone, and snapped a picture. Kat rolled her eyes.

With the leaves changing, the old-fashioned gas lamps, the cobblestones slick with rain reflecting the warm brick of surrounding buildings, the photo turned out pretty good.

Kat gave me a peck on the cheek when I showed it to her proudly. "You're a nerd."

"You're dating a nerd," was my weak comeback.

She tugged my arm but didn't walk away. I was the one holding the umbrella, after all. "Come on, I don't want to be late."

"Why are we going to the house anyway?"

"My father got an espresso machine, and he wants to show it off."

"You're kidding, right? I've had one since college."

"You know Phineas—frugal *and* out-of-date. He thinks it's the new rage."

Kat tugged on my arm, trying to dislodge my unconvinced feet from the cobbled beauty of Acorn Street.

"He knows I work in a coffee shop, right?"

"Don't start with me. I just do as I'm told." Kat quickened her pace.

Relenting, I matched her stride, ensuring neither of us got wet. When I began to walk faster, Kat followed my lead. Soon we were racing, doing our best to cut the other off. When Kat beat me to the front door, giggling, I whined, "You cheated! The umbrella got in my way."

Right then, her father opened the door. "I beg your pardon?"

Who still says that: "I beg your pardon?"

"Good morning, sir." I stifled a laugh and ignored the indignant look on his face. "What a lovely rainy day." I made a show of shaking droplets off the umbrella, and then collapsed it and stuck it in the umbrella stand on the porch. Umbrella stand! What century was this?

"Good morning, Cori. Kat." Phineas never opened his mouth when he spoke, and it freaked me out. I kept looking around him, expecting to see a man with his hand up Phineas's ass like a ventriloquist. Of course, his asshole would have been way too tight for anything like that. It was even hard to imagine someone so prim and proper taking a shit.

We walked into the kitchen, and I heard the shrill screech of the espresso machine. Kat's mom wore a pleated twill skirt and a white silk shirt with lace at the collar and cuffs. It made me want to burst into laughter. Phineas wore a suit and a tie—and he wasn't even going to church.

"Would you like an espresso, Cori?" asked Phineas. He

used my name every time he spoke to me. It annoyed me.

"Yes, please. How you liking your new baby?"

Phineas stopped in his tracks. "Pardon?"

He really had no clue what I was referring to.

Kat chimed in. "She means your espresso machine, Father."

He shook his head and replied. "It's a fine gadget, Cori."

Gadget. I was impressed that he used that word instead of appliance. He really was catching up with the times.

His thin lips slackened—his version of a smile. Then they tightened back up as if he had just sucked on a particularly sour lemon, pulling his face taut and draining all of the life out of it (and there wasn't much there to begin with). He resembled Lurch from *The Addams Family*, which was fitting because the house, although impeccably decorated with antiques and family heirlooms, hadn't seen the light of day for fifty years. They never opened the windows and the curtains always remained closed. All that was missing was the cobwebs, because Kat's mom was a tidy homemaker. She even crocheted thingamajigs for the couch and chair arms, and this house had many.

When Kat was a child, she had once opened her window and a wild finch flew in. Kat was tickled pink. She had always wanted a pet. But when her father found out, he chased the tiny creature around, swatting at it with a broom. Luckily, Phineas never made contact, but when the bird flew near the phone on her bedside table, it rang, and the finch dropped dead from a heart attack. To this day, Kat can't even see a finch without getting sad.

"How's school?" asked Mrs. Finn. She always treated me

like I was ten and a student, rather than like a professor.

"Fine, thank you, ma'am." I sipped my drink. It was putrid, and I tried not to make a sour face.

Phineas must have noticed and considered my dour look a compliment. "Glad to see you like it."

"Haven't quite had anything like it before, sir."

Kat nudged my foot.

Phineas handed Kat her coffee, and she looked at me like she was being forced to drink Castor oil. I smirked. What a delightful start to my day off.

Kat choked down some coffee, and tears formed in her eyes. "Mmmm ... this is good, Mother."

Phineas relaxed his lips again for a second before motioning for us to sit down at the kitchen table. After all of us sat, Phineas cleared his throat. "Cori, I asked my wife to arrange this meeting so we could talk about your billing."

Panicking, I wondered what in the hell I had done wrong.

"How are you liking it, Cori?" He lifted his dainty cup to his mouth and took a noiseless sip.

"I enjoy it, sir."

"Good." He set his cup down, again noiselessly. "That's good to hear, Cori." He stood and retrieved a basket of fruit from the kitchen counter, placing it in the middle of the table. "Would anyone care for some fruit?"

I passed. Kat took a banana, peeling it with trembling fingers.

"Well, Cori, I have some good news for you. I mentioned you to several of my associates, and they want you to handle their bills from now on, too."

I stifled a gasp. I was already billing for two doctors, and with everything else, my schedule was full. However, if there was enough, I could quit Beantown Café. But then I would be even more connected to Kat's father. This was a pickle.

"That's wonderful news, sir." I tried hard to make my voice sound somewhat cheerful.

"Yes, it is, isn't it, Cori?" He prattled off five names. Five more clients. How would I find time to teach, let alone to write?

Kat looked downcast but said nothing. Her expression mirrored how I felt on the inside: stifled.

"When do I start?" I knew I couldn't fight it. The only bright spot was that it would help me save money for the Italy trip. *Stay positive, Cori. Stay positive.*

"How does tomorrow work?" He locked his eyes on me. "Now, I hope I don't need to tell you that it's not just your reputation at stake, Cori."

"Not at all. I understand completely." I grabbed an apple and took an overzealous bite. "I won't let you down, Dr. Finn."

Kat's mother stared at the table the entire time, not showing any emotion. I felt for the poor woman.

I tried to envision what it was like going to bed with Phineas Finn every night. I imagined he lay on his back with his eyes closed like a corpse, never moving during the night. Before they had Kat, I guessed he had rigidly climbed on top of his wife once a week, thrusting his seed inside her before rolling onto his back without saying a word. Copulation was probably a disgusting act that neither partner enjoyed. When Kat was born, there were complications, and her mother nearly died. It wasn't possible for Mrs. Finn to fall pregnant again. Phineas probably felt relieved that he didn't have to denigrate himself further by forcing his wife into such a disgusting, "common" act.

I was pretty sure Phineas thought Kat and I lived like nuns. It was just too hard to imagine the Finn patriarch knowing the first thing about lesbian sex. After all, they never went to the movies and they only turned on the TV to watch the nightly news or documentaries on PBS. I bet the man never had a blow job in his life. To be honest, he probably didn't even know they were possible. I doubted the young Phineas had made any friends at high school or college to educate him.

"Shall we go, then, now that our business is concluded?" He looked to Kat, and then to me, his thin lips pursed together in a Phineas-smile. It gave me the heebie-jeebies.

Kat and I nodded meekly. I felt like a future-son-in-law in a 1950s sitcom: the rich father setting up the hopeful young man in business so he could provide for the daughter. It made me want to vomit. Thank God my parents weren't like this. When I stood, my knees felt wobbly. How had such a creature as Kat come from these two repressed, rigid people?

After we escaped her parents, Kat turned her sad, gray eyes on me and said, "Take me some place away from here, where I can let my hair down."

Being around her parents always suffocated her. She was a free spirit, an original. They wanted her to be a cardboard cutout.

It was noon, and I didn't have much time to prepare a getaway. I considered our family home in Cape Cod, but the place was full of rich snobs, and traffic on a Sunday would be brutal on the return journey.

"Okay, let's grab the train to Salem."

She shot me a look that asked, "Are you serious?"

I put both palms up. "I know it's a cheesy tourist town, but it's probably gearing up for Halloween. It might be fun, in a completely asinine way. Besides, I kinda want to go to The House of the Seven Gables. I haven't been in years."

I knew that would be the kicker. Kat loved that novel.

Smiling, she agreed, and I took her hand. She rested her head on my shoulder as we made our way to the station.

"Every time we leave your parents I try to imagine what it was like growing up in their house. It must have been hard. Phineas reminds me a lot of my grandfather." I learned early on not to call him her dad. She almost always called him Phineas. I think her father preferred it that way. Actually, I think he would have preferred if Kat had called him Doctor Finn, but he probably felt others would find that over the top. When it was just the four of us, she always called him Father— in a subservient tone. Around me, she called him Phineas, and her tone was always unpleasant.

"It was probably like you imagine. There weren't a lot of laughs. I wasn't allowed to have many friends. When I dropped out of college, I thought he would disown me completely. Phineas actually wanted me to move back home and live out my days as a spinster, locked up in that home. My father has no idea it's the twenty-first century. He doesn't know that women no longer patrol widow walks, awaiting the return of their husbands." Kat slipped her arm around my waist and pulled me close. "I know your family drives you crazy, Cori, but I envy you. When your mom accepted me and treated me like a daughter, it was wonderful. It might be one of the reasons I keep you around." She flashed me a smile and patted my arm lovingly.

"So, what you're saying is I have to keep my mom in the picture or its splitsville." I mussed her hair.

"And your aunt. I can't live without either of them. You know, I don't even think my parents are jealous that we spend a lot more time with your family. They probably don't even notice I'm not around. It wasn't like we talked all that much when I did live there." Her voice remained even, but I could tell it upset her. I wanted to take all of her pain away. Few people saw this side of Kat. They only saw the vivacious bombshell with a bubbly personality. Like the rest of us, Kat was human. She has her own demons to battle. I didn't completely understand all of her battles, but she was slowly letting me in.

We arrived at the train station and as I set about getting tickets, Kat wandered off to buy us some snacks for the twenty-minute ride. Neither of us ate much of our brunch, out of fear we would do something to upset her parents. I never felt comfortable around them. Even though I had been trained from a young age to know all my cutlery, glasses, and etiquette, I still panicked whenever I sat down across from Phineas. If I had grown up in his home, I would have died of starvation.

Standing on the grounds of The House of the Seven Gables, both Kat and I stared at the ocean. It was a stunning day. The azure sky was speckled with sporadic puffy clouds and sunlight sparkled off the Atlantic and illuminated a few boats that bobbed lazily on the horizon. The view was postcard perfect; both of us remained silent, enjoying it.

The tour of the home had been a mixed bag. Our guide was in her mid-forties, and she knew her stuff; however, she acted as though she had late lunch plans and rushed us through the house. It was still wonderful to wander through the old home, even if it wasn't the exact home Nathaniel Hawthorne had known. Over the years, many changes had been made to attract visitors.

"Do you ever wish we could leave everything behind and start afresh in a new place … a new country even?" Kat turned to me, her head cocked as she awaited an answer.

"Funny you should ask. Every time I stare at the ocean, I have a feeling there's so much out there and that I've barely seen any of it. I've never lived more than twenty miles from my childhood home. It's a shame, really." I kicked some of the pebbles near the water's edge.

"One day, I want to travel the world." Kat stood tall, her eyes fixed on the horizon. Her demeanor suggested she had every intention of following through on that desire.

"Deal. I'll add twenty more dentists and charge them double."

She looked at me, crestfallen. "I want to help you with the billing. I know my father wants me to stay out of it, but it's not right. Please, teach me how to do it."

I was stunned. I didn't know what to say. I thought she wouldn't touch that kind of work with a ten-foot pole. Not to mention that she usually avoided anything that had to do with Phineas.

"It's easy, really. I'm not sure why your father is so afraid someone might mess it up. Yeah, some claims need some follow-up with the insurance company, but mostly you just punch in the codes and submit them."

Kat slipped her hand through my arm and directed us back to town. "Do you mind if we visit the memorial for the victims of the witch trials?"

"Not at all. I think I remember the way."

When I was an elementary student, Salem had been a favorite destination for school administrators. The kids mostly loved it as well. I'd been to the memorial on many occasions, and to some of the witch museums, too. The pirate museum was a joke. All you did was wander through a warehouse featuring sets that resembled Disneyland but without the Walt Disney's props budget. Even as children, we knew it was hokey. It didn't stop us from buying hooks and eye-patches from the gift shop and growling like pirates on the bus ride home, though.

Still, there was something about this town. With all the shops catering to witchcraft and to the television show *Bewitched*, I loved Salem's quirky feel. Kat's seriousness slowly dissipated as she started to soak in the town's whimsy. Many of the houses were already decked out with Halloween decorations. Both of us loved the holiday and dressed up every year. Everyone in my family participated, even my stodgy father. Of course, he would normally dress as a doctor or something, but he tried. Phineas doesn't even hand out candy to trick-or-treaters.

The Witch Trials Memorial was established in 1992, and Elie Wiesel, a holocaust survivor, was present for the dedication during the Tercentenary celebration. The simplicity of it was brilliant: twenty granite benches sitting on the periphery of a small park, each bench inscribed with the name of the accused and the manner in which he or she was killed, along with the date. Twenty people, all ostracized by their friends, family, and neighbors. I didn't ask Kat why she wanted to see it, but I believed she felt a connection with the victims. With all of her privileges and her stunning looks, Kat still always felt as if she was on the outside looking in; that no one really knew her.

We walked around the perimeter, reading each inscription in silence. A few tourists were milling about, but mostly we had it to ourselves. We slowly made our way through the Burying Point, the cemetery situated right next to the memorial, before making it back to the city center.

"Want to have an early dinner and drinks?" I asked. The cookies we had on the train hadn't curbed my appetite, and after such a somber stroll, I needed a drink.

On Front Street, we strolled by a tourist trap that served lobster. "Since we'll be rolling in dough soon, can I buy you some lobster?"

Kat's face twisted into a smile. "It's been awhile."

The inside wasn't impressive looking, some tables and a bar, but they had seats outside and even though it was October, it was warm enough to sit outside.

We grabbed a table, noticing that a band was setting up on the opposite side of the sidewalk. Kat ordered a champagne cocktail with gin, sugar, and lemon juice. I got a Harpoon's Hard Cider. Something about autumn always made me crave cider. Since we were celebrating, I ordered Kat the calamari appetizer and some fries for myself.

"Maybe there'll be dancing." Kat's eyes sparkled, and she

stirred her drink with a plastic straw. It was in a plastic cup too. So high class. Phineas would not approve.

"I hope so. I happen to know a beautiful woman I would like to have as my dancing partner."

"Oooo ... that wasn't cheesy at all." She batted her eyelashes at me.

"Well, maybe it was, but it's true." I leaned over to kiss her cheek.

"I don't believe it! What are you two doing here?"

I turned to find Samantha and Lucy standing outside the rope that blocked off the restaurant's outdoor seating.

"A little sightseeing, actually. What are you two doing here?" I stood to hug them both. Kat didn't get up. She smiled, but her annoyance that we had run into them again was obvious and palpable.

"Lucy's parents live in town. We stayed the weekend, and we wanted some time away from the parental units." Samantha glanced over her shoulder. "Are they going to have live music? What do you say, Luce, shall we crash their dinner?"

Lucy looked uncomfortable at being put on the spot but was at a loss for words.

"Yes, of course, have a seat." I dashed off to steal a couple of unoccupied chairs from a nearby table. Kat stayed seated, but she did her best to hide her disappointment with a welcoming smile. I doubted she wanted company tonight at all, but the fact that it was Samantha made it even worse. But what could I do—send them away?

When they were seated, I motioned for the waiter to bring us more menus and water. Sam shouted for a beer. Lucy fidgeted with the drawstrings on her hoodie.

"Did you grow up in Salem?" I asked, hoping that if I got her talking the awkwardness would fade.

"Yeah," she mumbled.

"Her family has lived around here since the whole witch craze," said Samantha proudly.

"Really?" Interest erased the tension from Kat's face.

I felt a change in the atmosphere, and I let out a silent sigh of relief.

"Yeah," Lucy muttered again before finding other words to say. "One of my family members was found 'guilty.'" She made quote marks with her fingers.

"Oh, my, how horrible." Kat covered her mouth with one hand. "I've always been fascinated by the history here, but this is my first visit."

I looked at Kat, amazed. "You didn't go on any school fieldtrips here?"

"Fieldtrips? Do you think Phineas would allow that?" A flash of anger shot through her eyes. The flame tempered quickly and then extinguished, and she added, "My father is a bit stuffy."

I choked on my cider. "That's an understatement."

Kat playfully tapped my arm. "Not all of us have cool parents like yours."

"You think my parents are cool? Mom is a nut job and Dad can barely speak in full sentences around other people."

"Would you trade parents, then?" She pinned me with a glare.

"Not a chance in hell." I patted her hand.

Realizing we were neglecting our uninvited guests, Kat

turned to Samantha and asked, "How in the world did you get Cori to read *Twilight*?"

Samantha giggled. "You held up your end of the bargain, then." She turned to Kat and said, "Whiskey."

"On the train here, she had her nose buried in the book, and she didn't want to get off when we arrived." Kat ran her hand up my thigh, tickling me. It was good to see her back to her normal self, sort of.

"That's not entirely true, but"—I turned to Samantha—"they're at the ballet studio and …"

Kat stuck her fingers in her ears. "Don't say another word. I plan on reading it after you." She reached for my bag to pull out the book, but it wasn't *Twilight*—I could tell by the cover.

It was *Confessions of a Shopaholic*.

Kat dropped it like a lead weight, and fished out *Twilight* instead. She flushed and looked troubled, but she continued, "I bet I could get through this in a day." She flipped through the pages breezily.

Samantha clapped her hands together. "And then it will be your turn, Lucy."

"What?" Lucy sipped her water through a straw. "I'm not reading that!" Turning scarlet, she added, "Not that there's anything wrong with it."

"Oh, get off your high horse. Cori teaches English lit and Kat loves Wilkie Collins—and they're reading it."

Lucy stared at us as if we had termites crawling out our ears.

The waiter approached and all three of them ordered lobster. Being the odd man out, and the only vegetarian, I ordered the mac and cheese with tater tots on the side.

When the waiter asked if I wanted lobster on my mac and cheese, Kat said firmly, "She's vegetarian."

Kat didn't subscribe to my beliefs, but she defended them all of the time. The waiter tapped his pencil and asked if we needed anything else. Kat ordered a bottle of red wine, and for the first time, my heart didn't skip a beat. I have to admit that knowing my income was going to increase was a relief. Billing wasn't my choice, but it would be foolish to look a gift horse in the mouth. And if Kat actually helped, that made it even better. It felt like we were in this together. I mean we always had been, but even more so.

Samantha seemed uncomfortable. Unfortunately, the shoe was on the other foot. My money woes were getting under control just as hers were beginning. I saw Lucy comfort her, and I wondered if Samantha had confessed yet. My gut said no, but my heart hoped she had. Going through something like that alone would be tough.

"So, Lucy, how's Match.com going?" Kat dipped a ring of fried calamari into the lemon aioli sauce.

"Actually, pretty well." Lucy smiled shyly and squirmed in her chair. "I didn't think many hopefuls would want to meet up with a nerdy writer, but I've had several people ask me to coffee."

"Several? Do tell." Kat's eager face compelled her.

Samantha slurped her beer, and I sat there frozen like a deer in headlights, unable to think of a way to end this conversation.

After Lucy had described some of the women she had been conversing with, she said, "So far, I'm more flattered than interested."

Samantha's face lost some of its rigidity.

"Except for this one—"

"I need to pee!" interrupted Sam, and then she dashed inside.

Neither Kat nor Lucy paused to consider Samantha's body language. Could Lucy be that cold towards her ex, or was she just completely oblivious that Sam was still heads over heels in love with her? Lucy was book smart. I had checked out her novels on Amazon. She wrote thrillers—along the lines of the *Da Vinci Code*. From the excerpts I had read, she was quite good. But brilliant people tend to suck at the real world, especially when it comes to matters of the heart.

Samantha returned just as Kat and Lucy finished discussing the potential love match.

"So, Sam, have you reconsidered?" Kat asked, eyeing Samantha as soon as she sat down.

"What?" Samantha plunged some calamari into the sauce angrily. Even her fingertips were covered, I noticed. After popping the seafood into her mouth, she licked each finger dismissively.

"Match.com. Sounds like Lucy is having success. It's a shame we aren't getting you out there. I've had some luck setting people up." Kat's tone was upbeat, tempting.

Sam wiggled in her chair, unsure how to proceed. Then her eyes glimmered with something I hadn't seen before. "Sure, why not?"

I wanted to laugh out loud. Was she going for the jealousy angle? Rub Lucy's nose in the fact that others might want to be with her.

Looking over at Lucy, I tried to determine if I could detect any hint of hurt. I saw none. My heart fell into the pit of my stomach. Poor Samantha.

On the other hand, Kat's mood perked up.

Would this alleviate her fears? She had been joking about *Twilight* earlier, but I'm sure that, in her mind, my reading the book was a confession that I was crushing on Samantha. Was Kat rubbing it in my face? Was this her way of saying hands off? Or of trying to tell me Sam didn't want me. Women and the games they play. People hate the backstabbing in politics. Try lesbian romances.

I have two rules in life. One is never open a Facebook account. The other is never get in the middle of a girl fight. If necessary, I would break the first rule. But I'll never break the second.

The band's guitarist strummed a few cords and everyone at the table fell silent. Thank God. We came to Salem to help Kat relax, and now I was fretting about Samantha's feelings for Lucy and trying to steer my jealous girlfriend away from dating talk. It would have been more pleasant to walk across hot coals all night long.

The musicians were decent, covering songs from the eighties, but unfortunately there wasn't any room to dance. Instead, Kat leaned up against me, and I wrapped my arm around her shoulder.

In honor of the Red Sox, the band played "Sweet Caroline"—the song that is played at every Sox home game during the eighth inning. Many of the patrons stood to join in the singing, including Samantha and me.

Kat was slightly amused by us making asses out of

ourselves in public.

Lucy was shocked. How in the world had Sam fallen for such a straight-laced gal? Then again, Sam had told me Lucy was kinkier in bed. It was humorous to observe their differences, but I guess the same could be said about Kat and me. From the shocked look on many faces when they learned Kat was with me, I guessed most people thought we'd be a flash in the pan. So far, we'd been together three years, and my grandmother's ring was at the jewelers being resized.

When the song finished, I sat back down and kissed Kat on the lips. Samantha cheered, to my surprise. The beers were going straight to her head. Even Lucy tipped her glass in our honor.

The lobsters arrived, along with my mac and cheese. Both Kat and Samantha stole a tater tot as soon as the bowl hit the table.

"Ladies, hands off!"

"Why, Cori, I don't think you've ever said that to me before?" Kat faked a Southern belle accent.

"When it comes to my tots, hands off."

Kat waved me off and grabbed another one. I reached for my knife, brandishing it in her face with mock menace. The waiter chuckled as I requested two more orders of tater tots. He smiled and said that often happened. Here we were, grownups, fighting over tater tots.

"You can order me my own, but I still prefer your tots any day." Kat winked.

"How come you never say that to me?" asked Samantha.

At first, I thought she directed the question to Kat, but when I turned, I saw Lucy's face redden.

"Ah ..." was all she could get out.

Luckily, the band started a new song. Kat flashed me a quizzical look, and I shrugged innocently. Clueless, Lucy grabbed one of my tots and handed it to Sam. I was pretty sure she had missed the point completely.

"Ladies and gentlemen." The singer tapped the microphone to get our attention. "We appreciate all of you listening to us this evening, even though the Sox are playing. I wanted to let you know that just moments ago"—he stopped abruptly to get everyone's attention. "The Sox are going to the World Series!"

Samantha and I jumped up and hugged enthusiastically. Instantly, I knew I was in trouble. Turning quickly, I grabbed Kat's arm and pulled her to her feet before planting a kiss on her lips—a kiss I hoped would save me from an awkward conversation later. Lucy stayed in her chair while Samantha hugged some strangers at a nearby table.

For the rest of the evening, I dreaded the impending talk. Kat acted normal, playful even, but I knew the shoe was about to drop. I just didn't know when.

The train ride home started pleasantly. Kat nestled up against my shoulder and nodded off to sleep. I read *Twilight*. The train cruised through a few stops and neared Boston.

Then the train halted in between two stops. An announcement over the PA system informed us there was a small fire on the tracks. Great. Just great.

Kat roused herself, and looked around, confused. "Are we there?" Her voice was groggy.

"Not yet, sweetheart. There's a fire on the track up

ahead."

"Why aren't you reading the other book?" she asked testily. At first, I thought she was kidding.

"What's wrong with shiny vampires?" I teased, not sensing any doom.

"Does one of them have a shopping addiction?"

Alarm bells clanged in my head. "Hey, what are you implying?"

"Me? What are *you* implying? You left that book in your bag for me to find it." The sleepiness faded from her voice. Now, it was just full of anger.

"Do you really think I would do that?"

"I didn't—until I went into your bag tonight and saw it." She leaned away from me and crossed her arms.

"Samantha mentioned the book when she suggested *Twilight*. She said it was funny and lighthearted. I've been reading George Eliot—I need fun and lighthearted. There's no hidden message. How did I know you would go into my bag?"

She harrumphed. "Yeah, right."

"Listen, Kat, I would never buy anything to make you mad or to rub your face in it. I got the book because I heard it was funny. End of story."

"Why didn't you read it first? Why *Twilight*?"

I wanted to bang my head against the window. Was she seriously upset because I'd bought a book? I've never even called her a shopaholic. Never so much as implied it. As a matter of fact, I never complained about her shopping. No, instead, I worked out a way to get us out of debt without saying a word, and this was my thanks.

"Well, shiny vampires are cooler than shopping, in my

book." I smiled to cajole her, to get her to realize she was acting like an idiot.

It didn't work.

"Return the book," she demanded.

"What? Why? I haven't read it yet."

"I don't want it in my house."

*Her* house? What about *my* house—I mean *our* house?

"Let's talk about this later. You've obviously had too much to drink." I knew it was the wrong thing to say, but I couldn't take it back.

"Too much to drink! You sucked down ciders like they were water. And how many times can you make eyes at Samantha and think you'll get away with it?"

"Make eyes at Samantha? So now I'm a cheater AND a passive-aggressive asshole. Am I following your gist completely?"

Kat's expression suggested she didn't appreciate my sarcasm. "Glad to see we're on the same page."

There weren't many passengers on the train, but some people were eavesdropping on our fight, and I was embarrassed. "Can we just talk about it later?"

"Everything's always later with you. Later we'll talk. Later you'll write your book. Later, later, later!" She slammed her hands down onto her legs.

I'd had it. Standing up, I grabbed my bag and my copy of *Twilight* from her hands. She held on tight to the book, so when I finally pried it from her hands, it popped free and hit me on my chin.

"See you at home," I sputtered, and then barged through the train and sat two cars away. Seething, I took a seat and stared out the window. If there hadn't been that stupid fire, Kat and I wouldn't have fought—not yet, at least. We would be home by now, probably in bed.

# Chapter Twelve

The next night, when I approached the front door after class, the house was dark. I wondered if Kat decided to stay at my aunt's. By the time we got home from Salem the night before, neither of us were speaking, and I had spent the night on the couch. I had never done that before.

As soon as I opened the front door, I saw Kat sitting in the dark, drinking wine. The only light was from the fireplace.

Not knowing what to do, I stood in the doorway, dumbfounded. Kat eyed me and then motioned for me to have a seat. I obeyed.

"What's up with Samantha?" She peered over her glass as she sipped her red wine. The glass had several lipstick smudges on it already, and I wondered if she was on her first or second bottle.

"What? Why?"

"Is there a reason you won't answer the question?"

Her accusatory tone stunned me. "No, I'm just baffled why you want to know what's up with Sam—shouldn't we talk about last night?"

"I am. What's up with you two?" Kat tapped her wineglass with a fingernail.

"Kat, we're just friends. We've known each other a long time."

"Funny, because she only popped into your life recently, and now all of a sudden you two are BFFs. And she has a habit of always being around, such as the gay bar, Clammy's, Red Sox games, Salem—and God knows how many other times I haven't caught you." She didn't slur any of her words, but her eyes were foggy.

"Caught me! You make it sound like I'm having an affair."

"Are you?" Her voice was steady.

"Do you really think I suggested Salem yesterday so I could spend time with Samantha?" I deflected.

Kat sighed deeply. "My head says no. But … there is a part of me that worries."

"About what? Kat, you are totally off-base with this. Trust me. You have nothing to worry about."

"That's not how I see it, Cori. In fact, I'm wondering if I should just leave and not come back."

I pulled back as if I'd just been punched in the jaw. "You can't be serious." I glanced around to see if she had any bags packed. Was this the end? "Kat, you know me. I'm loyal to you, and to my friends."

"I also know your history."

"History—what do you mean history? I've never cheated on anyone in my life, including now." I tried to keep my voice under control, but it was hard to erase any hint of anger.

"What about your family?"

"So that's it! Roger is a cheater, so I must be, too. You're starting to sound like my mother," I muttered through clenched teeth.

"Your mother never had any proof."

"And you do?" I stared at her, incredulous.

She pulled out some papers I recognized as my cell phone records. She had printed out a record of all the text messages. Most were to and from Sam. I rubbed my face with both hands, hard. There was no way I wanted to end the conversation with Kat still doubting me, questioning us. But I had promised Samantha I wouldn't share her secret. Fuck! This was bad.

"Okay, I admit this looks bad—but it's not what you think. I just can't tell you."

"Tell me what?" Her tone was shrill.

I took the wineglass out of her hand and placed it on the coffee table. Taking both of her hands in mine I looked my girlfriend in the eyes. "Kat, I promise you, Samantha and I are just friends. Besides …" My voice trailed off. I had vowed I wouldn't tell a soul.

"Besides, what?" Kat's body stiffened, and she pulled her hands out of mine.

"Listen, I can't tell you. I promised."

"And she means more to you than me."

"What? Kat you know that's not true, and it's not fair." I pinned her with a look.

"So you won't tell me. Is she not into you but you're into

her?"

"Listen, you wouldn't want me to break a promise to you, would you?"

Her look said, "Knock it off and act like a grown-up."

"You're right, Samantha is not into me—" I raised my hand to silence her accusation—"and I'm not into her. She's going through a lot right now, and …"

"What's Miss Perfect going through?"

Wow! Kat's jealousy was shining through in full force tonight. Part of me found it amusing. I probably would have laughed if our relationship wasn't on the line over it. I had never done a thing to make her question me, or had I? I admit that the papers in front of us did not look good.

I bowed my head in defeat. "She doesn't want anyone to know."

"What? Was she passed over for a promotion? Harold is always talking about how well she does at work. How she'll take over the company someday. How she tips him more than anyone else. How she—"

"She was let go."

"What?"

"Sam was laid off. Do you remember that day I got drunk with her—that was the day it happened. She needed a friend, and that's all I am to her. That's all I've ever been to her, and that's all that I want. I love you, Kat. And only you."

Kat covered her mouth in shame. "Oh, Cori. I had no idea."

"That's what I was telling you—that you didn't know the full story. She's ashamed, and she doesn't want anyone to know." I thought for a moment and decided to drop a hint.

"Especially Lucy.'

"Lucy, why does she … oh." Kat scratched her chin. "Now I feel like an ass."

"I'm not saying another word. I feel shitty enough."

Kat rubbed my back. "Do you have feelings for her? I mean you spend so much time ..."

I sighed. "That's not it, Kat. It's easier talking to her."

This caused her eyes to well up, and she pulled her hand off my back as if she'd just been stung by a bee.

"I'm sorry, I didn't mean it like that. It's just, we can relate to each other. Once, I was on top of the world: basketball star, budding author, and people respected me. Now I serve coffee to a bunch of rich snobs who can't even take a second to say hello or thank you. Samantha has more wiggle room financially, but she can't stay unemployed forever. We both know what it feels like to be at the top and then to fall flat on our faces. It's humiliating."

Kat nodded, trying to understand. "Why can't you talk to me?"

"Everyone else has lost respect for me, even my own mother, and she's a loon running around hiring PIs and talking to psychics. I don't want to lose your respect. I mean, not more than I already have."

"What does that mean, 'more than I already have'?" Kat crossed her arms and leveled her stare so I couldn't escape.

"Come on, Kat. You can't be proud seeing me in a Beantown Café apron." I felt my own eyes well up.

"You could be a garbage collector and I would still respect and love you."

The thought made me smile. "Would you make me sleep

in a different room, though? I imagine it's hard to get the stink off."

Crinkling her nose, Kat slapped my shoulder. "That's what perfume is for. Gallons of it." She laid her hand on my thigh. "I want you to open up to me more. I'm not saying you have to tell me everything you say to Samantha, but just don't give me the cold shoulder because of your stupid pride."

Kat flicked the phone bill off the table. A tear dribbled slowly down her cheek. "I'm a mess. A hot mess."

I wrapped one arm around her, and she rested her head on my shoulder. "That may be the case, but you're *my* hot mess. And no matter what, I love you."

She made a half-giggle, half-sob sound. Placing her hand over my heart and gripping my shirt tightly, she said, "That's one of the nicest things you've said to me."

"Honey, if that's true, I'm more of an asshole than I thought. I love you, no matter what. I'm sorry our night was ruined yesterday. I swear to God I didn't know Samantha and Lucy would crash our dinner. Can I make it up to you and take you to dinner tomorrow night?" A thought crossed my mind. "Or better yet, I'll borrow Mom's car next Sunday and I'll take you to Lexington. I know you want to tour the Louisa May Alcott house. We can make a day of it, and have a nice romantic dinner, just the two of us. And we can even see her grave if you want."

Kat laughed and wiped her nose with her shirtsleeve. "Nothing says romance like a cemetery."

"In my defense, it's a beautiful cemetery." I nestled my head on top of hers.

"You really didn't know Sam was in Salem?"

I sighed in frustration. "I really didn't know. I should have guessed Lucy was from a weird place, but no, I didn't know we would run into them. Please you can't keep questioning my friendship with Sam. I know you and Harold spend a lot of time together."

"Harold! You can't possibly be jealous of Harold!" She chuckled.

"No, but I imagine you two talk about things you don't tell me. That's what friends are for."

She looked away guiltily. I'd said it just to prove a point, but it made me wonder why she was confiding in Harold and not me. "What do you and Harold talk about?"

"You would never want to hear it." She winked, but I could tell she wasn't completely comfortable. "Let's just say Harold has a lot of questions about things he's seen in movies."

"You mean porn."

"I think Harold's a virgin."

"Get out. I mean, I suspected, but still, he's twenty-seven. Does he have a crush on you?"

"Yes, I think he does. But I think he's really falling for this Amber chick." Kat's face twisted into a smile.

"Really? He doesn't talk much about her at work. At first he did, but not lately."

"Tough guys don't talk to the other dudes. And you, Cori, are one of his dudes. He asked me if I could talk him through his first time." Kat slapped her thigh and chortled.

"You mean, be in the room."

"Oh no. That's not his style. He wants us to have those earpiece things FBI agents use so I can whisper in his ear what to do next. Harold actually wants me to watch him and give him pointers. He's terrified. They haven't even kissed yet."

"You're making this up." I was laughing so hard my sides started to hurt. "Since we're being honest, what do you and my mother talk about?"

"Oh, that you'll never know." She winked at me.

# Chapter Thirteen

When I left Beantown Café, I was in an extra good mood. The Red Sox had won another World Series. More importantly, I had put in my two weeks' notice, and I meant never to go back after my final shift—not even as a customer. I only had four shifts scheduled over the next two weeks. I was almost home free. Time to celebrate with my stunning girlfriend.

I'd already texted her, inviting her to dinner. Kat had readily agreed and said she had a surprise for me. I envisioned her popping out of a cake, naked.

I didn't foresee showing up at the restaurant to find out Kat had planned a "Cori is ditching Beantown" party. And she had invited Sam.

When I saw Sam's bright eyes, I felt guilty that I was getting my shit together while she was still unemployed. Kat didn't plan it that way, I'm sure. At least I hoped. Kat was never the vindictive type, and now that she knew the whole truth, I'm sure the thought didn't cross her mind. But I was still surprised to see Sam there.

Walking up to the table, I couldn't hide my excitement. Yes I felt guilty about Sam, but it felt damn good to finally tell Beantown Café to shove it—hopefully for good. Kat threw her arms around me while Harold and Sam stood there grinning like fools. Sam was a good friend, and not the type to let her own situation put the damper on my mood.

When Kat released me, Harold shook my hand. "I'll miss you, Cori, but Kat assures me I'll see you more now that you won't be working all the time."

"I hope so. It'll be nice to get some sleep as well."

Sam eagerly threw her arms around my neck. "Congrats!" She didn't say anything else, but her hug was sincere.

I looked at Kat sheepishly while Sam hugged me, relieved to see not a trace of jealousy in Kat's eyes.

I felt a tap on my shoulder and was stunned to see Lucy and Amber. At first, I was puzzled as to why Kat had invited Lucy. Amber, Harold's girlfriend, I understood. But Lucy? I barely knew the girl, and vice versa. Why would she give two shits that I was leaving the coffee shop?

Since it was a Monday night, we had the entire back room of the restaurant to ourselves. The front of the joint only had one couple anyway. Good thing. The alcohol never stopped flowing. Even Harold found a drink he could tolerate: vodka mixed with grape Fanta. It wasn't a manly drink, and I had to chuckle to see Amber drinking a beer while her man had a "kid's" drink.

Everyone was in an excellent mood, and it was fantastic to feel free. I hadn't felt this good in a long, long time.

"Now I hope everyone saved room for dessert, because I ordered a cake especially for this occasion." Kat rose and tracked down our waiter. When she returned, the waiter carried a sheet cake lit up with sparklers. I felt like a giddy five-year-old on my birthday.

The waiter set the cake down in the middle of the table and hurried away. I saw writing on the cake, but couldn't inspect it too closely, since the sparklers were going off like it was the Fourth of July.

Kat tapped her wineglass with her knife. "Before we dig in, I have a couple of things I want to say. First, Cori, congrats on quitting Beantown Café. I know how much you hated that job. Second"—she turned to Samantha and my heart stopped—"I found out this morning, that congratulations are in order for you, Sam." Kat paused and glanced in my direction before looking back to Samantha. "Maybe Lucy wasn't supposed to let the cat out of the bag, but she did. You are now a director at Boston Mutual."

Sam's face flooded with color, and Lucy stood on her tippy toes to place a sweet kiss on Samantha's cheek.

I stood there in complete shock. The entire night I had felt somewhat guilty, but to learn that Sam had landed on her feet and hadn't told me ... no text or anything.

Maybe Sam sensed my thoughts. "I didn't want to say anything earlier, since this is Cori's night," she spoke up, staring into my eyes. "I found out this morning and told Lucy." Sam waggled a finger in Lucy's face. "I told her to keep it a secret."

Lucy flushed and confessed, "I'm sorry, but Kat has a way of getting me to spill secrets." She said it so confidently that it shocked the hell out of me.

Turning to me, Lucy added, "Cori, I bet she weasels everything out of you even before you know you have a secret." She raised her glass in my honor.

"Now, don't make me sound like a crazy girlfriend, Lucy." Kat placed her hand on Lucy's shoulder and whispered something in her ear. "But speaking of secrets," she said aloud. "I hope everyone is liquored up enough—Harold, how's the vodka treating you?"

Harold chirped, "Good." Then he hiccupped, getting a laugh out of the group.

"Alrighty, then. I have a game for us to play. Everyone has to whisper a secret to every guest here tonight. I promise not to weasel any of the secrets out." Kat leaned close to Samantha and whispered something in her ear. Sam's face paled completely and then flooded with color. I didn't want to know what Kat had said.

Samantha approached me, a silly grin on her face. "I'm not wearing any underwear," she whispered. Before I could respond, she moved on to Harold. I'm assuming she said the same thing, since Harold immediately looked eagerly down at her crotch. Did he expect her jeans to fly off magically?

Out of the corner of my eye, I saw Kat share her secret with Lucy, and again I wondered what was said. Lucy didn't blush. Instead, she looked more confident and winked at Sam. Sam did a double take and then whispered into Amber's ear. Amber looked at Samantha's crotch, too.

"Now, I do believe Samantha is telling the same secret to everyone," I teased.

Sam strutted around the table and stood next to Lucy. "You'll never know, Cori. No one is allowed to spill the beans."

"She says she's not wearing underwear," declared Harold, who then hid behind Amber.

"That's not a great secret. Neither am I," said Kat.

"Me neither."

I stared at Lucy in awe.

"Or me." Amber joined the fun.

Harold tried to peek down her jeans, but she swatted his hand away. "Not now. Later."

The look on Harold's face was priceless: both thrilled and terrified. I hoped Kat had already given him the birds and the bees talk and demonstrated how to do it using dolls.

To deflect the attention from Harold, Kat piped up. "What did Cori share?"

All eyes were on me. "I don't believe she's shared a secret with anyone," declared Sam.

I stuck my tongue out at Sam, who had ratted on me.

"I think, as punishment, Cori has to share one secret aloud to the entire group." My girlfriend looked pleased with herself at that.

I sucked in some air. "That's not fair, everyone else just said they aren't wearing underwear."

"How do you know it's not true?" asked Kat.

"It's hard to believe that four out of six of us aren't wearing any."

"Five," Harold said.

"Fine, five. If you can prove it, I'll share a juicy bit of gossip." I felt confident and flashed Kat a wicked smile.

"Deal. Will everyone confirm for Cori that their partner isn't lying? Harold is Amber wearing underwear?"

Amber pulled her jeans far enough away, and the look in Harold's eye told me she was definitely going commando. It didn't take long for everyone to report that I was the only one with any decency.

"Why do I have a distinct feeling my girlfriend set me up?" I glared at Kat, who feigned hurt.

"Secret, secret, secret …" Sam chanted. Everyone else joined in.

"Okay. I'm not wearing any underwear," I said.

"Liar!" Kat rushed over and ran her hand down my backside. Then she yanked my panties up, giving me a painful wedgie. "Now you have to confess two secrets."

"You can't just change the rules!" I cried.

"Cori, when will you realize I'm always in charge?" Kat strutted off to rejoin the group, by now all chanting "secret, secret" again. Then Kat blurted out, "Spill it, Ace."

There was no way out of this mess. Kat's veiled threat was clear. Would she possibly tell the group I liked it when she licked my butt? No. She wouldn't, would she?

Kat's smile told me she knew she had me in a corner.

Gritting my teeth, I revealed, "When I was in the third grade, I peed my pants in the playground."

Sam guffawed and covered her mouth with her hand. After a few seconds, she got control of herself and asked: "Is that why your nickname in high school was Pissdale?"

"I never clarified with those who called me that, but that

would be my guess," I reluctantly agreed.

"Good thing no one at Beantown Café found out. They would probably come up with worse names. And I thought Harry Pooper was bad," said Harold.

"You know they call you that?" I asked.

"Of course," he said, without a trace of annoyance in his voice.

"And it doesn't bother you?" I pushed.

"Not at all. Really, Cori, why would I care about those miscreants? They're going nowhere with their lives. I have 10,000 Twitter followers." He puffed out his chest like a warrior who had just slain a dragon.

I had to hold in a laugh. Twitter followers. He judged his self-worth by the number of Twitter followers he had.

Kat winked, telling me not to say anything and to just let Harold enjoy his moment. It was important to him. I had recently signed up to follow his tweets, and I was secretly impressed by how many of his fans interacted with him. He was like a literary tweeting rock star. Even Neil Gaiman tweeted him.

"All right, missy. That's one secret. What's the other?" demanded Lucy. I was blown away by her confidence. Had Kat put something in her drink?

"I have a tattoo that only one person has seen, and she's in this room." I stared defiantly at Kat. She knew I was lying, and I wanted to see what she would say.

"No way!" shouted Sam.

Amber eyed me doubtfully, but she didn't seem all that interested either. Maybe she was still impressed by the number of Harold's Twitter followers.

"I want to see proof," shouted Harold before swigging the rest of his vodka and grape Fanta. It was hard to take his swigging seriously when he was essentially drinking a glorified kid's drink.

Kat was speechless. She looked from me to Harold and then to Sam. She had put me on the spot, so I figured turnabout was fair play.

"She's not lying," Kat finally said.

I let out a victorious laugh and stifled a silent sigh of relief. I had no idea why I lied, but I wasn't good at sharing secrets, and I didn't like that Kat had tried to make me give out two. Maybe she sensed she had pushed me too far.

I wish I had lied about the peeing my pants one, too, but sadly that was true. I had forgotten the hateful Pissdale nickname, or pushed it out of my head.

Sam looked at me, impressed. "What's it of?"

"Ah ..." Nothing cool came to mind.

"A heart," said Kat, her way of getting even. She allowed me to pretend I had a tattoo, but she wouldn't allow me to have a kickass tattoo. I admired her move.

"Does it have a dagger through it?" Sam tried to help me amp up the cool factor.

"Nope." Kat responded before I could.

Laughing, I gave Kat a kiss and then whisked her away from the group briefly. When we were far enough away, I asked her, "Do you want to tell me what that was about—the whole secret bullshit?"

"I'm working on something."

"What? Embarrassing the shit out of me."

"Couldn't you come up with a better secret than I pissed

my pants? Seriously, Cori. I let you get away with the tattoo one."

"Very funny. Now tell me what you're up to."

Kat crossed her arms. For a moment, I wondered if she would actually spill. Then she put her palms up. "All right, but only because you were a good sport. I'm trying to get Lucy and Sam back together. My secret to both of them was that the other was still madly in love with them." She glanced back to the group. "From the looks of it, I think my plan is working."

I followed her gaze and watched Lucy flick a flag of hair off Sam's cheek. The gesture was brief, but it was full of tenderness.

Smiling, I turned to Kat. "I guess my embarrassment was worth it, then."

"How in the hell did you piss your pants?" Kat scoffed.

"I used to wait until the last second. It was like a challenge for me. That day, I gave up challenging myself when it came to bodily functions."

"You're such a nerd." Kat took my hand and led us back to the group.

"How did you convince everyone not to wear underwear?"

Kat smiled. "I only told two of them not to."

"Which two?"

Kat grinned, and then left me to rejoin the group.

# Chapter Fourteen

After my final shift at Beantown Café, I felt like a whole new woman. I sat at my computer, staring at a blank screen. Hours earlier I had come up with the perfect way to end my novel, but sitting with the document open, my fingers froze on the keyboard. Not a word came to mind. Not even a single consonant or a syllable.

Why was this happening? The first 60,000 words had come in a flood. I didn't think. I didn't hesitate. I just wrote. I hadn't written another word that was worthwhile since then. Oh, I tried, but as soon as I was done, I deleted whatever progress I made. It was garbage, complete and total poppycock! Stuff even Danielle Steele would have laughed at—and I wasn't even writing a romance. "Literary fiction" is the term these days, now that every book has to conform to a genre. I didn't like the phrase the first time I heard of it, and I still don't today. Did Dickens sit down and say, "I'm going to write some literary fiction?" Did Austen think, "I'll try writing a romance novel?" Charlotte Bronte: "Gothic, yes gothic!" I hated that everything had to fit into a genre.

A year ago, I was at least getting words on the screen. Now, I just stared, horrified by my inability to conceive any words. I tossed a baseball, the ball I had caught at the Sox game weeks ago, from hand to hand as I pondered my dilemma. I had experienced this same ennui in school, whenever I'd had a paper due. What helped was having a deadline. If I didn't turn the paper in I would get an F, and that thought forced me to write. I needed something I was terrified of. What terrified me?

Mom.

If I failed, my mom would never let me forget it. An idea struck me. Sitting up in my desk chair, I opened my email. Yet my fingers failed me again, and I didn't know how to start.

"I don't hear any clicking and clacking on the keyboard going on."

I turned in my chair, sighing heavily. "I just don't know, Kat. Maybe I'm not cut out to be a writer."

She sat down on my desk and picked up the baseball, examining the scuff marks on it. She seemed at a loss for words.

"Tell me why you write," she said finally.

I laughed. "That's just it, I don't write anything anymore. I can't even compose a fucking email."

"Okay." My tone obviously put Kat on edge, and she didn't try to coax me in her usual sweet-talk way. "Tell me why you used to write."

"Used to. That's a good way of putting it. Let's see ... why did I used to write?" Nothing came to mind

"Let's start this way. Why do you hate dental billing?"

"Are you serious?" I gave her my "don't be daft" look.

"Come on, you loathe doing it. I see it in your face every time you head in here. It won't hurt my feelings just because my father's a dentist."

"Its mindless work, and I need a challenge."

"I'm assuming that's the same way you felt about Beantown Café."

"Pretty much. I prefer billing over that, though, because I don't have to interact with customers in person."

"Do you like teaching?"

"Yeah, I guess." I shrugged.

"You guess. You either like it or you don't."

"I like it. It lets me share my passion for books."

"Is it what you want to do for the rest of your life?" She tossed the ball to me.

I caught it one-handed. "Yes, but ..."

"But, what?"

"Not just that."

"What else?" Kat smiled waiting for the answer.

"I want to write."

"Then write, Cori."

I sighed. "If only it were that easy."

"It is."

I started to say something, but she waved me off.

"Listen, if you truly have passion, you have to find a way to uncork it," she said. "The only thing stopping you is you." She reached over and tapped my forehead. "Get out of your head."

My computer chimed, and Kat nearly jumped out of her skin. Then she teased, "You see, even your computer knows it's time."

"Very funny, wise guy." I glanced at the screen. It was an email from my mother.

Groaning, I opened it. The email read: "When you start your blog, use this photo for your profile."

Mom had attached a photo of me sitting at my aunt's desk, writing notes on a pad of paper.

Kat grinned foolishly. "You see, everyone believes in you. Do you remember when you asked your mom if she blogged? When you left the room, she was thrilled that you were considering starting one. She actually said, 'Finally, she's taking it seriously.'"

"What does she mean, 'finally'?"

"Cori, stop! Just stop." She stood up and placed both hands on my cheeks. "Your mother loves you and she wants you to succeed. Your aunt loves you and she wants you to succeed. Your father loves you and wants you to succeed. And I love you, and I want you to succeed."

I stroked one of her hands lovingly. "What about my uncle?"

"He just wants to fuck every skirt he sees." She laughed, but her eyes conveyed sadness.

"You need to get out of your head. Open up—let those around you see who you really are," she added. "And let people who are close to you open up too. Stop slamming the door every time someone hints about having feelings, fears, desires, or whatnot. Let people in. Even your mother." Her eyes told me she wanted me to let her in as well.

I gently pulled her down onto my lap. Running my fingers through her hair, I said, "Thank you, Kat. How long have you wanted to say that to me?"

She pushed her head off my chest and stared into my eyes, "Oh, from the moment I met you. I love you, Cori, but you are a difficult person to get to know. If it wasn't for your mother, I would have left long ago."

"Ah, so you do have the hots for my mom. Is it the saggy boobs or the wobbly neck that does it for you?" I pinched her side gently.

"Neither. She reads cowboy porn."

I groaned. "Don't remind me." I put my palms up. "Not right now. Right now, I want to do this." I kissed her. When our lips met, I found her tongue was greedy to be inside me. Tasting her, I felt a release of emotions. Moments passed, and our desire intensified, yet I wanted to take things slow and not rush through the motions. I wanted to enjoy each blissful second. I pulled back to gaze into her gray eyes.

"What, do you need to work?" she asked sweetly, but her voice sounded disappointed.

"No, sweetheart. I just wanted to look at you."

I had never seen her eyes light up like they did just then. I ran my fingers down the side of her face and over the front of her shirt, never taking my eyes off hers. She was wearing one of my shirts, and I was glad because I could savor every button, undoing them slowly to prolong the moment. The idea of just ripping a shirt off over her head repulsed me. I wanted to reveal her body as if it were the first time.

Kat's expression conveyed that she understood. Still on

my lap, she watched me, her gray eyes sensually low-lidded as I undid the buttons. My fingers explored the milky skin along her neck. The second button gave me a glimpse of cleavage, but I held off and kissed her tenderly, my lips finding her neck and the base of her throat.

Kat let out a slight gasp. Just tasting her skin sent tingles down my body. I ached for her. Forcing the thought out of my mind, I continued my exploration.

Another button freed her breasts. She wasn't wearing a bra, and I felt my heart throb in my throat. I had always appreciated her size, but tonight, the tiny freckles dotting the tops of her breasts invigorated me. With one finger, I tried connecting all the spots. I left a single freckle on her left breast for last. Instead of caressing it with my fingertip, I kissed it softly. Then I put my tongue to it, licking it seductively. I felt Kat's body tense, wanting more but also enjoying the moment. Satisfied, I let my tongue stroke up to her nipple, and bit it playfully. She moaned, but I stopped abruptly to kiss her lips again. She kissed me back, passionately, clenching her fingers in my hair, holding the back of my head. We continued kissing for many moments.

When a lack of oxygen forced a breather, I leaned back against the chair, admiring the top half of her body.

Kat watched me watch her, amused.

"What?" I asked.

"You're looking at me as if you've never seen me naked before."

"Is that a bad thing?" I tickled the side of her face, and she placed her hand on top of mine, keeping it there.

"It's good." Her eyes bored into mine.

"Shall we move into the bedroom? I've only seen half of you."

Kat stood and took my hand, leading me into the bedroom, her hips twisting sensually the entire distance as she walked. She sat on the bed and began to remove the shirt completely.

"Patience, Kat. Patience." I stopped her.

"Whatever has gotten into you tonight, I like it."

"Well, relax and enjoy. Tonight is all about you."

Hours later, lying in bed, I asked, "What did you mean earlier, when you said if it wasn't for my mother you would have left long ago?"

Her head on my chest, she said, "She convinced me that if I stuck around I would finally worm my way inside, overcome your stubborn, independent streak." Kat drummed her fingers along my side.

Squirming, I shouted, "Hey, stop! That's not fair."

But she had me pinned, and she wouldn't stop tickling.

"I'm not stubborn, and I'm not independent."

That got Kat's attention. "Do you really think that?"

The look she gave me made my heart stop briefly. Had I really been so close to losing her right from the start?

"What evidence do you have that I'm too independent?"

"For the first sixth months we dated, you refused to stay over the entire night, saying you couldn't sleep unless you were in your own bed."

"Well, that's true!"

"Then why didn't you invite me to your place? For weeks I didn't even know where you lived."

"Oh, that's not true; I had you over for dinner."

Kat laughed. "And then you took me to a movie, and we went back to my apartment to fuck."

"Did I really do that?"

"Yes!" She slapped my shoulder, but at least she then placed her head back on my chest. "It drove me batty. Here I was falling head over heels in love with you, and you would let me in some and then push me away again."

"We moved in together," I argued. "You now live in my place—I mean, our place."

"You see!" Kat sat up. "You still think of this as *your* place, and I've been living here for two years." She pouted playfully.

"But you won, didn't you?"

"I won? What do you mean by that, Cori?" The playfulness left her voice.

I needed to backpedal, and fast. "I'm here, with you, and I couldn't be happier."

The smile returned to her face. "For the moment, yes."

Her words felt like a slap across the face. "I …"

Kat placed two fingers on my mouth. "Shush. Not tonight, Cori. I said my piece, and you actually listened. That's good enough for now. Baby steps."

Kat drifted off to sleep while I held her. My body was tired from the love-making, but my mind would not shut off. Was it possible I didn't know myself or what I had been doing?

An idea struck me like a hundred-pound pole, whacking me in the back of the head. I didn't know my main character. I didn't know her story. If I didn't know her story, how could I know the ending? That was it!

I kissed the top of Kat's head and gently wiggled free, not that she noticed. A sliver of drool snaked from her mouth, and to be honest, she looked lovely—drool and all.

A draft of my novel sat on my desk, and for months I had been tweaking it, molding it, trying to force it to be something it wasn't. I understood that now. Picking up the first sheet, I ripped it in half. Then I ripped it into fourths. I kept tearing it apart until the pieces were too tiny to bisect. Not done, I shredded the entire manuscript, feeding several pages into the shredder at once, all the while smiling like a woman possessed. I knew how to do it now, but before I could begin, I needed to obliterate the original.

Once I had completed that task, I switched on the computer to delete the file. For a second, my hand froze on the mouse.

Are you sure you want to delete this file? The console asked me.

Forcefully, I left-clicked the mouse.

Gone!

It was the first time in months I had felt good about writing, and all I had done was completely destroy my novel. Ah, life and its ironies. No matter, it was time to get to work.

The first tap of the keyboard was euphoric. The words poured from my fingertips onto the computer screen. Nothing stopped me for hours. Even when I noticed the dark sky giving way to the dawning of a new day, my fingers didn't stop.

"My, you are engrossed." Kat's sweet voice momentarily paused the words that flowed from my fingers. She placed both hands on my shoulders, leaned down, and kissed the top of my head.

"I'm sorry if I woke you." I nuzzled one of her hands with my chin, enjoying the warmth of her skin. I hadn't realized how cold I was.

"What's all this paper all over the floor?"

"My novel." I said casually.

"Your novel! You shredded your novel?" Kat's eyes bugged out at the mess.

"It's okay, Kat. Trust me. I'm writing a new one. One I can finish."

The tension left her body, and she leaned over my shoulder to peer at the screen. "You've already written over twenty pages."

"Really?" I squinted at the page number on the lower left-hand corner. "I hadn't realized. No wonder my back hurts." I stood and stretched.

Kat grinned and tickled my exposed stomach.

"You want some coffee?" I asked. "I'm going to need gallons to stay awake so I can help my aunt at the gallery today."

Kat looked away, staring at one of her paintings she had given me early on in our relationship. "Sure, but let me make it."

I didn't know why, but her tone upset me.

I tugged her arm, forcing her to look at me. "Is everything okay?"

"Of course," she said, and then glanced at the computer screen again.

"No, something's bothering you. Tell me, please."

"I just feel bad about how hard you work, and I—"

I raised my hand. "Shh … let's go to the kitchen and make some breakfast together. What time is it?" I glanced at the clock on the wall. "We have a couple of hours before we need to leave."

Kat started to speak, but I kissed her to keep her quiet. I was in a good mood, and I didn't want to talk about money problems or about her not working. I wanted this to be a good day. I could sense it.

## Chapter Fifteen

$I$ had always enjoyed helping my aunt set up a new exhibition. Unfortunately, I never picked up her ability to judge and critique art. When I wandered through the gallery, admiring all the paintings, all that came to mind was, "I like the color and the feel of them."

Kat beamed, looking lovely in her jeans and a Harvard tee she had stolen from me.

"You like them too?" I asked her.

Out of the corner of my eye, I saw my mom and aunt exchange a look.

Kat pulled me in for a hug. "I'm not sure, but I'm thrilled that you like them."

"Hey, now. Don't get any funny ideas. I've never been able to afford a single one of the paintings my aunt sells."

I thought that would make her smile disappear, but she

grinned even wider. "I'm counting on that."

"What do you mean?" Clueless, I looked to Mom and Aunt Barbara for help. They both pointed to Kat. "What's going on? Am I on candid camera or something? All of you are grinning like the Cheshire Cat, and I feel like I'm missing the obvious."

"Roger, can you bring that sign out here, please." My aunt barked her order, but she didn't stop smiling.

My uncle gleefully followed her instructions. Even Roger was grinning foolishly.

"Turn it around so we can see the artist's name," Barbara told him.

He turned the sign around painfully slowly.

I read the name.

Then I read it again.

Still staring at the sign, I read the name aloud, trying to fathom the meaning. "You?" I turned to Kat. "These are yours?" I motioned to all the paintings. "How? When?"

"You couldn't possibly believe I went shopping with your mother every day." Her voice sounded victorious.

"But you were never at home? You haven't touched your paints at home in … I don't know how long." I wanted to immediately retract those words. I didn't want her to know I had been keeping track of her.

"I wanted it to be a surprise." Her beautiful face grew serious. "Are you surprised?"

"Hell, yes! I'm surprised! Kat, I couldn't be prouder." My soft tone lured her into my arms.

Silently, my family left the room.

"But why didn't you tell me? I would have supported

you."

"I know, but I felt so guilty."

"Guilty? Why?"

"You've been working three jobs while I've been playing with paints." She wandered to the other side of the room and leaned against the wall. "That was difficult to live with. And then you started doing my father's billing; that nearly killed me."

"Honey, if you'd told me about this, I would have worked four jobs."

"I know. That's what I was afraid of. I barely saw you with your three jobs. And I know I haven't been much help with not working … and with my spending habits." She added as an afterthought, "I'm seeing someone about that."

"Seeing someone … you mean like a shrink?" I knitted my brows, trying to follow her meaning.

"Yes. Apparently I buy things to fill a hole, and I may have an addictive personality." She giggled nervously.

"A hole?"

"Growing up with my parents"—she looked at one of her paintings—"wasn't easy."

I couldn't even imagine growing up in the Finn household. "I didn't know … I mean about the shrink."

"The day I told my parents I didn't want to be a dentist, I ruined their lives."

I laughed uncontrollably. "I'm sorry, Kat, but that's the most ridiculous thing I've ever heard."

She laughed with me. "Yes, to normal people! But Phineas isn't normal."

"Are you two having sex in there, or can we come in?"

Mom shouted from the doorway.

"Mother!"

Kat shot me a look that said, "Remember what I told you last night."

"Yes we are, so stay out," I called.

My uncle rushed into the room. Did he really want to see us naked? What a perv.

My aunt shook her head in disgust, and my mother shot me a look of admiration. "You made a joke. A sexual joke, sorta?"

"Move on, Mother. Rome wasn't built in a day."

She put her palms up, acquiescing. "Not to ruin the moment, but I think you two should scoot so you can get ready for the opening."

"But what about our double date with Harold and Amber?" Then it hit me.

"I didn't want you to make other plans for this evening. No Red Sox games. No unexpected dinners with Sam. I wanted you to be here, with me."

"I feel foolish. I even sent him a text saying I'd see him later."

"You will. He's coming."

"What? You told Harold, and you didn't tell me!"

The look she flashed me turned me on. Confidence suited her.

I pulled my mother to one side. "How much money do I owe you?"

"What are you talking about, Cori?"

"Kat's therapy. I know her parents aren't paying for it, and the money hasn't come out of my account." I crossed my arms.

"Kat's like a daughter to me. I won't accept a dime from you." She walked off in a rush, but I dashed after her.

"Mom, wait."

She spun around, ready to do battle.

"I started my novel over. I promise you I'll have the first draft done in four months."

"You are full of surprises today. Any chance I can talk you into joining our book club?"

"Not a chance in hell."

"Good, I was afraid you were becoming a stranger to me. Keep an open mind, but stay true to yourself. That's all I've ever wanted from you."

"You could have told me that sooner."

"Yes, but where's the fun in that." She smiled. "Besides, you're just like your father. You wouldn't have listened to me anyway."

"Speaking of that, where is Dad?"

"At home—working. He's decided to open his own business. He's not that handy anyway. Better he stays at home. Do you remember the time he rewired the lights?"

"Yes. I'm still afraid to turn on a light switch. That bolt of electricity hurt more than when my knee blew."

"Your hair stood on end for hours." Mom smiled at the memory. "Have you started your blog yet, missy?"

"Not yet, but soon."

"You better do it before the end of the week, or I'll put you over my knee and spank you."

"Oh, please, Mother. I'm half a foot taller than you."

"Yes, but I'm cunning. Now go get ready for tonight. Kat

and I picked out a dress for you to wear." Her malevolent smile returned. "And a stunning pair of heels."

"Heels!"

"Yes, and you'll wear them. It's Kat's night, not yours. Besides, we both know you love to dance in heels, like Ginger Rogers."

I let out a rush of air. "All right, but when it's my night to celebrate, I'm making you two wear sweats out in public."

"Deal."

Harold, dressed in a black suit and white socks, made a beeline for us, dragging poor Amber on his arm. When he reached us, he dropped Amber's arm like a lead weight and pumped Kat's hand enthusiastically with both of his.

"Congratulations, Kat. They're amazing." He motioned to the paintings surrounding him.

"Thanks, Harold." My girlfriend pried his hands away delicately and placed one of his hands back on Amber's arm. Harold continued to grin like a fool. I don't think he even noticed what Kat had done.

Amber patted his arm. "He's been gushing the entire time, telling everyone he knows the artist."

To my surprise, Kat didn't act embarrassed. "Thanks." She turned to me, all smiles. "I have my first raving fan."

"Second." I raised Kat's hand to my mouth, and kissed it.

"Third." Samantha appeared before us, with Lucy by her side. Lucy had an arm around Samantha's waist like a lover. I arched my eyebrows to catch Sam's eye. She confirmed their romance by blushing and looking down at the floor instead of at my face. They were dating again.

Kat's sly look also confirmed my suspicion.

Everything in my life was falling back into line. It felt good.

Kat wandered off to mingle with some of the guests, and my mother approached, beaming.

"Did you two have a quickie before getting changed? You know, if you're doing it right, it should only take seven minutes to get Kat to climax."

I glared at her. "None of your beeswax."

Kat and I did have sex, but I wasn't going to admit that—and it lasted longer than seven minutes.

Instead, I said, "I've booked our tickets to Italy. We'll be gone for the first week of January. I'm hoping you can arrange for everyone else to show up, as a surprise, after I give her the ring. I'll know she'll want you there. With the success of Kat's show, I feel confident she'd be ready for me to pop the question."

"And you?" Mom raised an eyebrow.

"I wouldn't have it any other way."

My mother stared, dumbfounded. "So my independent child really is getting engaged?"

"God, I hope so. Kat is a hot mess, but she's mine."

"And you are hers," said my mother. "You're perfect for each other. I knew that the first time I saw you with her."

Kat turned to smile at me. I lifted my champagne flute, saluting my soon-to-be fiancée. Kat nodded, with a look in her eye that meant we wouldn't be getting any sleep tonight. Life was good.

## Epilogue

Quickening my pace, I pushed through the crowded Financial District, swearing under my breath as I checked my watch again. Five minutes late.

*Move aside people, seriously.*

I shoved past two businessmen who had stopped in the middle of the sidewalk to chat.

Dread inched up from my gut. Being late was part of it. But truth be known, it was mostly that I was heading to the one place I swore I'd never return to. Every time I thought I was done with Beantown Café, something lured me back. A scene from *The Godfather* flashed through my mind. "Just when I thought I was out … they pull me back in."

As I approached, I could see the coffee shop was hopping. I'd almost hoped no one would be there. I sighed, dragged my apron from my bag, and put it on. The fucking cherry-red apron I swore I'd never put on ever again. Kat had chuckled this morning when she'd seen me folding it into my bag. She thought it was cute. Yeah, real cute.

"Cori! Over here." Harold waved from behind the counter.

I tried my best to act normal. This was just another day. Nothing special.

"Do you remember how to do this?" He smiled. "It's packed. I'm going to need a hand."

I nodded. Remember? I still had nightmares about the place. Of course I remembered.

He pushed me towards the cash register. I sighed heavily and prepared for the onslaught.

"Ladies and gentlemen, the program will start shortly," announced Harold. "If you haven't had a chance to order a drink yet, please come to the counter now." He pointed to me.

I plastered a well-practiced fake smile on my face. "What can I get you?" I asked the first customer.

A frizzy-haired woman looked down from the large menu that hung behind me and started to order, but then stopped abruptly. "You look familiar. Do I know you?"

Before I could speak, Harold jumped in with, "She used to work here ... and now she's back." He nudged my arm, grinning.

More than a dozen customers ordered and moved aside, waiting for their drinks. As I closed the drawer to the cash register, without looking up, I asked the next person in line, "What can I get you?"

"Hey, I know you!"

My head snapped up and I rolled my eyes at Mom and

my aunt. "Like I said, can I help you?"

Mom looked to Aunt Barbara. "Didn't this person write a book or something?"

"Huh, now that you mention it, I think she did," my aunt confirmed. "But I don't remember her name."

"Very funny you two. Are you going to order?"

"Four cappuccinos, please. Bean Supremes." Mom started to hand over the cash, but I shook my head.

"Oh no, this is on the house."

"Well, well, well—look at the coffee house big shot." Mom winked and moved to the side.

Harold chuckled and tapped me on shoulder, gesturing for me to follow him.

"It's like riding a bike." He beamed at me.

"You're enjoying this, aren't you?"

He held up his cell phone, revealing a photograph of me waiting on Nell Tisdale. "I'm going to hang this up on the wall." He pointed to the wall on the far side. "Right between Kat's paintings."

"Oh that's perfect, Harold." Kat strolled up and looped her arm through mine. "You ready for the big night? Look at the crowd!"

I stepped from side to side, like a child who had to pee.

"You'll be fine." Kat tried to reassure me. "If you get nervous, just picture everyone naked."

Sam and Lucy were right by Kat's side, nodding.

"And just to help you imagine that, I think you should know we're going commando," Lucy whispered at me with a wink.

Harold's eyes nearly boggled out of his head as Lucy

257

pulled at the waistband of her jeans to prove it. His girlfriend, Amber, swatted his arm.

"That's my cue." Harold excused himself and walked to the makeshift stage in front of the gathering crowd.

I felt my pulse quicken and rubbed my sweaty palms on the apron as I slipped it off. This time, I didn't allow myself the luxury of thinking I'd be removing it for the last time. I didn't want to jinx myself.

Much sooner than I wanted, I heard Harold boom, "Ladies and gentlemen, if I could have your attention, please." He paused dramatically. "I would like to introduce our guest tonight, who is launching her first novel. Some of you may recognize her, since she just took your coffee order." He winked at me.

A few chuckles followed, and the frizzy-haired customer said loudly, "I thought she looked familiar."

Ignoring the crowd's laughter, Harold continued. "It is with great pleasure that I welcome Boston's newest literary sensation, and my good friend, Cori Tisdale."

Despite the applause, my feet refused to budge. Kat shoved me with her shoulder, nudging me toward the front of the room.

"Good luck." Sam thrust a book into my hands and gave me a thump on the back.

"Cori has agreed to read from her novel, and then will answer some questions." He motioned for me to take over.

I cleared my throat, feeling like an amateur speaker. *My first official book reading.* I tapped the microphone.

"Uh, before I begin, I would like to say a few words. First, I would like to thank Harold, the manager and my loyal friend, for arranging this event. Looking at all of you is—to be frank—intimidating as hell." I fidgeted with the book in my hand, taking in all of the people. All of the chairs were full, and many more people stood sipping coffees behind them. It was a packed house.

"The first time I heard Harold had such a Twitter following," I continued, trying to keep the waver from my voice, "it was hard for me to fathom. But seeing all of you here, thanks to his efforts, shows me just how much pull he has in the literary world." To prove my point, the front door opened and several more people poured in.

Harold bowed, and the crowd appreciated it.

"Next, I would like to thank my mother, Nell Tisdale. Some of you may know of her—she wrote a book or two." I waved a hand dismissively.

More laughter followed, and Mom nodded, mouthing "Bravo."

"My mother and my aunt"—I pointed to them in the crowd—"have supported me from the beginning. I would like to tell them—in front of all of you, so I have witnesses—that I love them, even if they are both a pain in the ass."

"Takes one to know one," my mother shouted.

Aunt Barbara shushed her but it was hard to control my laughter. Mom was trying so hard not to take over and be the star of the evening.

I thanked my father and Uncle Roger, too, who both nodded sternly, proud smiles on their faces.

"I apologize for dragging this out. I promise I won't turn it into an Oscar speech, but before I read from my novel, I have to give a shout-out to my beautiful wife, Kat Finn, who was the inspiration for …"

Not wanting to choke up, I raised the novel. Slipping on my reading glasses, I cracked the book open to the first page, "Chapter One …"

# Author's Note

Thank you for reading *Confessions from a Coffee Shop*. If you enjoyed the novel, please consider leaving a review on Goodreads or Amazon. No matter how long or short, I would very much appreciate your feedback.

You can follow me, T. B. Markinson, on twitter at @50YearProject or email me at tbmarkinson@gmail.com. I would love to know your thoughts.

# Acknowledgments

I would like to thank my editor, Karin Cox. I am extremely grateful for all the hours she spent hunting for my mistakes, and for her wonderful suggestions on how to improve the final product. Thank you to my beta readers, who assisted me in the early stages. Jeri Walker did a fabulous job proofreading, giving me peace of mind. Cindy Taylor has been extremely instrumental with all of my books. I can't thank her enough for her belief in me and for her friendship. Lastly, my sincerest thanks go to my partner. Without her support and encouragement, this novel would not exist.

# About the Author

T. B. Markinson is an American writer living in England. When she isn't writing, she's traveling the world, watching sports on the telly, visiting pubs, or taking the dog for a walk. Not necessarily in that order.

Printed in Great Britain
by Amazon